WEB OF DESIRE

As she followed Gary through the hall, Mandy felt genuinely relived to discover that he was married. She had John hanging around, and was beginning to hope that she'd meet other men. She didn't want to be tied down to anyone in particular. She was sure that her web-design business would soon pick up and she'd be able to afford to get out more. If she could buy a car and . . . But, right now, she had Gary to entertain.

'What is it about dirty panties that turns you on?' she asked him as she sat in the armchair.

Settling on the sofa, he grinned. 'Everything,' he said, chuckling. 'The smell, the feel of the wet material . . . The idea of you wearing them all night and all day turns me on. They must be really wet and beautifully scented by now.'

'Yes, I think they are,' she breathed. 'Tell me what you really like doing.'

WEB OF DESIRE

Ray Gordon

This book is a work of fiction.
In real life, make sure you practise safe, sane and
consensual sex.

First published in 2008 by
Nexus
Thames Wharf Studios
Rainville Rd
London W6 9HA

A catalogue record for this book is available from the
British Library.

www.nexus-books.com

Typeset by TW Typesetting, Plymouth, Devon

Printed in the UK by CPI Bookmarque, Croydon, CR0 4TD

The paper used in this book is a natural, recyclable product made
from wood grown in sustainable forests. The manufacturing
process conforms to the regulations of the country of origin.

ISBN 978 0 352 34167 9

Distributed in the USA by Holtzbrinck Publishers, LLC,
175 Fifth Avenue, New York, NY 10010, USA

Symbols key

 Corporal Punishment

 Female Domination

 Institution

 Medical

 Period Setting

 Restraint/Bondage

 Rubber/Leather

 Spanking

 Transvestism

 Underwear

 Uniforms

One

Mandy was twenty-two and not unattractive. Tall, slim and with long black hair, she should have been enjoying her life, but she was feeling increasingly despondent. The web-design business that she'd set up from home had been running for two years, but it barely generated enough income for the essentials, let alone for luxuries. She'd heard stories about people making a fortune on the internet, but it wasn't as easy as she'd thought. It seemed that everyone wanted something for nothing, and they were unwilling to part with their cash.

As she lugged her shopping to the bus stop she wondered whether she'd ever be able to afford to buy a car. It was early days, she thought, checking her watch and looking down the road for the bus. Maybe, after three or four years, the business would pick up and the money would start rolling in. A car would make things so much easier, she thought as a Mercedes pulled up at the bus stop. Having to take a bus everywhere was a pain. And it was no fun in the winter with the wind and rain . . .

'Mandy?' the blonde in the Mercedes called through the open window. 'Mandy Jones?'

'Paula,' Mandy breathed, stooping to look at the girl in the driving seat. 'How are you?'

'I'm fine. Want a lift?'

'Thanks. That would be great.'

'Put your bags on the back seat and get in.'

Mandy dumped her shopping in the back and breathed in the aroma of the leather upholstery as she sat beside her old school friend. Paula had obviously done well, she thought, eyeing the Mulberry handbag on the dashboard. Feeling rather ashamed to be picked up at a bus stop, Mandy covered her own tatty handbag with her denim jacket. Paula was wearing a dark skirt and matching jacket with a white blouse. Her long blonde hair crimped, her make-up impeccable, she'd turned out to be an attractive – and obviously successful – young woman.

'So, how are things?' Paula asked her, pulling out into the traffic. 'Oh, where do you want dropping off?'

'Anywhere by Lockwood Park will be fine,' Mandy replied, not wanting to give the address of her small maisonette in the less salubrious part of town.

'God, we haven't seen each other since school. So, are you married, got kids, divorced?'

'Not married,' Mandy replied. 'No kids, either. How about you?'

'No time for marriage,' the other girl replied with a giggle. 'I've been having too much fun to settle down and tie myself to a kitchen sink.'

'Yes, and me,' Mandy breathed. 'It's great to see you after all this time. Are you still in touch with anyone from school?'

'Not really, but I have seen Kay Burnshaw working in the local supermarket. Fancy ending up as a checkout girl. Mind you, she never was very bright. How about you – do you work?'

'I have my own business,' Mandy replied proudly. 'It's web design.'

'Oh? Does it pay well?'

'Er . . . yes, yes it does. What do you do?'

'I run my own business,' Paula said, tapping the steering wheel impatiently as she pulled up at the traffic lights. 'Import and export.'

'Sounds interesting.'

'The money's interesting, and I get to travel abroad. California, Tokyo . . .' Putting her foot down as the lights turned green, Paula smiled at Mandy. 'I should be going to Thailand soon. Now, that *will* be fun.'

'Thailand? Wow, I wish I was going.'

'I always mix pleasure with business, Mandy. That's the secret of success. Here we are, Lockwood Park.'

'Thanks, Paula. It's great to see you after all this time.'

'Hey, we'll have to meet up for a drink. How about this evening?'

'Well, yes, all right.'

'The wine bar in the high street? Say, seven o'clock?'

'Yes, I'll be there.'

'It's lovely to see you again, Mandy. We'll have a few drinks and catch up on the latest news.'

'Great. I'll see you later, then.'

As she climbed out of the car and took her shopping from the back seat, Mandy bit her lip. Money was going to be a problem. All she had was the ten-pound note she'd put by for her mother's birthday present. She really couldn't afford to go out drinking, but it would be nice to meet Paula and chat about old times. When she got home she dumped her bags on the floor and gazed at her reflection in the mirror.

Twenty-two years old and broke, she thought dolefully, recalling the luxury of Paula's Mercedes.

3

Wandering into the lounge, she looked at the second-hand sofa and the threadbare carpet. What with the mortgage and other bills, things hadn't been easy. But she had faith in her web-design business, and she was sure the day would come when the hard work would begin to pay off. Eyeing the brown envelope on the kitchen table as she put the shopping away, she knew that time was running out. She was getting behind with the bills and, unless she started making money soon, she'd be in dire trouble.

Mandy went into the dining room, switched on her computer and checked her emails. She shook her head despondently. A man wanted a web site designed for his landscape-gardening business, but he didn't have a great deal of money. He'd listed his questions. Could Mandy do him a deal? Could she design something simple on the cheap? Could he pay by monthly instalments? This was typical, Mandy thought, replying to his email. Didn't he realise how long it took to design a web site? Even a simple design would take several hours, but she needed the money and offered to design a site for a cut price.

Her father had always said that she shouldn't lower her price. He reckoned that her services should be expensive, giving the punters the idea that they were paying for something special. He was right, she knew. But she was afraid that she'd get no business at all if she followed his advice. His analogy was that a coffee table for sale in a backstreet shop might be fifty pounds, and in a posh shop the same table would be two hundred. Not having a head for business, Mandy didn't know what to do.

It was approaching seven o'clock. Mandy dressed in a turquoise miniskirt and white blouse. She looked good, she thought, eyeing her reflection in the dressing-table mirror. But she didn't feel good. She applied her make-up and tried smiling, but her smile failed to conceal her pained expression. It was worry, she knew. Worry over the business and her lack of money. She'd often thought of selling her flat and moving in with her parents, but that would be admitting defeat. The way things were going, though, she might not have a choice.

Mandy grabbed her handbag and walked the short distance to the wine bar. It made a pleasant change to go out, she thought as she wandered into the bar. The sound of people joking and laughing cheered her up. She couldn't remember the last time she'd been out for a drink. It must have been at least a year ago, maybe two. She ordered a vodka and tonic, took her drink to a corner table and checked her watch. Ten past seven. Hoping that Paula wasn't going to let her down, she watched a group of men standing at the bar. They were chatting and laughing, reminding Mandy of her teenage years when she'd go out on Friday nights with her friends.

She'd met her first love when she was eighteen. John was good-looking and great fun to be with. But he'd run off with another girl and had left Mandy heartbroken. Alan came along and, after a year, he did the same thing. Mandy had decided that men were a waste of time and had put all her efforts into her web-design business. But two years without a relationship – two years of celibacy – had left her introverted. She'd locked herself away in her own little world and had thought only of her business. She really had to make an effort to get out and meet people before she became a total recluse, she thought as Paula breezed into the bar.

'Sorry I'm late,' Paula said, walking to the table. 'One of my boyfriends wanted to see me this evening and he wouldn't take no for an answer.'

'That's OK,' Mandy said. 'Get a drink and we'll have a chat about old times.'

Watching the girl walk up to the bar, Mandy sighed as she recalled her friend's words. *One of my boyfriends* ... How many men did Paula have? she wondered as she eyed her friend's red miniskirt and white crop top. The last thing Mandy wanted was several men hanging around her. One man would be nice, though. A male friend to share the odd evening with, go out for a meal now and then and ...

'He looks all right,' Paula said, joining Mandy at the table and nodding in the direction of a young man standing at the bar. 'I wouldn't mind getting inside his trousers.'

'Yes,' Mandy breathed, unsure what to say in response to Paula's crude remark.

'Mind you, I have enough men hanging around at the moment. How about you? Are you screwing anyone?'

'Well, I ... I do have a boyfriend,' Many lied.

'What's he like? Has he got money?'

'Well ...'

'Always make sure they have money. That's the first rule, Mandy. A man without money is about as much use as a man without a cock.'

'That's a good way of putting it,' Mandy said, with a giggle.

'It's true, isn't it? By the way, someone said that you were working in a café. I'm going back a couple of years, so I can't remember who it was that told me. But I do remember thinking that they must have been wrong. I mean, who'd work in a greasy-spoon café?'

'Yes, I ... I did for a while,' Mandy admitted sheepishly. 'Actually, I didn't work there. I mean ... I *did* work there, but I was only helping out a friend.'

'Oh, right.'

Mandy felt her face flushing as she recalled her time at the café. The pay had been awful, but she'd worked there for eighteen months because she couldn't find a decent job. Luckily, her parents had given her the deposit for her flat and had even helped out with the mortgage a couple of times. But, even with their help, things hadn't been easy. Recalling the late nights she'd worked at the café, the times she'd got home at midnight, she gazed at Paula and pondered on her success. It was funny to think that the two of them were the same age and had had the same education, and yet Paula had done so well for herself.

'I meant to ask you earlier,' Paula said. 'Why were you waiting for a bus? Don't you have a car?'

'No, I ... I don't need a car,' Mandy replied. 'Working from home, I don't need to go anywhere.'

'I don't know how you can survive without a car,' Paula breathed, her blue eyes frowning. 'Lugging your shopping home on a bus every week must be dreadful.'

'I don't go shopping,' Mandy returned, deciding to retaliate. 'I mean, I did today but ... I get my boyfriend to do that.'

'Really?'

Mandy giggled. 'I'm far too busy to traipse around supermarkets and catch buses,' she said, sipping her drink. Round one to me, she thought happily. 'Surely you don't do your own shopping?'

'God, no. I have a cleaning woman. She also does the shopping.'

Mandy didn't want to play a game of one-upmanship, but she couldn't admit to doing her own shopping and lugging carrier bags home on a bus every week. Paula obviously lived in a different world. Mandy knocked back her drink and reflected dolefully. A Mercedes, a cleaning woman, travelling abroad ... Wondering where she'd gone wrong, she went to the bar and ordered another vodka and tonic. She was going to run out of money if she wasn't careful. She could only afford four drinks, and would have to pace herself.

'Allow me,' the man who Paula had pointed out said, taking his wallet from his jacket pocket.

'Oh, thank you,' Mandy breathed. 'That's very nice of you.'

'You're a very nice girl. I'm Gary, by the way.'

'I'm Mandy, pleased to meet you.'

'Er ... are you staying with your friend for the evening or ...'

'Yes, yes, I am.'

'Maybe we could have a drink together one evening?'

'Well, er ...' Mandy bit her lip and glanced at Paula. 'I'm not sure.'

'You must think me rather quick off the mark. It's just that I've been watching you and ... well, if you don't ask, you don't get. How about tomorrow evening?'

'Maybe,' Mandy said hesitantly. 'I'll have to see what I'm doing.'

'Here's my number.' He passed her a business card. 'Give me a ring, OK?'

'I will,' she said, gazing at the card. Gary Moore, accountant. 'Thanks. Well, I'd better be getting back.'

'Ring me tomorrow, OK?'

'OK.'

Returning to the table, Mandy couldn't believe that she'd been asked out. And it had happened so quickly. He was in his late twenties and very good-looking, and Mandy wondered whether she should phone him. Feeling confident as she sat opposite

8

Paula, she grinned. Paula's eyes darted between the man and Mandy, and she was obviously curious. Round two to me, Mandy thought, sipping her drink and waiting for the inevitable question.

'Do you know him?' Paula finally asked her.

'Gary? Yes, yes, I do,' she replied triumphantly.

'Why didn't you say so when I pointed him out earlier?'

'I didn't realise that you were talking about Gary. I thought you meant that other man.'

'Is he an old boyfriend, or what?' Paula persisted.

'Sort of,' Mandy replied mysteriously.

'He's very good-looking. Why don't you ask him to join us?'

'He's with his friends. Besides, I want to catch up on your news and chat about the old days.'

'Do you still see him?'

'I'm seeing him tomorrow evening. So, tell me about your business. What is it that you import and export?'

As Paula rambled on, Mandy kept one eye on Gary. Returning his smile, she felt her stomach somersault as she imagined going out with him. Things couldn't have turned out better, she reflected. Chatting to a handsome young man when Paula was watching ... Luck was definitely with her, she thought happily. If only she could afford to get out more. It would be nice to go out and meet people and enjoy life for a change. All work and no play wasn't a good thing. All work, and no pay.

'And that's how I got where I am today,' Paula said, breaking Mandy's reverie.

'Sounds interesting,' Mandy commented.

'Do you have your own house?'

'Yes, I do,' Mandy replied. 'Well, it's a flat, a maisonette.'

'Oh, I couldn't live in a flat,' Paula returned. 'Don't you find it claustrophobic? I don't know what I'd do if I didn't have a garden. Especially in the summer.'

'I don't have time for gardening.'

'Neither do I. That's why I have a man who comes round once a week. He cuts the lawn and keeps things nice. I really couldn't be without a garden.'

'I was thinking about moving,' Mandy lied as the alcohol went to her head. 'But I decided to stay where I am because I don't have the cash at the moment.'

'It doesn't cost much to move house.'

'No, no . . . I don't want another mortgage.'

'Oh, I see. Well, er . . . you must be doing well if you're thinking of buying a place for cash.'

'It won't be for a while, yet. What's your house like?'

'Very small,' Paula replied, much to Mandy's surprise. 'I rent out my big house,' she added. 'I decided to live in the smaller one because I don't need six bedrooms. I'll get another drink. I won't be a minute.'

Fortunately, Gary called out goodbye as Paula took her empty glass up to the bar. The last thing Mandy had wanted was for Paula to start chatting to him. This really was a game of one-upmanship, Mandy reflected. *I don't need six bedrooms.* She'd always got on well with Paula at school, and she felt that they were still good friends, but she didn't like having to lie to the girl. At least she'd not had to lie too much about Gary. She was going to see him tomorrow – that was no lie.

'He really is dishy,' Paula said, placing her drink on the table and retaking her seat. 'You don't want to let that one go.'

'I like to keep him hanging around,' Mandy breathed. 'He has his uses.'

'I'll bet he has. I'll tell you what I'm going to do when I go to bed tonight.'

'What's that?'

'Get my vibrator out and enjoy several good orgasms.'

'Oh, er ... right,' Mandy stammered, wondering what to say.

'My vibro is better than any man.'

'I used to think that, until I met Gary,' Mandy said, with another giggle.

Mandy enjoyed the evening and swapped phone numbers with Paula before leaving the bar. She felt a little apprehensive about going out with Gary, but she knew that she shouldn't back out. It was time she had some sort of friendship with a man. Her thoughts turning to sex, she imagined Paula using a vibrator. Mandy had masturbated regularly throughout her teens, but the urge had left her a couple of years ago and she'd neglected her feminine needs.

Back at her flat she made herself a cup of coffee and checked her emails. The landscape gardener had accepted her offer and had sent several photographs for the web site. At least she'd make a little money. She climbed the stairs to her bedroom and slipped out of her clothes. Eyeing her reflection in the full-length mirror, she reckoned that she had a pretty good figure. Her long dark hair framed a pretty face and cascaded over her well-formed shoulders. Her breasts were small but firm and nicely pointed and she was slim with shapely hips. No, she wasn't bad looking at all. Maybe the time had come to rediscover her sexuality.

Sprawled out beneath the quilt in her double bed, Mandy wondered what it would be like to use a vibrator. She hadn't given a thought to sex for so long that she'd forgotten what an orgasm felt like. Her fingers toyed with the swelling lips of her vulva, pulling and kneading the soft cushions of flesh rising either side of her wetting sex crack. She parted her legs wide and ran her finger up and down the hot valley of her vagina. She was surprised by the hardness of her clitoris, the wetness of her opening vaginal entrance. Her vaginal muscles tightening, her juices of desire flowing, her clitoris calling for her intimate attention . . . Whether it was the effect of the alcohol or the thought of going out with Gary, she had no idea. But she felt sexually alive for the first time in years.

Her sensitive clitoris responded to her intimate caress and she breathed heavily, arching her back as the sensations permeated her young womb. Maybe her life was about to change, she mused dreamily as she reached beneath her thigh and slipped two fingers into the wet sheath of her tight vagina. Meeting up with Paula had opened her eyes to the world outside. Working from home and rarely going out, she'd become insular in her thinking. All work and no play, she reflected. All work and no money. No sex.

Her clitoris pulsated and her rhythmically contracting vagina gripped her thrusting fingers. Her orgasm came quickly and shook her young body to the core. Whimpering and writhing in ecstasy as her climax peaked, Mandy knew instinctively that her life was about to change. Chatting to Paula, meeting Gary . . . Her eyes had been opened, not only to the world outside but to her femininity.

'Yes,' she breathed as her naked body shook uncontrollably in the aftermath of her self-loving. Realising how much she missed sex, she slipped her wet fingers out of her sated vagina and pulled the quilt over her trembling body. She recalled her early days of masturbation as she licked her pussy-wet fingers and tasted her orgasmic juices. She used to spend her nights masturbating in her bed, fingering her tight sex sheath and savouring the aphrodisiacal taste of her hot cream. At least she'd rediscovered the pleasure of masturbation, she reflected dreamily as sleep engulfed her.

Mandy woke at nine with a start. She'd been dreaming about Gary, his hard cock slipping deep into her tight vagina, his throbbing knob splattering her ripe cervix with sperm. Sitting up in her bed, she looked about her and smiled. Maybe Gary would be fucking her before long, she thought with a rising sense of wickedness. Her inner thighs sticky with her dried sex milk, she slipped out of bed and recalled her amazing orgasm. Feeling as if her feminine desires had woken after two years of sleep, she ran a fingertip up and down her opening vaginal slit and smiled. Her clitoris was swollen, again calling for her intimate attention, and she knew that her nights of masturbation had returned with a vengeance.

After a shower, Mandy dressed in a miniskirt and loose-fitting blouse and checked her emails. The landscape gardener had written again. He'd sent payment in full and was obviously keen to get his web site up and running. Mandy poured herself a cup of coffee and munched on toast and marmalade as she got down to work. Although the money wasn't good, she felt invigorated. Maybe her orgasm had sparked her enthusiasm. Whatever it was, she worked solidly for several hours and finally sat back to admire her creation.

The landscape gardener was delighted and couldn't praise Mandy enough, which boosted her confidence no end. When a plumber emailed her that afternoon asking for a quote for a web-site design, she stuck to her price. Maybe things were changing for the better, she thought when the man accepted her price and sent the money up front. All work and no play was fine, as long as the money rolled in. But she had to make time for Gary. Gazing at his card, she grabbed the phone and punched in his number.

'I didn't think you'd ring me,' he said in surprise. 'I mean, I'm glad you did. But I thought . . .'

'I know what you mean,' she cut, in with a laugh. 'How about meeting in the wine bar this evening?'

'Oh, er . . . Right, yes.'

'Seven o'clock?'

'Yes, great. I really didn't think . . . I mean, an attractive girl like you . . .'

'There's no need for flattery, Gary. I've said that I'll meet you, so there's no need to sweet-talk me.'

'No, no, I wasn't. This has come as a bit of a surprise, that's all. So, tell me about yourself.'

'Later, we'll talk later. I'll see you at seven.'

'Yes, right. OK, I'll look forward to it.'

Heart racing, Mandy replaced the receiver and punched the air with her fist. 'Yes!' she shouted. Things really were beginning to look up, and it was all due to Paula. Had it not been for Paula, she'd never have gone to the wine bar. Had it not been for Paula, she'd never have met Gary or masturbated or . . . Wondering what to wear, she dashed up the stairs to her bedroom and flung her wardrobe doors open. Not too tarty, she told herself, eyeing her miniskirts. There again, not too conservative. Finally deciding on a knee-length skirt and blouse, she spent several hours getting ready. This was going to be a good evening, apart from one problem. She had no money. She didn't like the idea of having to rely on Gary to buy her drinks, but she had no choice.

Arriving at seven-fifteen, she noticed Gary standing at the bar. Dressed casually in jeans and an open-neck white shirt and with his dark hair swept back, he looked good. But Mandy felt self-conscious, and wondered whether she looked all right herself. She wasn't used to socialising, and she knew that this was going to be awkward. Already having second thoughts, she bit her lip and began to panic. It had been so long since she'd been chatted up and asked out that she had no confidence in herself. Just act normally, she reminded herself as she walked up to the bar and stood beside Gary. Just be yourself.

'Hi, Mandy.' he said, his face beaming. 'Drink?'

'Vodka and tonic, please,' she replied, perching her rounded buttocks on a stool.

'Wow, you look great.'

'Thanks.'

'I didn't think you'd turn up.'

'You didn't think I'd ring you, and then you didn't think I'd turn up. Have you no confidence?'

'No, yes ...' he stammered. 'It's just that, an attractive young girl like you ...'

'Let's not go there again,' she said, giggling as he ordered her drink. 'I did phone, and I did turn up.'

'Ice?' the barman asked her.

'Please.'

'So,' Gary breathed, looking Mandy up and down. 'Here we are.'

'You're not shy, are you?' Mandy asked him.

'Well, yes, I suppose I am.'

'Good, that makes two of us. My heart has been banging and my stomach churning all day. It's silly, isn't it?'

'Not at all. To be honest, I've felt the same. Every time the phone rang, I thought it might be you. So, here we are.'

'Let's sit at a table,' Mandy suggested, slipping off her stool and taking her drink from the bar. 'We don't want to bore the barman by saying, "So, here we are" all evening.'

Feeling more confident as she followed Gary to a secluded corner table, Mandy thought it odd that he was so shy. He was very good-looking, and she'd imagined he'd have several girlfriends on the go. Perhaps he's a virgin, she giggled inwardly as she sat opposite him at the table. But he must have had sex at *some* time in his life, she thought. Maybe he was playing at being shy? Maybe he was a married man and . . .

'Do you come here often?' he asked her. 'Sorry, that sounds stupid. It's like saying, what's a nice girl like you doing in a place like this.'

'I'll bet you say that to all the girls,' she quipped. 'Seriously, this is only the second time I've been here. I work from home and don't have a great deal of time for socialising.'

'No men friends, then?'

'Not for a couple of years. How about you?'

'I was in a long-term relationship, but . . . That was ages ago.'

Mandy enjoyed Gary's company and decided to see him again. Nothing heavy, she thought, downing her fourth vodka. It would be nice to have him as a friend, someone to meet up with and chat to a couple of times each week and . . . and have sex? Recalling Paula's various comments about men, she wondered whether Gary had money. She also wondered whether to keep him hanging around and use him for sex. Her clitoris stirring, emerging from beneath its fleshy hood between her swelling vaginal lips, she imagined Gary making love with her. Was that what she wanted? she wondered as he glanced at his watch.

'Are you worried about the time?' she asked him.

'No, no,' he replied, smiling at her. 'Well, I do have an early start in the morning.'

'Do you want to go?'

'Not yet.'

'I thought you might ask me back to your place for coffee. That's the usual line, isn't it?'

'Yes, I suppose it is,' he said, chuckling as he again checked his watch. 'But I live with my mother, so . . . well, it's not easy.'

'You could come back to my flat. It's not exactly a mansion, but I do have a kettle and some coffee.'

'Well, I . . . Is it far?'

'Not really. You don't have to, Gary. If you want to get home to your mum, that's OK.'

'Let's have coffee at your place,' he said, finishing his drink. 'There's no hurry.'

Leaving the bar, Mandy wondered why he hadn't been very keen to go back to her place. It seemed odd that he'd wanted to get home to his mother, and she began to think that he might be married. The last thing she'd wanted was to become a married man's mistress, but she reckoned that it might have its advantages. No strings, no ties . . . Gary didn't say much as they walked along the street, which Mandy thought odd. Maybe he did live with his mother, she reflected, opening the door to her flat. Not all men were adulterous bastards, were they?

Filling the kettle as Gary looked up at the kitchen clock, she thought that he was either incredibly shy or didn't fancy her. She'd made all the moves. She'd done most of the talking, and it had been her idea to go back for coffee. Shuffling his feet and saying nothing, he seemed nervous. Was his wife waiting for him? she wondered, taking the cups into the lounge and indicating for him to sit on the sofa. She thought

17

about asking him whether he was married as he sat down. If she was going to see him again, she wanted to know where she stood.

'This is a nice place,' he said, obviously trying to strike up a conversation.

'It's dreadful,' she said, placing the cups on the coffee table and standing in front of him. 'It's too small and I hate the area. Anyway, I'm hoping to move soon.'

'Really?'

'I want a house, not a flat.' Pushing her hips forward, she wondered whether he'd make a move as he gazed at her naked thighs. 'Where do you live?' she asked him. 'Locally, I suppose?'

'Not far.'

'Where is "not far"?'

'A few streets away. Cannon Road.'

'Yes, I know it. They're nice houses, quite big.'

'It's OK.'

Sitting in the armchair opposite him, Mandy reckoned that Gary wasn't interested in her. This was the first man she'd been out with in two years and he wasn't interested. She'd never come on strong to a man, never made any sexual advances, but she felt that she had to catch up with Paula. The alcohol relaxed her, stripping her of her inhibitions, and she parted her thighs just enough to display the triangular patch of her tight panties hugging her swelling sex lips. She knew that Paula would question her about her evening with Gary and she didn't want to have to lie. She wanted to say that Gary had taken her in his arms and made love to her, but . . .

'Mandy,' Gary began, glancing at the wall clock.

'Don't tell me,' she sighed. 'You have to get back to your mother?'

'Yes. I mean, no . . .'

Watching as he left the sofa and knelt in front of her, she wasn't sure what to do as he parted her knees and gazed longingly at her tight panties. This was all rather quick, she thought, wondering whether she'd gone too far with her panty-flashing. Pulling her short skirt up and pressing his face into the damp material of her panties, he breathed in her girl-scent. It was strange that he'd had a sudden change of mind, she thought, as he sucked her outer lips through the white cotton crotch of her panties. And it was strange to think that she was allowing him to do this even though she'd only just met him.

Her clitoris swelling, her juices of desire flowing, Mandy closed her eyes and parted her legs wide. It had been so long since a man had attended her feminine needs. Gary wasn't so shy after all, she thought happily, as he kissed and licked the creamy-smooth flesh of her inner thighs. Pulling her panties aside and licking the puffy lips of her vulva, he slipped his wet tongue into her sex valley and tasted her lubricious pussy milk. Mandy writhed in the armchair, her breathing fast and shallow as his tongue repeatedly swept over the sensitive tip of her erect clitoris.

She hadn't realised how much she'd missed sex, until now. After two years of celibacy, she was desperate to feel the hardness of a cock stretching her neglected vaginal sheath open, the smoothness of a swollen knob pressing against her ripe cervix. Was Gary's cock hard and ready for her pussy? Were his balls full and ready to be drained?

'I'm coming,' Mandy breathed shakily as her clitoris swelled and pulsated beneath his snaking tongue. Her vaginal muscles tightening, her womb rhythmically contracting, she let out a rush of breath as her orgasm erupted and shook her young body to the core. Gary thrust two fingers into her sex-wet vaginal duct and massaged her creamy inner flesh, adding to her incredible pleasure as he sucked on her pulsating clitoris. If Paula could see her now, she thought, digging her fingernails into the arms of the chair as she cried out. There'd be no need to lie to her.

Oblivious to her surroundings as her climax gripped her, she imagined Gary's solid cock driving deep into her sex-hungry pussy, his knob battering her cervix as he pumped out his creamy spunk. He slipped his fingers out of her sated vagina. Teasing the last ripples of orgasm from her solid clitoris with his sweeping tongue, he pressed his mouth to her gaping vaginal entrance and sucked out her orgasmic cream. This was sheer heaven, Mandy thought as she quivered and writhed in the armchair. She'd definitely be seeing Gary again.

She opened her eyes and frowned as he covered her swollen pussy lips with her panties. She gazed at his solid cock which he held in his hand. To her surprise, he began wanking the huge organ. Wasn't he going to drive his fleshy shaft deep into her tight vagina?

He gasped suddenly and his spunk jetted out, raining over the wet crotch of her panties. Rubbing his purple knob against the cotton material, he tried to sustain his orgasm.

Reckoning that he'd not had sex for so long that he couldn't hold back, she watched his orgasmic liquid soak into her panties. She'd wanted him inside her, but there'd be other evenings, she thought, as he drained his balls and finally sat back on his heels.

'That was quick,' she said, smiling at him.

'That was amazing,' he breathed, gazing at her sperm-splashed panties.

'It was messy,' she returned with a giggle. 'I was hoping that you'd—'

'I have a thing about spunking on panties,' he cut in. 'Will you do something for me?'

'Well, that depends on—.'

'Don't take them off. Leave your panties on until I see you again.'

'Well, I . . . When will I be seeing you? I'm not going to wear dirty panties for two weeks.'

'Tomorrow evening, if that's OK?' he said, standing and zipping his trousers. 'I'll come round here.'

'I'm not sure whether . . .'

'Ring me tomorrow. You have my office number.'

'What's your home number?'

'I don't have a phone at home. I mean, there is one but . . . It's my mother's phone.'

Leaving the armchair and pulling her skirt down to conceal her sperm-soaked panties, Mandy was now sure that he was married. She also reckoned that his request for her to keep her panties on was rather odd. But she'd enjoyed her orgasm and was looking forward to their next meeting. Watching Gary gulp down his coffee and check his watch again, she decided that she wasn't bothered about his marital status. She'd enjoyed her evening with him and, if he had a wife waiting at home, that was his problem. Determined to be more like Paula, she led him to the front door and grinned.

'Bring a bottle of vodka with you,' she said, opening the door.

'Yes, yes, I will,' he breathed, kissing her cheek. 'Ring me tomorrow, OK?'

'Yes, I will. Thanks for a lovely evening.'

'Thank you, Mandy. I'd better go.'

Closing the door, Mandy shook her head and sighed. The first man she'd been out with in two years had wanked and spunked on her panties, and wanted her to keep them on until the following evening.

Returning to the lounge and sipping her cup of cold coffee, she wondered what other peculiar fetishes Gary had. Although the evening hadn't been at all as she'd expected, she'd enjoyed an amazing orgasm and had watched a man wank and spunk over her panties. It had been different, she mused. And most pleasurable.

Two

The following morning, after she'd had a shower, Mandy gazed at the sperm-starched panties on the floor in the corner of her bedroom. She'd wear them for Gary that evening, she decided, taking a clean pair from her dressing-table drawer. Fetish or not, there were limits to what she'd do for him. There was no way she was going to wear dirty panties all day just to please a man. Besides, he wouldn't know that she hadn't worn them.

Dressed in a miniskirt and T-shirt, she went downstairs and checked her emails. To her amazement, two more potential customers had contacted her asking for quotes. Again sticking to her price, she replied and hoped for the best. The landscape gardener had been happy, and now it was time to get to work on the plumber's web site. Settling at her desk with a cup of coffee, she hoped that her business was going to take off at long last. Having spent two years promoting her work, she thought that it would be nice to start earning some decent money.

Two years without sex, she mused, recalling Gary sucking on her erect clitoris and bringing her to a massive orgasm. But she still hadn't had full-blown sex. When Gary turned up that evening, she'd make sure that he pumped his spunk into her tight pussy rather than all over her panties. A fuck at last, she thought happily, grabbing the phone as it began to ring.

'Hi,' Paula said. 'How are you?'

'Hi, Paula. I'm fine. It's nice to hear from you.'

'How did you get on with that dishy man last night?'

'Oh, the usual,' Mandy replied with a giggle. 'A few drinks and then an evening of sex.'

'Lucky you,' Paula sighed.

'What did you do last night?'

'I . . . I stayed in, for a change. Several men rang me, but I felt like an evening at home. I thought we might go out this evening for a drink?'

'Oh, er . . . I'm seeing Gary again this evening. Maybe we can meet up tomorrow evening?'

'Oh, all right. What about meeting for lunch? I'm free between one and two today, so . . .'

'I can't today, Paula. I've got a lot of work to do on a customer's web site. He's paid up front, so I'd better get it done today.'

'You *are* keeping busy. OK, I've just had an idea. How about a foursome this evening? We could all meet in the wine bar. You and Gary, and . . .'

'He's coming here for the evening. Sorry, Paula.'

'That's OK. Ring me when you're free.'

'I will, I promise.'

'Oh well, enjoy your evening.'

'I will, thanks.'

'Don't wear out that sweet little cunt of yours, will you?'

'Er . . . no, no, I won't.'

Mandy frowned as Paula hung up. She'd sensed jealousy in her voice. Or had it been annoyance? Mandy couldn't neglect her work or change her plans for the evening just to meet up with Paula. Besides, the girl had said that she had several men on the go so she shouldn't be short of company. Perhaps she wanted to chase after Gary? *Don't wear out that sweet little cunt of yours* . . . Paula's crude words played on her mind, Yes, she *was* jealous. Although, with several men phoning her friend and wanting to take her out, Mandy couldn't understand why.

Beginning work on the plumber's web site, Mandy reckoned that Paula was lonely. It was all very well having a string of men on the go, but that was no substitute for a decent relationship. Wondering whether she'd be better off in a long-term relationship herself, Mandy again considered Gary's marital status. In a way, she hoped that he *was* married. It would be fun to be the other woman for a change, she thought wickedly. Her previous boyfriends had screwed around behind her back, so it would make a nice change to be a married man's bit on the side.

Working on the computer and imagining Gary's rock-hard penis slipping into her tight vagina, Mandy felt her young womb contract. His wife would be waiting at home while he drove his cock deep into Mandy's wet pussy and flooded her sex sheath with his spunk. He might go home and fuck his wife but the woman would have no idea that he'd fucked and spunked in another girl. She forgot about the web-site design, slipped her hand up her short skirt and felt the wetness of her tight panties.

'God,' she breathed as the doorbell rang. Dashing through the hall, she checked her hair in the mirror. Her face flushed, her hands trembling, she realised that she was sexually aroused as never before and she'd only been *thinking* about Gary. She took a deep breath as the bell rang again. She'd only been thinking about his solid cock driving deep into her tight pussy and . . . 'God,' Mandy murmured again as her clitoris emerged from beneath its pinken hood and called for her intimate attention.

'John,' she murmured, opening the door and facing her ex-boyfriend. 'What are you doing here?'

'I was just passing,' he replied, smiling at her. 'I thought you might ask me in for a coffee.'

'Well, I . . . I suppose so. How did you get my address?'

'I asked around. It's been a long time, Mandy,' he said as she led him into the kitchen. 'How are you?'

'I'm fine. I must say that I'm surprised to see you here after what happened.'

'Water under the bridge,' he said with a chuckle.

'Are you still with her? The slut, I mean.'

'Carol? No, no, we split up ages ago. It's really good to see you, Mandy. I . . . I was wondering whether you'd like to go out for a drink one evening?'

'No, John,' she returned firmly. 'After the way you treated me, I do *not* want to go out for a drink with you.'

'Are you seeing anyone?'

'Yes, I am.'

'Oh, right. It's a shame the way things turned out. We were good together, Mandy.'

'Yes, we were. Until you started screwing that slut behind my back.'

'OK, so I made a mistake.'

'On reflection, I don't think we *were* any good together. I've had several proper men in my life since we split up, since you cheated on me, and I now realise how good sex can be.'

'Oh, thanks. That's nice, I must say.'

'It's true, John. With you, it was over in minutes and I was left wondering what it was all about.'

'You used to come.'

'I faked my orgasms, John. Anyway, I don't want to talk about the past. Do you want a cup of coffee?'

'Er . . . no, no, thanks. I was hoping that . . . that we'd at least be friends.'

'We can be friendly, if that's what you want.'

'Actually, I wasn't just passing. I've moved into a flat down the road.'

'Really? You always said that this was a scum area. After we'd split up and I bought this place, I remembered you saying that this was a scum area.'

'Yes, well . . . it's not that bad.'

'So, do you have a girlfriend? Who are you attempting to satisfy at the moment?'

'Mandy, you weren't that good in bed. You say that you've had several proper men. Well, I've had several proper women. Women who enjoy giving blow-jobs.'

'I never did that with you because—'

'You wouldn't even try it, Mandy. You were such a prude.'

'I love cocksucking,' she lied. 'One of my men calls me his blow-job queen, so I must be pretty good.'

'One of your men? How many have you got?'

'Enough to keep me happy.'

'A blow-job queen? I don't believe a word of it.'

'I have work to do, John. I've been civil to you, I've offered you coffee, and now I have to get on with my work.'

'I know you too well, Mandy. You *don't* have a string of men, do you?'

'Yes, I do. I don't care whether you believe me or not.'

'I was hoping that we could start again, start afresh.'

'After what you did, you want me to . . .'

'I'm still in love with you, Mandy. I haven't stopped thinking about you since . . . since we parted.'

27

'You don't know what love is, John. All you ever wanted was sex, and now you say that I was no good in bed and you expect me to . . .'

'I *do* know what love is, Mandy. I'm in love with *you*.'

Kneeling in front of him, Mandy tugged John's zip down and hauled out his flaccid penis. I'll bloody show him, she giggled inwardly, trying to bring herself to take his cock into her wet mouth. Wanking his shaft, she felt his cock stiffen in her hand as he gasped. This was completely out of character, but she felt that she had to prove something to John. Perhaps she was trying to prove something to herself, she mused as she slipped the tip of her wet tongue into the small opening of his fleshy foreskin and tasted his salty knob. This was the first cock she'd taken into her mouth, she reflected dreamily as she probed his sperm-slit with the tip of her tongue. She was twenty-two years old, and this was her first blow job. But, since meeting Paula, she'd changed. She wanted to live as well as work, and this was a good start.

Perceiving that she could build up John's hopes and then dump him as he'd dumped her, she made her plans as she retracted his fleshy foreskin and sucked his purple knob into her hot mouth. Savouring the salty taste of his swollen knob, she realised that she still had feelings for John. But this was a means to an end, she reflected. He needed to be taught a lesson. She'd arrange to see him, have a drink with him, suck his knob and have sex with him and talk about getting back together – and then dump him. For the way he'd treated her, destroyed her life, she'd destroy him.

John gasped as he gazed down at Mandy's full lips enveloping his solid cock. Obviously unable to believe what she was doing, he stammered something unintelligible as his penis twitched and his knob swelled within her gobbling mouth. Mandy was also unable to believe what she was doing as she ran her tongue over the velveteen surface of his bulbous glans. She was behaving like a common slut, but loving every minute of it. She'd suck Gary's cock that evening, she decided. He was a young man, and should be able to pump his spunk into her mouth as well as her cock-hungry vagina. The evening was going to be very interesting.

Sucking on John's ripe knob and wanking his solid shaft, she pulled his trousers down to his knees and cupped his heavy balls in her free hand. He clutched her head, gasping and trembling as Mandy expertly worked on his rock-hard penis. She *would* become a blow-job queen, she thought happily, as she took his knob to the back of her throat and sank her teeth gently into his veined shaft. She'd allow Gary to fuck her pretty mouth and spunk down her throat. To keep up with Paula and her sexual antics, she'd become a blow-job expert. A cumslut?

John was going to fill her mouth with his creamy spunk, she thought as she ran her tongue around the rim of his bulbous knob. He'd praise her, tell her that he loved her, ask whether he could see her again . . . She'd agree and suggest that he call round for a meal one evening. She'd take him to her bed and show him that she was far from prudish. Then, after a few weeks, she'd dump him.

'God, I'm coming,' he breathed, rocking his hips and fucking her pretty mouth. 'Mandy, I'm . . . I'm coming.'

'Mmm,' she moaned through her nose, waiting for her first-ever taste of spunk.

'God, you're good. I'm coming . . . Now, now.'

He held her head tight as she swallowed hard, drinking the spunk from his orgasming cock. Savouring his male cream, she wondered why she'd never sucked his cock before. She had been a prude, he was right. But she hadn't deserved to be tossed aside like a broken toy. She'd loved John and had hoped they'd marry one day. But he'd deserted her for a filthy slut. The tables had turned, at long last.

'You *are* a blow-job queen,' John gasped as she sucked the remnants of his spunk from his deflating cock. 'God, that was amazing.'

'I love the taste of spunk,' Mandy said, rising to her feet and smiling at him. 'I can't get enough of it.'

'Mandy,' he began, tugging his trousers up. 'Is there any chance that we might get back together?'

'Yes, I think there is,' she breathed softly, her dark eyes sparkling lustfully.

'I've really missed you. Now that I'm living a few doors away, perhaps we could—'

'Give me time, John,' she cut in. 'I think we're going to be good together, but give me time.'

'So, do you have someone else?'

'No, I don't.'

'I thought not. Things will be great, I promise you. How about going to bed now?'

'Not now, John. I lead a busy life and I have things to do.'

'Shall I come round this evening?' he persisted. 'We could go out for a drink and then go to bed and—'

'I'm seeing an old school friend this evening,' she said, interrupting him. 'I'll see you tomorrow night, if I'm free.'

'Here's my phone number.' Taking a pen from his pocket, John wrote the number on the back of an envelope. 'Ring me any time. If you want to come round, I'm at number twenty-two.'

'OK,' she said. The taste of sperm lingered on her tongue and she felt her clitoris swell. 'I have things to do now so . . . I'll ring you.'

'Great. It's good to be back together, Mandy. I really have missed you.'

'And I've missed you,' she lied, leading him through the hall to the front door. 'I'll ring you, OK?'

'OK. Bye.'

Realising that things had changed so much since she'd bumped into Paula, Mandy smiled as she closed the front door and went into the lounge. Never had she dreamed that she'd be licked to orgasm by a man she'd met in a bar, and then suck John's cock and drink his spunk. She was beginning to live. She slipped her wet panties off and settled on the sofa with her thighs parted. Spreading her swollen outer lips and slipping a finger into her tight hole, she gasped when she felt how wet she was. The taste of sperm still lingering on her tongue, she closed her eyes and pictured John's cock pumping spunk into her thirsty mouth as she massaged her inner flesh.

Two men in two days, she thought dreamily, as she slipped a second finger into her tightening sex sheath. Two men, and yet she hadn't felt a cock inside her yearning vagina for two years. Opening her eyes as she had an idea, she grabbed a banana from the fruit bowl on the table beside the sofa. She peeled back the skin and, feeling wicked, she slipped the end of the fruit between the fleshy lips of her pussy. A substitute cock, she thought as the fruity phallus drove deep into the wet heat of her contracting vagina. Gasping as her clitoris swelled and her muscles tightened, she closed her eyes and pictured John's solid cock stretching her tight pussy to capacity.

Working the banana in and out of her contracting vagina, Mandy listened to the squelching sounds of

31

her pussy juices as she trembled uncontrollably on the sofa. Wondering why she'd neglected her feminine needs for so long, she lifted her left foot and dangled her leg over the arm of the sofa. Her outer lips opened wide and the banana induced her juices to flow in torrents. She let out whimpers of sexual pleasure as the fruit massaged the sensitive tip of her eager clitoris. Her young body alive with ripples of sex, her breathing fast and shallow, her heart banging hard against her chest, she cried out as her orgasm erupted and her vagina crushed the thrusting banana.

Her nostrils flaring, she repeatedly rammed the hot banana deep into her vagina until she'd mashed the fruit to a pulp. Massaging her pulsating clitoris and driving two fingers into her fruity vagina, she couldn't believe the strength and duration of her massive orgasm. There must have been more to her sexual awakening than talking to Paula, she reflected as her young body shook violently. Gary had licked her to orgasm and she'd sucked the spunk from John's throbbing knob, but now she felt that she'd become a nymphomaniac. Why the massive and sudden change?

Her fingers massaged the last ripples of sex from her deflating clitoris as she scooped out the hot pulped banana from her sex duct and tasted the blend of fruit and her pussy milk. Sucking her fingers clean and swallowing the creamy cocktail, she finally lay quivering on the sofa in the aftermath of her incredible self-loving. What had changed her? she mused dreamily. She felt like a teenage girl who had just discovered the delights of her young body. But why?

Mandy hauled herself off the sofa, climbed the stairs to her bedroom, grabbed the sperm-starched panties from the floor and slipped them on. The crotch immediately soaked up her flowing cream and she knew that Gary would be pleased with her. She felt dirty, like a common whore, as she went downstairs and sat at her computer. Her panties were hot and sticky, the outer lips of her vagina glued to the wet material as she worked on the plumber's web site. She'd tell Gary that she hadn't taken her panties off all day. She'd tell him that she'd slept in them and creamed them for him. Although the notion excited her and her clitoris once more called for her intimate caress, she managed to finish the web site by six o'clock.

After a light meal, Mandy was ready for Gary. Her panties soaked with a cocktail of creamed banana and milky girl-juice, she was looking forward to an evening with her new man. With another woman's man? Repeatedly checking the time as she paced the lounge floor, she was also looking forward to her first session of full-blown sex in two years. But, when seven o'clock came and went, she began to feel despondent. By eight, she reckoned that Gary wasn't going to turn up. Wondering whether to phone John and invite him round, she breathed a sigh of relief as the doorbell rang.

'Sorry,' Gary said, stepping into the hall and passing Mandy a bottle of vodka. 'I couldn't get away from work.'

'I was about to go out,' Mandy sighed. 'I didn't think you were going to turn up. Do you often have to work late?'

'No, no. It's just that we have a big project on at the moment.'

'I've got a lot of work on at the moment, too,' she said, leading him into the kitchen and pouring two glasses of vodka and tonic. 'Oh, I take it that you want vodka?'

'Yes, yes that's fine. I can't stay for long, I'm afraid.'

'Does your wife think you're at work?'

'Yes, she . . . er . . . I mean . . .'

'I'm not stupid, Gary,' Mandy cut in with a giggle. 'All that rubbish about living with your mother and you can't use her phone . . .'

'I shouldn't have lied to you, Mandy. It's just that you're such a beautiful girl and . . . I'm sorry.'

'Don't apologise, Gary. I suppose I knew all along that you were married.'

'You don't mind?' he asked her hopefully. 'That I'm married, I mean.'

'It wouldn't get me anywhere if I did mind, would it? To be honest, I don't want any ties. As long as we both know where we stand, that's fine.'

'Oh, right. Well, that's a relief.'

'Tell me about your wife. What's she like?'

'She's a prude.'

'I used to be a prude,' Mandy said, giggling as she sipped her drink.

'I can't believe that. Are you still wearing the panties?'

'I am. And I haven't taken them off once.'

'That's good. Shall we go into the lounge?'

As she followed Gary through the hall, Mandy felt genuinely relieved to discover that he was married. She had John hanging around, and was beginning to hope that she'd meet other men. She didn't want to be tied down to anyone in particular. Again wanting to be more like Paula, she was sure that her web-design business would soon pick up and she'd be able to afford to get out more. If she could buy a car and . . . But right now she had Gary to entertain.

'What is it about dirty panties that turns you on?' she asked him as she sat in the armchair.

34

Settling on the sofa, he grinned. 'Everything,' he said, chuckling. 'The smell, the feel of the wet material . . . The idea of you wearing them all night and all day turns me on. They must be really wet and beautifully scented by now.'

'Yes, I think they are,' Mandy breathed. 'Tell me what you really like doing.'

'Wanking into the material. I love spunking over your panties, but you must be wearing them at the time.'

'Don't you want sex with me?'

'Well, no. I mean, I'll lick your pussy and everything. But when I come, it must be over your panties.'

'Is that what you do to your wife's panties?'

'God, no. She wouldn't understand.'

'And, I do?'

'Yes, I think so. You're so easy to talk to, Mandy. By the way, I'm not really shy. I was hesitant yesterday because . . . well, I'm married and I didn't think you'd understand.'

'I'd guessed that you were married, Gary.' Mandy felt in control as the other woman, and decided to use Gary for sex. 'So, where shall we start?' she asked him impishly, cocking her head to one side. 'Perhaps you should begin by examining my dirty panties.'

He leapt off the sofa, knelt between her parted feet, yanked her short skirt up and gazed longingly at her soaked panties. Mandy's arousal soared as she looked down at her dirty panties and imagined Gary sucking on the sodden material. She was learning about sex, she mused as he pressed his face into the bulging crotch and breathed in her girl scent. Not just sex, but real sex, dirty sex.

'If your wife could see you now,' she said, giggling as he licked the wet crotch of her tight panties. 'She'd think you're a dirty little boy.'

'She'd think more than that,' Gary breathed.

'She might spank you for being a naughty boy.'

'She'd kill me, more than likely.'

Closing her eyes as Gary moved her wet panties aside and ran his tongue up and down the length of her cream-dripping girl slit, Mandy imagined her ex-boyfriends sneaking off with other girls and screwing them behind her back. Now that she was the other woman, a married man's bit on the side, she couldn't get hurt, she thought happily. Where there was no love, there could be no pain. She'd been in love before, she thought as Gary drove two fingers deep into her contracting vagina. She'd loved and made plans for the future and . . . and been betrayed. She'd enjoy friendship and real sex with Gary, she decided. Cold sex, without the pain of love.

'Fuck me, Gary,' she breathed, shocked by her crude words.

'No, I want to spunk over your panties,' he replied through a mouthful of vaginal flesh.

'Put your cock in my cunt and fuck me,' she ordered him. 'Do it, or I'll talk to your wife.'

Gary frowned, obviously wondering whether she was serious as he hauled out his erect penis and retracted his fleshy foreskin. Obviously deciding not to take any risks, he slipped his swollen knob between the sex-dripping petals of her inner lips. Mandy gasped as his ripe plum entered the tight sheath of her neglected vagina. The first time in two years, she thought excitedly as his cock shaft stretched her wet duct open to capacity. His swollen glans finally pressed hard against her ripe cervix and she gazed down at her outer lips stretched tautly around the root of his solid organ. She smiled.

As Gary rocked his hips, repeatedly driving his purple globe deep into Mandy's trembling body, she dug her fingernails into the arms of the chair and arched her back. The squelching sounds of sex resounded around the room as she breathed heavily and swivelled her hips to meet the thrusts of his penis. Her vaginal muscles tightening, gripping his cock as if never wanting to let it go, she whimpered in her sexual delirium as she enjoyed her first cock in two years.

She'd missed this, Mandy reflected as Gary pulled her wet panties further aside and increased his fucking rhythm. His swinging balls battering the rounded cheeks of her bottom, her inner lips rolling back and forth along his veined shaft, she vowed to never again neglect her feminine needs. She'd make up for two lost years, she decided, her young body jolting with the adulterous fucking. She'd fuck Gary and John and drink their spunk and . . . and live the way Paula lived. She'd embark on an exciting life of sex with different men, she thought as her young body rocked with the illicit fucking.

Thinking that she could now compare John with another man, she imagined him driving his solid cock deep into her tight sex sheath and spunking against her cervix. Two men on the go, she reflected, as Gary gasped and his eyes rolled. Two men, two hard cocks . . . Her arousal soaring, Mandy opened her blouse and exposed the firm mounds of her pert breasts, her elongated nipples. Gary leant forward, sucking her milk teat into his wet mouth as he increased his fucking rhythm. How interesting it would be if John happened to walk in and witness her crude act, she thought wickedly.

As Gary sucked on each ripe nipple in turn, Mandy opened her legs further and rocked her hips to meet his thrusts. She could feel her inner lips rolling back and forth along his pussy-slimed shaft, her lower stomach rising and falling jerkily as his knob repeatedly battered her cervix. She was ready for his spunk now – her contracting vagina was thirsty for his orgasmic milk.

'I'm coming,' Gary announced, much to Mandy's delight. 'God, I'm coming.'

'Come inside me,' Mandy breathed. 'I want to feel your spunk inside me.'

'No, no,' he gasped. 'Your panties . . . I want to—'

'In my cunt,' she cut in, wrapping her legs around his body. 'Fuck me like you've never fucked before and spunk in my tight cunt.'

Gary tried to pull away, but Mandy gripped him with her legs as his sperm jetted from his throbbing knob and flooded her contracting vaginal canal. Her solid clitoris massaged by the pussy-wet shaft of his thrusting cock as she repeatedly pulled him towards her with her feet, she cried out as her orgasm erupted and rocked her young body to the core. Her clitoris pulsating, pumping its pleasure into her trembling body, the cocktail of her orgasmic juices and his fresh sperm spraying from her bloated vagina and splattering her inner thighs, she let out a cry of pleasure as Gary sank his teeth gently into her erect nipple.

Entwined in lust, lost in her incredible pleasure as she rode the crest of her cock-induced climax, Mandy vowed again never to neglect her inner desires, never to deny her vagina the pleasure of a thrusting cock. She'd use Gary, and John, she mused in her sexual frenzy. She'd use them to satisfy her increasing thirst for crude sex. Once she'd primed John, set him up to believe that he'd be with her for ever, she'd drop him and crush him beneath her foot.

'God,' Gary finally gasped, stilling his deflating cock deep within her sperm-flooded vagina as she dropped her feet to the floor. 'You really are amazing.'

'And you're not so bad,' Mandy breathed shakily. 'You don't know how much I needed to be fucked. If fact, *I* didn't know how much I needed it.'

'The trouble is . . .' Gary began, his knob absorbing the inner heat of her spasming vagina. 'The thing is . . .'

'Go on,' she sighed. 'What is it now?

'I've never committed adultery before.'

'What are you talking about?' she said, frowning at him. 'You committed adultery with me last night.'

'No, no – that wasn't adultery.'

'What the hell was it, then?'

'You see, I only spunk over girls' panties. I've never had sex with another girl. I've never committed adultery.'

'You're weird,' Mandy said, giggling as she imagined him wanking over girls' panties. 'How many girls have allowed you to spunk over their panties since you've been married?'

'Only three. I mean, you're the fourth. I feel bad now that I've actually committed adultery.'

'I feel *good*,' Mandy murmured as he slipped his sperm-dripping penis out of her drenched pussy and stood up. 'I've never felt better, Gary. I want you to fuck me every night from now on. I want you to—'

'I'd better be going, Mandy,' he cut in, his expression pained as he bit his lip.

'Already? Wouldn't you like another drink or . . .'

'No, no. God, I feel as guilty as hell. Bloody hell, I've cheated on my wife.'

'You're mad, Gary,' she said, laughing as he zipped his trousers and concealed his adulterous cock. 'So, would it be all right if your wife allowed another man to spunk over her panties? If that's not adultery, that would be OK?'

'Well, no, not really.'

'Hang on. let me get this right. It's all right for you to wank and spunk over my panties, but if another man did that to your wife that would be adultery?'

'Well . . . oh, I don't know. Mandy, will you leave your panties on again? They will soak up the spunk and—'

'Yes, yes, if that's what turns you on,' she interrupted him, concealing her dripping crack with the wet material. 'Do you have any other peculiar fetishes that I should know about?'

'Yes, there is one. But I'll leave that until we get to know each other a little better.'

'How intriguing. OK, you'd better run back to your little wife and leave me here all alone.'

'I'll see you tomorrow, OK?'

'You want to commit adultery again?'

'Yes, I suppose I do. God, you're so tempting, Mandy. You're beautiful and sexy and dirty and . . . I just want to fuck you all the time.'

'What about your wife? Don't you want to fuck her?'

'Yes, of course. But she's not like you. I mean, she's . . .'

'Not a dirty little slut? Give me your address, Gary. I want to walk past your house and take a look.'

'No, Mandy. It's too risky.'

'Your address, Gary. If you want to see me again, if you want to spunk over my panties and fuck me again, write it down on that pad by the phone. There's a pen next to the pad.'

Scribbling on the pad, Gary turned and frowned at Mandy. He was obviously in two minds as to whether to trust her or not, but he wanted to see her again, and spunk over her panties. Mandy grinned as he moved to the lounge door and mumbled something about a messy divorce if she went to his house. She'd got it made, she mused, following him to the front door. She was the other woman now, the bit on the side, and she loved the notion.

'You won't cause trouble, will you?' he asked her, opening the front door and turning to face her.

'Of course I won't,' she replied, giggling as he frowned at her again. 'You give me what I want, and things will be just fine.'

'I hope so, Mandy.'

'What's your wife's name?'

'Jennifer. Mandy, if you . . .'

'You'd better get back to Jennifer, Gary. Get home before she becomes suspicious.'

'Yes, yes, I will.'

'Will you fuck her tonight?'

'No, I . . . I don't know.'

'If you do fuck her, then think of me. Imagine that you're fucking my tight little cunt as you slip your adulterous cock into her pussy and spunk her. I'll ring you tomorrow, OK?'

'You're a wicked girl.'

'And that's the way you like me?'

'Yes, yes – I do.'

'I get worse,' she said, giggling again. 'I can't wait to discover your other little fetish. And I have one or two of my own that might interest you.'

'You're an angel.'

'A wicked angel. Go to your wife now, Gary. I'll keep my cunt hot and wet for you.'

'Thanks, Mandy. You're great. Bye.'

Mandy was amazed by her crude words as she closed the front door. Walking into the kitchen and pouring herself another vodka and tonic, she raised her glass and smiled. 'To me,' she said, feeling very pleased with herself. With two men on the go, she was catching up with Paula. All she needed now was some money, a car, a house . . . She had a long way to go, she mused, taking her drink into the lounge and settling on the sofa. Wondering what Gary's other fetish was as her wet panties filled with a blend of girl cream and spunk, she sipped her drink and made her plans.

Three

Mandy rang Paula the following morning and suggested that they meet for lunch. Paula was keen to catch up on the latest news and tell Mandy about the new man in her life. He was good-looking, he had money and a fast car and a house in the country . . . Mandy didn't think she'd ever be able to catch up with Paula as the girl rambled on about her latest conquest. She seemed to attract one rich man after another, and Mandy wondered what her secret was. How come she had so many men chasing after her?

Hoping that she could learn from Paula, Mandy worked all morning and then walked into town. Reaching the café, she reckoned that Paula's secret was her looks and her money. She was extremely attractive and a successful businesswoman. She had money, a nice car, she'd travelled the world . . . But, above all, she had charisma. Smiling as Paula arrived, she thought how good her friend looked in her matching skirt and jacket. It was no wonder that men chased after her.

'So, where did you meet this new man of yours?' Mandy asked Paula as they sat at a table outside the café.

'I didn't feel like staying in last night so I went to a bar,' Paula said excitedly. 'I'd only just ordered a drink when he came over and started chatting me up. He is really dishy, Mandy. And I mean *dishy*. We went out for a meal and then I went back to his place in the country and stayed the night.'

'Wow,' Mandy breathed. 'I'll bet you're glad you didn't stay in.'

'I'm a social creature,' the other girl replied, with a giggle. 'I have to be out and about having fun and sex. So, how did *your* evening go?'

'Great. Gary spent the night with me and . . . well, we didn't stop screwing until the sun came up.'

'Sounds good. You must be shattered?'

'Not at all. I'm used to late nights.' As she ordered a ham salad when the waiter arrived, Mandy wished that she really had screwed until the sun had risen.

'I'll have the same, please,' Paula said, gazing at the waiter's tight trousers. 'I'm in a dilemma, Mandy,' she sighed as the waiter left. 'Do I see Josh tonight, that's my new man, or do I see Greg? Greg is one of my other men.'

'See them both,' Mandy said, grinning at Paula.

'Now, that's an idea. I've gone to bed with two men before and it's absolutely amazing. You should try it, Mandy. Two men, two hard cocks, two tongues . . .'

'I have tried it,' Mandy lied.

'Really? Tell me about it.'

'I was shattered in the morning, I can tell you that.'

'I'll bet. So, did they take turns or did you have them both at once?'

'Well, they . . .'

'You haven't had sex until you've had two cocks in your pussy at the same time. The first time I tried it . . . Wow, what an experience. So, did they double-penetrate you?'

'Er . . . yes, yes, they did,' Mandy breathed softly, wondering how far to take the fantasy.

'There's nothing like a double fucking,' the girl whispered. 'The first time I had two cocks was when I'd been to a business thing and these young men . . .'

Mandy began to wonder whether she really wanted to catch up with Paula as the girl rambled on about her illicit double fucking with two men. It was one thing having several men on the go, but to go to bed with two . . . Unable to imagine two cocks forced into the tight sheath of her pussy, Mandy reckoned that Paula was a sex-crazed nymphomaniac. Her mind wandering, she pictured herself naked in her bed with Gary's knob pumping sperm into her gobbling mouth as John flooded her tight pussy with his spunk. It would be an experience, she mused. But not one that she wanted.

'I know what men want,' Paula continued. 'And, more importantly, I know what *I* want. I have a few rules. If a man doesn't make me come, I won't see him again. If a man has no money, I won't bother with him. You have to have rules, Mandy.'

'Oh, I do,' Mandy murmured as the waiter placed two ham salads on the table.

'And, when you find a man who's good in bed, you have to know how to keep him hanging around. As you probably know, most men like shaved pussies.'

'Er . . . yes, I . . .'

'I've been shaving for years. In fact, I started shaving when I was still at school.'

'Yes, me too,' Mandy said softly, trying to imagine her pussy without any hairs veiling her sex crack.

'Actually, I use cream. A razor is too harsh on my skin. I expect you've found the same.'

'Yes, yes, I have. So, it looks like we're both doing well on the men front.'

'We're young, Mandy. Men like young girls, especially older men. I went with a man of sixty-eight a few weeks ago. What's the oldest man you've screwed?'

'Er . . . well, I'm not sure,' Mandy murmured, wondering where Paula's sexually deviant escapades would end. 'One of my men was in his sixties.'

'I'll bet he loved getting his hands on a young girl like you. The guy I went with had a lot of money. He'd take me to a hotel and we'd spend the afternoon fucking and coming and . . .'

Eating her salad as Paula related the sordid details of her time with the old man, Mandy again wondered how far to take her lies. The game of one-upmanship was becoming ridiculous. But it didn't really matter. Reeling off a load of fictitious stories about her non-existent sexual escapades was perfectly harmless. And, in a way, it was fun. She could dream up as many stories as she liked about her past, and Paula would never discover the truth.

Paula was still rambling on as Mandy finished her meal. Two men in a bed, screwing a married man in the lounge while his wife was upstairs, sucking on two cocks at once . . . Her amazing tales were never-ending. Mandy didn't think for one minute that the girl was lying, not even when she mentioned a gang bang with three men. She had no reason to lie. With her own business and her Mercedes, it was pretty obvious that she was a successful businesswoman. And a successful man-eater.

'I'd better get back,' Paula said, finally finishing her salad and checking her watch.

'Yes, and me,' Mandy breathed. 'I have a lot of work on at the moment.'

'We'll have to go out on the pull one night, Mandy. How about tomorrow?'

'Er . . . yes, that should be OK.'

'I'll ring you and we'll sort it out. Right, I'd better go.'

Stacking the plates and tidying the table as Paula left, Mandy realised that the girl hadn't paid for her

46

lunch. Taking her credit card from her handbag, she sighed. Although the money was beginning to come in, she couldn't really afford to pay Paula's bill. Paula had been in a hurry, she reflected as the waiter took her card. She hadn't deliberately left without paying, had she?

Walking home via Cannon Road, Mandy stopped outside Gary's house and looked at the neat garden. The front door was open and there was a car parked in the drive, and she wondered whether Gary was at home. She hid behind a bush as a young woman emerged from the house and opened the car door. Mandy reckoned that it was Jennifer, Gary's wife. If only she knew what her husband got up to behind her back, she mused, eyeing her short skirt and long legs. With long blonde hair and a perfect figure, she was extremely attractive. But she was a prude, Mandy thought, recalling Gary's words.

Walking on, Mandy wondered what it would be like to be married and live in a beautiful house. Jennifer was lucky, she thought. With a good-looking husband bringing in the money, they probably enjoyed holidays abroad and ... But her husband screwed other women on the side. No, that wasn't for Mandy. Wondering whether his wife had any idea of his infidelity, she recalled the devastation she'd endured when she'd discovered that John had cheated on her. There was no way she was going to fall in love again, she decided as she reached her flat.

Two more potential customers had contacted Mandy about web-site design, and she was feeling increasingly positive about her business. Replying to their emails, she stuck to her price and hoped for the best. She was about to switch her computer off and make a cup of coffee when another email arrived. It was from a large company, Gregson Associated Plastics, and they wanted an equally large web site. Mandy read the email several times and realised that this would be a massive job. Go for it, she thought, replying with a rough estimate of several thousand pounds. At the very worst, they could only say no.

Wondering whether to ring Gary and tell him that she'd see him that evening, Mandy imagined John arriving and making up a threesome. Two cocks, she thought, her clitoris stirring, her vaginal juices flowing between the swelling lips of her pussy. As she filled the kettle for coffee, she recalled Paula's remarks about shaving her pussy. Was that what men really liked? It was something she'd never even dreamed of doing, but now she wondered whether she should try it.

She bounded upstairs to the bathroom, slipped her drenched panties off and tugged her short skirt up over her stomach. Her black pubic curls concealed her sex crack and she wondered what Gary would say when he saw her hairless pussy. Would he like it? she wondered as she massaged hair-removing cream into the fleshy lips of her vulva. What would John think? She knew that she was doing this to keep up with Paula and she began to wonder how far she'd go in the game of one-upmanship. Would she allow three men to join her in her bed and triple-fuck her just because Paula had?

Allowing the cream to do its job for fifteen minutes, she realised that Paula had become her role model. The girl seemed to have so much excitement in her life. Rather than stay in for the evening, she'd gone to a bar, met a rich man and spent the night at his country house. Paula had some nice clothes, she thought, wondering whether to spend a little money on a new skirt and top. Not having a social life – or

48

any money – she hadn't bought any clothes for over two years.

'God,' Mandy breathed, washing the cream and curls away from her pussy. Her hairless sex lips swelling, her naked crack opening, she gazed wide-eyed at her exposed vulva. It was too late now, she thought, drying her hairless sex-lips, tugging her panties up her long legs and lowering her skirt. There was no turning back now. What if Gary didn't like it? What if John . . . She left the bathroom, her sex-soaked panties caressing her hairless outer lips, bounded down the stairs and grabbed the ringing phone.

'Hi, it's me,' Paula said. 'When I got back to the office I realised that I'd left you to pay the bill.'

'That's OK,' Mandy replied, with a chuckle. 'I can afford it.'

'No, no, it's not right. Look, I'm leaving the office now. I'll come round with the money.'

'Honestly, Paula, it doesn't matter.'

'Give me your address and I'll be there about four.'

Mandy needed the money, but she didn't want Paula seeing her flat. She'd make up some excuse about the old furniture, she decided, finally giving the girl her address. Replacing the phone, she bit her lip as she looked around the lounge. The carpet was threadbare, the sofa had seen better days, and the curtains looked as though they'd been there for fifty years. What would Paula think? What on earth would she say? There was nothing she could do, she decided as she straightened the sofa cushions. There was no way she could hide the fact that she lived in near-poverty.

As she tidied the kitchen, Mandy wondered whether to close the lounge door and take Paula into the dining room. Her computer and the desk looked all right and the table and chairs weren't too bad. This was the end of the game, she knew as she paced the floor. There'd be no more one-upmanship once Paula had seen the flat. There again, she hadn't claimed that she lived in a penthouse. She'd lied about her sexual encounters, but not about her flat. Answering the door when Paula arrived, she invited the girl in and led her into the dining room.

'Sorry about the state of the place,' she said softly.

'I can see why you want to move,' Paula said, looking around the room.

'Yes, I . . . I've put all my furniture into storage,' Mandy said, having an idea.

'Into storage? Why's that?'

'I'm going to rent the flat out. That's why I've bought all this old furniture.'

'Oh, I see. So, have you found a house?'

'I'm still looking, but there is one I'm very interested in.'

'I must say I was surprised to find that you live in this area. I thought you'd have a posh flat somewhere.'

'No, no. I bought this place purely to rent it out. I'm only living here temporarily. So, where's your house?'

'The small house, the one I live in, is in Church Road.'

'Yes, I know it,' Mandy said, wandering into the kitchen and switching the kettle on.

'It's not much, but it's all I need.'

'What number is it? Only, I had a friend who lived in Church Road.'

'I don't invite people round.'

'Why not?'

'Well, because it's only my base, somewhere to live. I work all hours and I'm abroad a lot so . . . It's just a place to sleep.'

Placing the coffees on the kitchen table, Mandy felt that Paula wasn't telling her everything. She'd talked about a gardener, and a cleaning woman who also did her shopping. So why not invite people round? It wasn't as if she was short of money, so what was the problem?

'I'd love to see your garden,' Mandy persisted. 'It must be really nice with a gardener looking after things.'

'The garden *is* nice,' Paula replied abstractedly. 'Anyway, when am I going to meet Gary?'

'Gary? Well, I don't know. I don't see a great deal of him.'

'We really must go out in a foursome. I'll bring one of my men and . . .'

'I don't have much spare time,' Mandy sighed. 'I might be doing a web site for a large company soon, so I'll have to get my other work out of the way. I suppose we could meet at the wine bar one evening.'

'Does Gary have a friend? I mean, another man he could bring along.'

'I don't know. Why?'

'I thought it might be fun if I went on a blind date. You know, Gary brings a friend along and I . . .'

'I'll have to ask him, Paula. Yes, he has friends, but I don't know whether they'd want to go on a blind date.'

'It would be a laugh. Anyway, it was just a thought. Right, I'd better be going.' Finishing her coffee, Paula left the table. 'Ring me, OK?'

'Yes, I will,' Mandy said, following her to the front door.

'Fix something up with Gary, and let me know.'

Closing the door, Mandy frowned. A blind date? Why on earth would Paula want to go out on a blind date? Realising that Paula hadn't given her the money for her lunch, she shook her head and sighed. Something wasn't right about the girl, but she couldn't put her finger on it. Paula had her own business, a beautiful car, two houses, men chasing after her . . . It didn't make sense. Unless her thirst for new sexual conquests was unquenchable?

Deciding to walk to Paula's house, Mandy grabbed her keys and left the flat. Noticing Paula turn the corner, she frowned as she walked briskly after her. Where was her car? she wondered as she turned the corner. Still, it was a lovely day, so maybe she'd decided to walk. Mandy was intrigued and now she wanted to take a look at the girl's house. She'd seen Gary's house, and now wanted to check out Paula's place. Sure that the girl was hiding something she watched her turn along Church Road and open a front gate.

The house was small but well maintained, with a beautiful front garden, and Mandy couldn't understand why Paula didn't invite people round. She felt guilty for following her friend, but curiosity had got the better of her. Reckoning that the Mercedes was in the garage, she decided that Paula had been honest and really did use the house as a base. Working all hours and travelling abroad, she probably didn't spend much time at home. And she preferred to go out in the evenings, so she probably didn't want to bother with entertaining people at home. Deciding to walk home though the park, Mandy became aware of her wet panties rubbing against the hairless lips of her pussy. Unable to believe that she'd removed her pubic hair, she pondered again on her transformation since meeting Paula.

She sat on a bench in the park, feeling pleased that things were improving. The business was picking up, she had two men on the go . . . But her sexual transformation had been incredible. From a celibate prude to a nymphomaniac – she'd changed beyond belief. Looking up at the sun shining in a clear blue sky, she felt positive about the future. If her estimate for the large web site was accepted, she'd be able to afford some new clothes. If things carried on like this, there was a chance that she'd be able to buy some decent furniture and, possibly, a car.

Recalling her schooldays, Mandy remembered meeting Paula in the park. They'd play about on the swings, explore the woods . . . They'd been carefree days, days of happiness and no money worries. Paula used to say that she was going to be rich, and it seemed that her dream had come true. Mandy had never dreamed, and she thought that might have been her problem. If there are no dreams, they can't come true, she reflected.

'Mandy,' a man said as he approached. 'I haven't seen you since you left home.'

'David,' she said softly, looking up at her parents' next-door neighbour. 'How are you?'

'I'm fine. I was only saying to your dad the other day that I haven't seen you in ages.'

'I suppose I should go and see mum and dad,' she sighed. 'The weeks seem to pass so quickly and I never get time to go and see them.'

'You're looking good,' he said, gazing at her short skirt, her naked thighs. 'Mind if I join you?'

'No, not at all.'

David was in his late forties, and Mandy had always got on well with him. He'd never married, and Mandy's father had said that he was loaded. As David talked about her parents, Mandy's thoughts turned to Paula. If she met David and discovered that he had money, she'd be trying to get off with him. But Paula wasn't going to meet him, and Mandy wondered whether it was a good idea for her to meet Gary. Paula was a man-eater, and would be best kept away from Mandy's male friends.

'You might think this rather forward of me,' David began, gazing into Mandy's dark eyes. 'But . . . would you like to come out for a drink one evening?'

'Well, I . . . I don't know,' Mandy breathed.

'I know I'm old,' he said, chuckling.

'No, no, it's not that.'

'I only mean as a friend, Mandy.'

'Oh, I see.'

'Good God, I didn't mean anything else.'

'Well, I . . .'

'I've always liked you and . . . To be honest, I've always enjoyed your company. When your dad used to invite me round to his barbecues, you were always so friendly and . . . As I said, I enjoy your company.'

'All right,' Mandy said, smiling at him. 'I'd love to go out for a drink with you.'

'That's great. You tell me when you're free, and I'll pick you up.'

'I'm free this evening.'

'Right, well, that's settled.'

Giving him her address, Mandy thought that it would be nice to have David as a friend. Although Paula had talked about screwing older men, that wasn't what Mandy wanted. David was a family friend. Sex wouldn't come into it. Besides, she had Gary and John to use for sex. There was no point in soiling her friendship with David. Wondering where he'd take her that evening, she decided to wear her knee-length skirt and a blouse.

'About seven o'clock?' David asked her.

'Yes, I'll be ready,' Mandy replied. 'Don't mention it to my parents. I mean, they might get the wrong idea.'

'Don't worry, I won't even tell them that I've seen you. I was on my way to the bank, so I can't stay. I'll see you later.'

'I'll look forward to it, David.'

As she watched David walk away, Mandy imagined her parents discovering that she'd been out with him. If they heard that she'd been out for a drink or a meal with their middle-aged neighbour, they'd be bound to come to the wrong conclusion. Recalling the times he'd been round to the family barbecues, she knew that her parents would think him a pervert if they discovered that he was taking her out. He'd watched her grow up, he'd given her birthday presents . . . No one would know of her new friendship, she decided. Not even Paula.

David arrived at seven in a Mercedes, which Mandy thought was a coincidence. It would be great if Paula could see her now, she mused as she settled on the leather seat. A middle-aged man with money and a nice car . . . Paula would be extremely envious, Mandy thought as David drove off. Again unable to believe how her life had changed in such a short time, she was looking forward to the evening. David knew her life history, and there'd be no sexual advances. Just a lovely evening out with a good friend, she thought happily.

'It's great to see you after all this time,' David said. 'You've been away from home for two years now, haven't you?'

'That's right. Two years struggling to pay the mortgage on my flat and trying to get my web-design business off the ground.'

'You're young, Mandy. You have all the time in the world. I don't know whether you're into country pubs, but I know of one down by the river which is rather nice. I thought we might have a drink and then wander along the river bank, seeing as it's such a nice evening.'

'Yes, that sounds good. It'll be nice to get out of town for a change.'

'I suppose that at your age you go clubbing most nights.'

'No, I . . . I don't get out that often.'

'Really? Well, I hope you enjoy the evening with me. I've always liked the countryside. Even during my teens, I preferred the country to the town. My friends would go clubbing and I'd go for walks and find a nice country pub or . . .'

As David talked about his love of the countryside, Mandy felt at ease in his company. It was nice to go out as friends, she mused again as he pulled up outside the pub. Leaving the car and following him, she thought how much nicer this was than the wine bar in town. It was good to get away from people. But the pub was busy, the tables outside were all taken, and she began to think that it hadn't been such a good idea. She'd hoped to spend the evening having a quiet chat with David, and she was pleased when he suggested they go for a walk before having a drink.

'No boyfriend, then?' David asked her as they walked down to the river bank.

'No, not really,' Mandy sighed. 'To be honest, I don't know that I want a permanent relationship.'

'As you know, I never married. I suppose the right girl never came along but, apart from that, I could never see myself settling down.'

'You must have had girlfriends?' Mandy said as they followed the bend in the river.

'Oh, yes, I've had girlfriends. But I've never had a meaningful relationship. I'm too old to find a girl now.'

'You're not old,' Mandy said, with a giggle.

'I've always liked younger girls and I'm far too old to attract them now.'

'Girls of my age?' Mandy prompted him.

'Well, yes. I mean . . . don't get me wrong, I'm not trying to score with you. I find you incredibly attractive, and very sexy . . . What I mean is . . .'

'I know what you mean, David.'

Sitting on the short grass in a secluded spot by the river, Mandy felt flattered. *Incredibly attractive, and very sexy . . .* His words playing on her mind as he sat next to her, she felt her clitoris stir beneath its fleshy hood. This wasn't supposed to be a sexual relationship, she reminded herself as she gazed at him. He was wearing an open-neck shirt and tight trousers and was very good-looking. He was also great company – but he was a friend of the family. As his gaze lowered to her naked legs, she again felt her clitoris stir.

'Are you seeing anyone at the moment?' she asked him.

'No, I've not been out with anyone for over two years.'

'There's something about two years,' Mandy sighed. 'I left home two years ago, I started my business two years ago and . . . and that's when a long-term relationship ended.'

'You've not had a boyfriend for two years?' he asked softly, frowning at her.

'Well, I've had the odd encounter. But nothing to speak of.'

'A young and attractive girl like you . . . I find that amazing, Mandy.'

'Amazing or not, it's true. I suppose I've been busy and haven't ventured out a great deal.'

'Haven't you felt lonely?'

'Not really. I suppose I haven't thought about it, until now.'

'I'm sure you'll find a young man and fall in love before long.'

'I don't think I want that. Not yet, anyway.'

'What about girlfriends? Surely you have girlfriends you go out with?'

'There is one, but she's always chasing after men. She's great fun but . . . All she talks about is men and her sexual conquests. To be honest, I don't know what I want.'

'You have all the time in the world, so don't worry about it. Right, shall we walk back to the pub and have a drink?'

'No, not yet,' Mandy murmured. 'Let's stay here for a while.'

'You like it here?'

'Yes, yes, I do. I always liked playing in the woods when I was young. The family picnics were great. The woods, open countryside, the river bank . . .'

'I remember you going off in the car with your mum and dad. It's funny to think that I've watched you grow up and now we're out together.'

'I used to like it when you came round. You were always fun to be with.'

'You are sweet,' David said, leaning over and kissing her cheek.

Mandy's stomach somersaulted as she breathed in his aftershave. It was only a friendly kiss, she reminded herself, returning his smile. Or was he making a sexual advance? Lying back on the short grass, the evening sun warming her young body, she felt at ease with David. Perhaps it was because he was an older man, she reflected as he placed his hand on her knee. Her womb fluttered as he moved his hand up her leg. She was sure now that he wanted her body.

'Mandy, you're beautiful,' he breathed, leaning over and kissing her full lips. 'I'm sorry, I shouldn't have done that.'

'It's OK,' she murmured, losing control of her inner desires. 'Do it again.'

His hand slid up beneath her skirt as he locked his lips to hers. He massaged the swell of her pussy lips through the tight crotch of her panties. Mandy breathed heavily through her nose as his tongue met hers. This wasn't what she'd wanted or expected, but . . . Moving her panties aside, David eased a finger deep into the contracting sheath of her vagina and massaged her inner flesh. She quivered as she breathed in the scent of his aftershave again. An older man, she thought, recalling Paula's words. But he was a friend of the family and . . . Kissing her neck, he moved down and sank his teeth gently into her erect nipple through the thin material of her blouse, and she quivered again.

Mandy writhed on the grass as he slipped his finger out of her tight vagina and tugged her panties down her long legs. Kicking her shoes and panties off, she parted her legs wide as his hand ran up her inner thigh to the hairless lips of her vulva. She'd never dreamed that she'd be having sex with the man she'd lived next door to for most of her life. If her parents discovered that she was now having a sexual relationship with him, they'd go mad. David certainly wouldn't tell them, she mused dreamily as he massaged the solid nub of her sensitive clitoris. No one would discover her affair with a man old enough to be her father.

'You've shaved,' David gasped in surprise .

'Yes, I . . . Is that OK? I mean, do you like it?'

'God, yes. I've always thought it a shame to cover the beauty of the female form with hair. You really are beautiful, Mandy.'

'I don't think I'm beautiful,' she replied, giggling.

'Well, *I* think you are. I've watched you grow into a stunningly attractive young lady. I must admit that I've had naughty thoughts about you. But I never dreamed that I'd be with you like this. I remember one of your dad's barbecues when you were wearing a short skirt and I gazed at your legs and . . .'

Arching her back as David continued to massage the solid bulb of her clitoris, Mandy wasn't listening to him. Her clitoris began to pulsate and she wondered what sex would be like with an older man. How big was his cock? she wondered in her sexual delirium. He'd said that he'd had his naughty thoughts. Had he imagined fucking her? Had he tried to look up her skirt at the barbecues? She'd never imagined that the neighbour she'd known for so many years would one day be masturbating her.

'What were your naughty thoughts?' she asked him as she writhed on the short grass beneath the evening sun.

'I used to look at your naked legs,' he murmured, increasing the pace of his massaging rhythm. 'I'd look at your naked thighs and sometimes I'd be lucky enough to glimpse your tight panties.'

'Tell me more,' she gasped. 'What did you think?'

'I'd see you come home from college and I'd gaze at your short skirt, your tight blouse. My thoughts were very naughty.'

'Tell me.'

'I'd picture your sweet little pussy nestling between your slender thighs. I'd imagine that I was licking your tight crack, tasting your hot milk and . . .'

'I'm coming,' Mandy breathed shakily. 'God, I'm . . . I'm coming.'

Her young body shaking uncontrollably, her breathing fast and shallow, she cried out as her clitoris swelled beneath his massaging fingertips and erupted in orgasm. Waves of pure sexual ecstasy welling from her contracting womb and crashing through her convulsing body, she parted her legs to the extreme and lifted her naked buttocks clear of the ground. Her juices streamed from her neglected vagina and ran down to the delicate brown tissue surrounding her anus. She was desperate for the feel of David's wet tongue between her splayed thighs.

Maybe he wasn't into oral sex, she thought as her pleasure finally began to fade. Recalling Gary, the way he'd tongued her wet vagina and sucked her clitoris to orgasm, she hoped that David had some surprises in store for her. Three men, she thought, as she remembered John's purple knob pumping sperm into her gobbling mouth. Maybe one would be good at oral sex, one good at fucking, and one ... John wasn't particularly good at anything, she mused as she recovered from her amazing orgasm.

'How about going for that drink now?' David said. 'Or would you rather stay here?'

'I'm not interested in the pub,' she murmured.

'You're young, Mandy. I don't want to take advantage of you.'

'*I* might be taking advantage of *you*,' she said, chuckling softly.

'Well, I really don't think that you'd want to take advantage of an old man like me.'

'All right, then, you go ahead and take advantage of me. I'm yours, David. Do what you want with me.'

Moving between her splayed thighs, he kissed the hairless mound of her mons. His tongue slipped into her well-creamed vaginal slit and teased the sensitive tip of her swelling clitoris as he drove two fingers into the tight duct of her pussy and expertly massaged her inner flesh. Mandy writhed again, her lubricious juices lubricating his thrusting fingers as he sucked the solid protrusion of her clitoris into his hot mouth.

David was good at massaging her clitoris to orgasm, Mandy thought as her thighs twitched and her head lolled from side to side. He knew how to use his fingers, his mouth and tongue. But did he know how to pleasure a girl with his solid cock? Wondering again about having several men, each with their own particular sexual expertise, she recalled Paula's comments on having two men pleasure her. But Mandy wasn't a whore. She could never imagine allowing two men to use her young body. Picturing two solid cocks, one pumping sperm into her mouth, the other flooding her tight pussy with spunk, she grabbed David's head and cried out as her clitoris pulsated within his wet mouth.

'Again,' she gasped. 'God, I'm coming again.' Her young body shaking uncontrollably as she writhed and whimpered in the grip of her powerful climax, Mandy held David's head tight and ground her open vulva hard against his face. Her swollen clitoris pulsating within his wet mouth, her vagina gripping his thrusting fingers, she once more imagined his solid cock gliding in and out of her tight sex sheath. Desperate for the feel of his rock-hard organ thrusting deep into her, she finally pushed his head away as she came down from her amazing pleasure.

'No more,' she breathed. 'God, no more.'

'You're beautiful,' David murmured, licking his pussy-wet lips as he sat upright between her splayed legs. Slipping his fingers out of her fiery vaginal duct, he smiled. 'You'd better rest for a while and then we'll go and have a drink.'

'No, no,' she gasped. 'I want you to fuck me.'

'I'm too old for you, Mandy. You don't want some old bugger like me . . .'

'I *do* want you,' she persisted. 'I want your hard cock fucking my tight little cunt.'

Her crude words sent her arousal soaring and she half-opened her eyes, watching David through her long lashes. Unzipping his trousers, he grabbed his solid cock by the root and slipped his purple plum between the splayed inner lips of her hungry pussy. His cock shaft driving into her contracting sex sheath, his swollen knob meeting her ripe cervix, he locked his dark-eyed stare to hers and smiled.

'I never thought I'd be doing this,' he said. 'I've watched you over the years, fantasised and dreamed and . . . this is a dream come true, Mandy.'

'If I'd known how you felt . . .'

'You were too young. But you're too young now. I find it hard to believe that you want an old man like me.'

'Stop worrying about our ages. We're together, we're loving, so enjoy it.'

Withdrawing his solid cock and then driving again into her young body, David let out a low moan with every thrust. In a sexual frenzy, Mandy wrapped her legs around his back, allowing him a deeper penetration of her young vagina. The sensitive tip of her erect clitoris massaged by the wet flesh of his veined shaft, she reached another mind-blowing orgasm as he threw his head back and pumped out his fresh spunk. Squirming beneath him, digging her fingernails into the soft grass as he increased the pace of his shafting rhythm, she knew that she'd be meeting him again.

This wasn't just cold sex as it had been with Gary, she reflected as she rode the crest of her orgasm. There was something more to this. Perhaps it was his age? Her young body shook and writhed and her vagina overflowed with his creamy sperm. If he discovered that she had other men, that she'd used other men for crude sex ... This relationship was special, she decided as her orgasm began to fade.

'Sorry I was so quick,' he gasped, stilling his deflating cock deep within the spermed sheath of her vagina. 'I just couldn't hold back.'

'It was heavenly,' Mandy murmured, her eyes rolling as she drifted down from her orgasm. 'You're amazing, David.'

'You look beautiful with your shaved pussy. You look young and ... You must think I'm a dirty old man.'

'You must think I'm a slut.'

'God, no. Not at all. Why say that?'

'David, you're not a dirty old man. OK, you're old enough to be my father. But what the hell does that matter?'

'You're right, I'm being silly. It's just that it's not every day a beautiful young girl like you ... Would you like to see me again?'

'Yes, very much. I think it's time for that drink now.'

Slipping her panties up her long legs and concealing her sperm-oozing pussy slit, Mandy clambered to her feet and adjusted her clothes. Running her fingers through her long dark hair as David straightened his shirt, she felt happy. Thinking again that there was something special about their relationship, as they walked back to the pub she began to wonder whether to keep Gary and John hanging around. Now that she had David she didn't need other men.

Sitting outside the pub with David, Mandy sipped her vodka and tonic and pondered on the future. Playing games of one-upmanship with Paula wasn't going to get her anywhere, she decided as she gazed into David's dark eyes. Making up stories about sexual conquests and earning lots of money was a waste of time. She'd keep Paula as a friend. But the games would have to stop. She had David now, so there was no need for silly games.

Four

Mandy leapt out of bed the following morning and grabbed her dressing gown as the doorbell rang. Bounding down the stairs, she hoped that Gary hadn't called round for early-morning sex. She'd have to tell him that she wouldn't be seeing him again, she decided as she checked her reflection in the hall mirror. And she wanted John out of her life, too. She'd arranged to see David again that evening, and she didn't want other men getting in the way.

'John,' she said as she opened the front door. 'It's rather early. I'm not even dressed yet.'

'Sorry,' he said, walking past her into the hall. 'I have to speak to you, Mandy.'

'I'll make some coffee,' she sighed, closing the door and wandering into the kitchen. 'Do you realise that it's only seven-thirty?'

'I saw you last night, Mandy,' he said accusingly, leaning in the kitchen doorway. 'You were at the Riverside pub with a man.'

'Yes, that's right. We went out for a drink.'

'I thought we were going to get back together?'

'We are, John.'

'But . . . you were out with some old guy.'

'That's David, the man who lives next door to mum and dad. He's a family friend.'

'Oh, I . . . I see. Do you often go out for a drink with him?'

'He comes out for a drink with us now and then.'

'Us?'

'Mum, dad and me. We were all there.'

'I didn't see your parents.'

'They must have gone into the pub. You should have joined us.'

'I was with . . . I was with a friend.'

Pouring the coffee as John sat at the table, Mandy concealed a grin. John was worried, he was upset, and he'd probably been up half the night wondering who the man was. Payback time, Mandy thought happily as she placed the cups on the table. Sitting opposite John, she allowed her gown to fall open just enough to display the brown teats of her elongated nipples. Coming up with an idea, she decided to worry him further.

'David and I go out for a meal together on the odd occasion,' she said, watching John for a reaction.

'With your parents, you mean?' he asked her, gazing at the firm mound of her exposed breast.

'No, just the two of us. I've known him most of my life and we've become good friends.'

'You never mentioned him when we were together, Mandy.'

'It's only during the last year or so that I've got to know him really well.'

'Not *too* well, I hope.'

'He's been helping me run my business.'

'You always said that you wanted to do something with web sites.'

'And that's what I'm doing. I'm good at the design, but I don't have a head for business. That's where David comes in.'

'So you two work together as well as go out with each other?'

'Yes, we do. I mean, we don't actually work together full-time. He's round here a lot and we . . .'

'Have you ever been to bed with him?'

'John . . . if we're going to get back together, I don't want you to start questioning me. David and I are very close friends. We get on well, we work together, and we go out for a meal now and then.'

'I wasn't questioning you, Mandy. I was just curious, that's all. When are you seeing him again?'

'He's phoning me later today.'

Concealing her breast with her dressing gown and sipping her coffee, Mandy pondered her decision to dump Gary and John. She didn't want to lose David, she thought as she recalled his hard cock driving deep into her tight vagina. She didn't want him to think she was a slut. But she'd be safe enough as long as he didn't discover that she had other men. Besides, if she was going to be more like Paula, she'd have to have several men on the go. Torn between her feelings for David and her attraction to Paula's lifestyle, she wasn't sure what to do. Was it possible to lead two separate lives? David would only see one side of Mandy, he'd only know the sweet little girl who used to live next door. It didn't matter what Gary thought, seeing as he was married.

'I thought you might have come round to my place by now,' John whined. 'It would be nice to spend an evening together.'

'I don't have a great deal of spare time, John. What with running my business and other commitments . . .'

'Is David a commitment?'

'I wouldn't say that he's a commitment,' she replied with a soft laugh.

'What is he, then?'

'John, if you're having a problem with David, I don't see that we're going to get anywhere.'

68

'I'm not having a problem with him. It's just that it would have been nice if we'd spent the evening together.' He looked down at his cup of coffee and sighed. 'You've changed, Mandy,' he murmured.

'Have I?'

'Yes, you have. You used to be . . . oh, I don't know. You used to go along with things I said. If I suggested that we go out for a meal, you'd agree. If I wanted to stay in, you were happy to do that.'

'I was weak and subservient, John. Now I'm my own woman. I have my own friends, I run my own business, I have my own flat . . .'

'Sounds like you're too busy to fit me in.'

'Not at all.'

'So, when will I see you?'

'I'm pretty busy today and I have to see David this evening.'

'You *have* to see him?'

'About my business plans, John. We have to go through some plans to do with my business and . . . I meant to ask you, how come you've bought a flat a few doors away from me?'

'It was just coincidence. Well, as you're so busy I'd better go.' John didn't look at all happy as he finished his coffee. 'If ever you do get a free moment, let me know.'

'You don't have to go, John. I'm not starting work yet so do why don't you stay for a while?'

'Oh, right.'

Refilling the coffee cups, Mandy decided to allow him a glimpse of her hairless pussy. She knew that he'd question her when her gown opened, exposing the naked lips of her vulva. He'd probably believe that she'd shaved for David or some other man, and the idea of riling him excited her. He'd treated her badly in the past, dumped her for a slut, destroyed

69

her plans for a life together with him . . . Now it was her turn to destroy him. Paula would fuck him and dump him, she reflected, as he gazed wide-eyed at her hairless vulva.

'When did you shave?' he asked her.

'Oh, sorry,' she breathed, giggling as she pulled her gown together. 'I shaved because I prefer it that way.'

'Does David prefer it that way?'

'I don't know – you'll have to ask him.'

'What? You mean he's seen you naked?'

'I was joking, John.'

'Mandy, I don't want you hanging around with him.'

'Hanging around? What do you mean?'

'Well, seeing him all the time and . . .'

'David is a family friend, John.'

'Now that we're back together, I want things to be like the old days. You're my woman and I don't want you going to pubs with other men.'

Like the old days? Mandy reflected, retaking her seat at the table. Doing as she was told, not allowed friends, staying in while John went out with his mates . . . Like the old days when John was screwing a slut behind her back? Smiling at him, she sipped her coffee and once more allowed her gown to fall open and expose the rise of her young breasts. She'd go along with him, she decided. She'd play the subservient woman and follow her master's orders to the letter. Reaching across the table and holding his hand, she smiled at him again.

'OK,' she said. 'I liked the old days. I won't go out with David. I'll have to speak to him about the business, but I can do that on the phone.'

'That's good, Mandy. I want us to have a secure relationship. I want to know that you're here for me, not out with some other man. We'll see each other this evening. You'll have to cancel your meeting with David. I'll be round at seven, OK?'

'Yes, I'll phone him and tell him that I can't see him.'

'Good. This is going to work out well, Mandy. Just like the old days.'

'Yes, just like the old days.'

Mandy was seething with anger, but she didn't show it. Squeezing John's hand and grinning, she did her best to appear happy. He was a bastard, she thought as he suggested they went up to her bedroom. *You'll have to cancel your meeting with David.* His words playing on her mind as she led him to her room, she knew what Paula would do in this situation. Paula was clever, resourceful, and she was Mandy's role model. She'd fuck John, use him and his money – and then dump him.

Slipping out of her dressing gown and sliding beneath her quilt as John undressed, Mandy knew that David's spunk was still swimming around in the wet heat of her tight vagina. She hadn't taken a shower, and her pussy would be bubbling with David's sperm. Joining her in the bed, John settled between her parted legs and kissed the hairless lips of her vulva. Licking her opening sex crack, his tongue entering her jism-brimming love hole, he commented on how wet she was.

'You've obviously missed me,' he breathed, his tongue lapping up the flowing cream. 'Just thinking about having sex with me has made you really wet.'

'You're right, John,' she gasped as he sucked out the blend of her love milk and David's sperm. 'Being with you has made me feel so horny.'

'I love your bald pussy.'

'Shall I tell you why I shaved?'

'Yes.'

71

'I did it for you, John. I remembered you saying that you liked smooth pussies, so I did it for you.'

'We're going to be great together, Mandy.'

'Just like the old days?'

'Yes.'

'That's good. Now, suck out my pussy juice and swallow it.'

Listening to John slurping and sucking, Mandy closed her eyes and recalled David's solid cock pumping spunk into her contracting vagina. Writhing on the bed as her clitoris swelled, she recalled Gary licking and sucking between her splayed thighs. Gary had sucked her clitoris to orgasm, David had tongued her hot vagina and taken her to orgasm, and now John was attending her feminine needs. Things were working out nicely. Her business was looking good, and she was well on the way to catching up with Paula's rampant sex life.

'You're mine,' John breathed, his wet tongue sweeping over the sensitive tip of her erect clitoris. 'You belong to me now, Mandy.'

'Yes, yes,' she gasped. 'I've missed you so much.'

'I'll sell my place and move in with you. You'd like that, wouldn't you?'

'Yes, yes. God, you make me feel so good.'

'I could move in this evening. I'll bring a few things round and move in this evening.'

'I'd like that, John. I've prayed for the day to come when we could get back together.'

'There was nothing with David, was there?'

'Of course not. I've never given myself to another man, John. Since the day we parted, I've been waiting for you to come back to me.'

Imagining that it was David between her splayed thighs, licking and sucking on her solid clitoris, Mandy reached her mind-blowing orgasm and writhed uncontrollably on the bed. Arching her back and grinding her open sex valley hard against John's face, she felt her young womb contracting as her climax peaked and rocked her naked body to the core. John must have thought that he was good in bed, she mused as she once more recalled David's rock-hard cock shafting her tight vagina. It was John's tongue sweeping over her pulsating clitoris, but it was the thought of David that brought Mandy her incredible pleasure.

'You're amazing,' she gasped as her orgasm began to fade. 'God, how I've missed you.'

'I've missed you too, Mandy. Do you want my cock now?'

'Yes, yes. It's been so long since . . .'

'You should have asked me to come back ages ago.'

'Yes, I wish I had. Make love with me now. Make love, just like the old days.'

The solid shaft of John's penis entered the wet heat of her tight vagina as she closed her eyes and recalled again David's beautiful organ. David was kind, considerate and loving, she reflected. John was a bastard. His cock slid in and out of her contracting pussy and he gasped and moaned as he fucked her. That's all this was, she thought. Nothing more than a fuck. *You should have asked me to come back ages ago* . . . This really was just like the old days, Mandy reflected as John pumped his spunk into her hot vagina and finally collapsed on top of her naked body.

Rolling onto his back, he lay beside her and talked about the future. Mandy listened to *his* ideas, *his* wants and needs, *his* plans. He'd move in that evening, and she would cut all ties with David because she needn't bother with her web-design business now. He'd have her phone number changed so that people from the past couldn't contact her. They were going to start again, meet new people and . . . Again, Mandy concealed a grin as she made her own plans.

'What time this evening?' she asked him.

'Have dinner ready at seven,' John ordered her. 'Oh, you'd better give me a key.'

'OK, I'll have one cut today.'

'Good. This is going to be great, Mandy. As I said, forget about your web-site thing. I'll have your phone number changed once I've settled in. We can do that tomorrow.'

'OK, that's fine.'

'Steak and chips would be nice this evening. You can go shopping this morning. You'd better stock up the fridge with lager and I'll need . . .'

Just like the old days, Mandy thought again as John went on about his needs. Watching him dress, she realised just how much he'd used her in the past. She'd done everything for him, from cooking and washing to cleaning and ironing his shirts . . . Not any more, she thought as she slipped back into her dressing gown. *You can go shopping this morning.* And you can go to hell, she giggled inwardly.

'I'll see you this evening,' he said, kissing her cheek before leaving the room. 'Don't forget the French mustard.'

'I won't,' she called as he bounded down the stairs. 'The meal will be on the table at seven.' Hearing the front door close, she slammed her bedroom door shut. ' "Don't forget the French mustard",' she whined. 'I'll give you fucking French fucking mustard. You fucking bastard.'

After a shower, Mandy dressed and had eggs and bacon for breakfast. Taking her coffee into the dining room, she sat at her computer and grinned as she read the email from the plastics company. They'd accepted her rough quote for a web site and wanted to meet her to discuss the design. *Forget about your web-site thing* ... 'Bastard,' she breathed as she replied to the email. *I'll have your phone number changed* ... 'Fucking bastard.'

Mandy worked until four o'clock and then rang David. He was delighted to hear from her and said he was looking forward to the evening. 'I won't be free until nine,' she said. 'Sorry, but I have some business to deal with.'

'That's OK,' he replied. 'Business must come first.'

'If you'd like to come round at nine, we could have a drink or something.'

'I'll be there at nine, Mandy. But only if you're sure.'

'Of course I'm sure, David. I'm just sorry that I can't make it earlier.'

'Don't apologise,' he said, with a chuckle. 'It's your life – I don't own you.'

'Great, well ... I'll see you later.'

Replacing the receiver, Mandy recalled his words. *It's your life – I don't own you.* John would never think that way, she thought angrily. *Don't forget the French mustard.* Grabbing the phone, she punched in Gary's number. Listening to the ring tone, she wondered why Paula hadn't contacted her. She was probably too busy taking men to bed, she mused. And taking their money.

'It's me,' she said as Gary answered. 'Your bit of rough on the side.'

'Hi, sexy,' he breathed. 'You're not rough, you're beautiful.'

'Don't talk crap, Gary. You only want me so that you can spunk on my panties.'

'And suck your clit,' he returned, laughing gently.

'You can do that this evening, OK?'

'I can't, Mandy. We're going over to see the wife's parents this evening.'

'Then put it off.'

'I wish I could.'

'Be here at six-thirty, Gary. I need you here at six-thirty.'

'Look, I'll see what I can do. We're not going over until eight, so—'

'Be here, or I'll go and see your little wife and tell her about your panty-spunking fetish.'

'You need me that bad?'

'Yes, I do.'

'Great. OK, I'll be there at six-thirty.'

Grinning as he hung up, Mandy tossed the receiver into its cradle and punched the air with her fist. This was going to be perfect, she thought as she paced the lounge floor and made her plans. Three cocks in one day. John, Gary, and then David. Paula was going to be left behind, she thought as she went up to her room. Taking a pair of stockings and a suspender belt from her drawer, she rummaged through her clothes and chose a red miniskirt and a loose-fitting blouse. Red stilettos, she decided as she dressed. And no bra or panties.

Mandy walked into the lounge and answered the phone. She was pleased to hear Paula's voice.

'How are you?' she asked the other girl.

'Bored,' Paula replied. 'I thought we might go out this evening.'

'I can't, Paula. I've got Gary coming round and later another friend is coming to see me.'

'Another man?'

'Yes, that's right. Maybe we could arrange something for tomorrow evening?'

'Two men in one evening?'

'Three, if you count my ex-boyfriend. He came round this morning.'

'For sex?'

'Of course, Paula. I don't have men round for anything else.'

'God, you *are* doing well. Where do you find all these men?'

'Same places as you, I suppose. Bars, clubs . . .'

'Did you arrange anything with Gary about a blind date?'

'Er . . . no, not yet.'

'It would be great to go out in a foursome one evening, Mandy. Surely you can fix something up?'

'You have enough men on the go. Can't you bring one of them along?'

'I like new men,' Paula said, chuckling. 'Men I haven't fucked before. I meant to ask you, are you into spanking?'

'Spanking?' Mandy echoed. 'Well, I . . .'

'There's nothing like a good spanking. I love the feel of a leather belt across my bum. It's an amazing experience. Have you ever been whipped?'

'Yes, of course,' Mandy said, forcing a giggle. 'I love it.'

'We'll *have* to go out in a foursome one evening, and then all go back to your place for sex.'

'Yes, good idea. Look, I'd better go. I have to get ready for this evening.'

'OK, let me know when you've fixed something up.'

'Yes, yes, I will. Bye.'

Shaking her head as she replaced the receiver, Mandy imagined Paula having her naked bottom whipped. The girl was incredible, she thought as she clenched her own buttocks. Was there *anything* she wasn't into? Unable to see herself deriving pleasure from a gruelling whipping, she realised again that she'd never catch up with Paula and her sexually deviant lifestyle. She'd be talking about water sports next, she thought, giggling inwardly as she imagined a man peeing over her naked body. Spanking and whipping was something she'd never experience, she decided. She'd just have to lie to Paula about that particular fetish.

Gary arrived on time, carrying a bottle of vodka. Eyeing Mandy's stockings and red stilettos, he remarked on her beauty as he followed her into the kitchen. Mandy poured the drinks, reckoning that he thought she'd dressed up just for him. She was going to have to use him, she thought as she led him into the lounge. He was a married man and he was using her for sex, so what the hell? Paula used men and now Mandy was going to do the same. My role model, she reflected, recalling the girl's various comments about men.

'What colour are your panties?' Gary asked her as she sat on the sofa.

'I'm not wearing any,' she replied, parting her thighs and displaying the hairless lips of her vulva.

'God, you've shaved.'

'Do you like it?'

'Yes, very much. I love hairless little cunts. But if you're not wearing any panties . . . I need to spunk on your panties, Mandy.'

'We're not playing that game tonight, Gary.'

'Oh? So what game *are* we playing?'

'We're going to play Fuck the Slut.'

'But I want to spunk on your panties. Just put some on for a while and then you can take them off and we'll—'

'I want you to do my arse, Gary,' she cut in unashamedly. 'Have you ever done that?'

'Well, no – no, I haven't. God, you've become a right little . . .'

'Slut?'

'No, I don't think you're a slut.'

'I am, Gary. I'm a slut for this evening, OK?'

'If you say so.'

'I do say so. Now, take all your clothes off.'

Leaving the room as Gary slipped out of his clothes, Mandy opened the front door. Her juices of arousal trickled from her opening sex crack and ran down her inner thighs, and she'd never felt so excited as she bounded up the stairs and grabbed her lipstick from the dressing table. Payback time, she thought happily as she returned to the lounge to find Gary naked. Lifting her short skirt, she passed the lipstick to Gary and bent over.

'I want you to write the word "slut" on each buttock,' she instructed him.

'Slut?' he echoed, gazing at her rounded bum cheeks.

'Don't you know how to spell it?'

'Yes, of course.'

'Then write it.'

'If you say so.' Scrawling the red letters across each buttock, Gary laughed. 'What's this for?' he asked her as she stood up.

'Now write it just above my pussy,' Mandy said, lifting up her skirt.

'I wish you'd tell me what this is about,' he muttered, kneeling in front of her and inscribing the letters just above her hairless pussy-slit.

'You'll find out,' she said, standing and checking the time. 'I could have done with two men,' she breathed. 'Not to worry. OK, stiffen up your cock ready for my cunt.'

After she'd dragged the armchair into the centre of the room, Mandy opened the lounge door and checked the time. Gary watched her, frowning as she looked around the room. He was obviously confused, but Mandy couldn't tell him about her plan. Slipping her skirt off and leaning over the back of the chair, she ordered him to drive his solid cock deep into her pussy. Wasting no time, he slipped the purple head of his penis between her open inner lips and drove his cock fully home.

'Is this the game?' he asked her, grabbing her hips and pressing his lower stomach hard against her naked buttocks. 'I'm going to get lipstick all over me. What's this about, Mandy?'

'You'll find out any minute now,' she replied. 'Now that your cock is well creamed, take it out of my pussy and force it deep into my tight little bum-hole.'

'Whatever the game is, I like it,' Gary said, withdrawing his pussy-wet penis and pressing his purple plum hard against the brown ring of her anus. 'I've never done this before,' he gasped as his swollen knob slipped past her defeated anal-sphincter muscles. 'God, you're so hot and tight.'

'And you're big,' she breathed, clinging to the arms of the chair as his solid prick drove deep into her hot rectal duct. 'Talk dirty to me. Tell my I'm a slut and you love arse-fucking me.'

Grimacing as Gary rocked his hips, Mandy gasped and trembled. She'd never experienced anal sex, and she thought that she was going to split open as his knob repeatedly drove deep into the dank heat of her bowels. The delicate brown tissue of her anal ring rolled back and forth along his veined shaft as he fucked her, and she felt her copious juices of lust flood from her gaping vaginal entrance and stream down her inner thighs. This was perfect, she thought, hoping that John would arrive on time.

Gary growled his crude words, calling her a filthy tart, a dirty little arse-slut, a cum-loving whore. Mandy's arousal soared as she listened to his running commentary on the crude arse-fucking, and her clitoris swelled and pulsated in the beginnings of her orgasm. Glancing at her watch, she grinned. Seven o'clock. *Don't forget the French mustard.*

'Here it comes,' Gary cried, increasing the speed of his shafting rhythm as his spunk jetted from his throbbing knob.

'Don't stop,' Mandy gasped, slipping her hand between the chair back and her hairless vulva and massaging her solid clitoris. 'I'm . . . I'm coming.'

'Filthy little arse-whore,' Gary breathed, the sound of his lower stomach slapping Mandy's naked buttocks resounding around the room. 'A filthy little slut like you needs a damned good-arse fucking.'

'Give it to me. Fuck my arse and spunk deep in my bowels.'

Writhing in the grip of her orgasm, Mandy felt Gary's sperm lubricating her anal cylinder as he pistoned her tight rectum. Her clitoris pulsating wildly beneath her vibrating fingertips, the squelching sounds of illicit sex filling her ears, she shook uncontrollably as her orgasm peaked and rocked her young body. Two cocks, she thought, imagining a second rock-hard penis shafting the neglected sheath of her contracting vagina. Two cocks, three, four . . .

'Fuck me,' she gasped, her head resting on the armchair cushion, her long black hair veiling her flushed face. 'Fuck my arse and fill me with spunk.'

'Dirty little whore,' Gary breathed, his swinging balls battering her swollen vaginal lips. 'Filthy arse-fucking slut.'

Wondering whether her tight holes could accommodate two solid penises as her climax finally began

81

to wane, Mandy realised that she was plunging deeper into a pit of depravity. Never had she dreamed that she'd be committing such a crude sexual act, never had she thought that she'd be screwing three different men in one day. But she knew that she couldn't help herself as sperm streamed from her inflamed rectal duct and flowed in rivers down her inner thighs.

Finally hauling her trembling body upright as Gary slipped his deflating cock out of her sperm-brimming anal canal, Mandy clung to her lover for support as she swayed on her trembling legs. Her heart racing, her hands shaking, she felt dizzy in the aftermath of her incredible orgasm. Anal sex would have to be explored further, she mused, wondering why John hadn't arrived. Although she believed that her plan had failed, she'd loved the sensations of a huge cock filling her rectal sheath to capacity.

'I've seen enough,' John said, standing in the doorway.

'John,' Mandy gasped. 'I ... I thought we said eight o'clock.'

'What the hell ...' Gary began, grabbing his clothes and dressing hurriedly.

'That sums you up,' John said, pointing to Mandy's lower stomach. 'Slut, that's just what you are. I've been here all the time, Mandy. I agree with that guy: you're a filthy, dirty, spunk-loving, fucking slut.'

'Now you know what it feels like to be cheated on,' Mandy retorted. 'Now you know how I felt when I discovered that you'd been screwing a slut behind my back.'

'I thought we were putting all that behind us and starting again?'

'I *am* starting again. I'm starting again with David when he calls later. I fucked you this morning, I've just fucked Gary, and I'll fuck David later. Three beautiful cocks in one day. Well, two beautiful cocks, since I don't count yours as anything special.'

'Filthy slut,' John breathed, walking to the front door.

'"Don't forget the French mustard",' Mandy called.

'What the hell was all that about?' Gary asked as he finished dressing.

'The game I told you about,' Mandy replied, with a giggle. 'Fuck the Slut.'

'You knew that he'd turn up, didn't you?'

'Yes, that's why—'

'You could have told me, Mandy. Bloody hell, if I'd known that some guy was going to turn up . . .'

'You wouldn't have participated in my plan, would you? I'm sorry, Gary. I used you, and I'm sorry.'

'Who was he?'

'Just someone I knew a long time ago.'

'And you've got some other guy turning up later?'

'Yes, I have. I use men, Gary. I use them for pleasure and . . .'

'Actually, I quite like being used,' Gary said, grinning at her. 'Especially if it means fucking your tight little bottom-hole. When did you first get into anal sex?'

'Just now,' she replied.

'You mean I'm the first?'

'Yes, and it was amazing. We must do it again, Gary.'

'Definitely. What was that about French mustard?'

'Nothing for you to worry about. Take your belt off.'

'What?'

'Your leather belt – take it off. You haven't got to get back to your sweet little Jennifer yet, have you?'

83

'Not just yet.'

'Good. Take your belt off.'

Watching as Gary unbuckled his belt, Mandy felt a quiver run through her young womb. She might as well make an effort to catch up with Paula, she thought, recalling the girl's words. *I love the feel of a leather belt across my bum.* Was she just trying to catch up with Paula? she wondered. Or did she harbour a latent genuine desire for the feel of a leather strap across the naked cheeks of her firm buttocks? What had started out as a game of one-upmanship was unearthing deep-seated desires. Retaking her position over the back of the armchair, she ordered Gary to whip her naked buttocks gently. She had to experience a gentle thrashing, she thought, imagining John returning and witnessing the degrading act. But she doubted that she'd ever see him again.

'Are you sure about this?' Gary asked Mandy, standing behind her with the leather belt swinging from his hand.

'Just do it gently,' she whispered.

'OK, but you must tell me when you want me to stop.'

'Just do it, Gary.'

The leather met her naked buttocks, jolting her young body, and she let out a rush of breath. The second lash was slightly harder, smearing the red lipstick and leaving a red stripe across the pale flesh of her bum cheeks. Lashing her tensed buttocks progressively harder, Gary was sure that she'd ask him to stop as she squirmed and yelped like a dog. But, as her pussy milk streamed down her inner thighs and her gasps became whimpers of pleasure, he knew that she was enjoying the experience. The belt swished through the air and landed across her tensed buttocks with a loud crack, and he grinned as Mandy asked him to thrash her harder. Begging for more, she clung to the arms of the chair as he repeatedly lashed the reddening cheeks of her firm bottom.

Realising that David would see her glowing bum cheeks, Mandy wished that she hadn't agreed to him coming round later that evening. She could hardly tell him that she'd been thrashed with a leather belt, she thought as a loud crack resounded around the room. David was special, and she didn't want him to think of her as a common slut. Begging for more as Gary thrashed her harder, she knew that she was a slut. This had nothing to do with one-upmanship, this had nothing to do with Paula . . . Mandy had become a slut.

As a gush of hot urine streamed down her inner thighs and splashed on the floor, Mandy knew that she'd become hooked on thrashing. She recalled her father threatening to thrash her when she'd been young, but he'd only been joking. Had he spanked her, had she tasted the delights of a naked-buttock thrashing, she'd have been hooked years ago. Had she experienced anal sex in the past, she'd have become a slut long before. At least she was now discovering her darker side, she reflected as her clitoris swelled and demanded attention.

'No more,' she cried as her flow of urine stemmed.

'You really are incredible,' Gary said, lowering the belt to his side. 'I wish you were my wife.'

'No, you don't,' she gasped, hauling her trembling body upright. 'I'd be screwing other men behind your back, and you wouldn't like that.'

'I'd watch you,' he said, slipping his belt on. 'I'd watch other men fuck you and—'

'Would you like that?' she cut in, cocking her head to one side.

'Yes, I would. And I'd like to join in. I've heard about girls getting fucked by two cocks. It would be great, Mandy.'

'I might be able to arrange that,' she said huskily as Gary checked his watch.

'Really?'

'I've never had two cocks, but it is something that I've been thinking about.'

'Let me know when, and I'll be here. Right, I'd better get going.'

'I'll ring you.'

'You're beautiful, Mandy.'

'I'm a slut,' she replied. 'Go on, get out of here.'

'OK, I'll see you soon.'

As Gary left the room, Mandy grinned. The evening had been quite eventful, she reflected happily as the front door closed. She'd given John the shock of his life, experienced anal sex and a damned good thrashing ... Grabbing the ringing phone, she was pleased, and a little worried, to hear David's soft voice. Glancing at the wall clock, she knew that she was going to have to put him off as he asked her how she was.

'I'm very tired,' she replied. 'I was wondering whether we could—'

'I'm sorry to let you down,' he cut in. 'But I can't make it this evening.'

'Oh, right.'

'I'm so sorry, Mandy. Something has cropped up and I have to deal with it. How about tomorrow?'

'Yes, yes, that's fine. As I said, I'm feeling very tired. An early night will do me good.'

'You sleep well and I'll ring you tomorrow.'

'I will. Thanks, David.'

Replacing the receiver, Mandy breathed a sigh of relief. She needed a shower, the carpet had to be

86

cleaned, and she was feeling tired. Locking up, she climbed the stairs and slipped beneath her quilt. Her buttocks stinging, her thighs sticky with a blend of pussy milk, spunk and urine, she closed her eyes. She'd shower in the morning, she thought as sleep engulfed her. She'd shower, clean the carpet, straighten the lounge . . . and get fucked again.

Five

Mandy found a note on the front doormat the following morning. It was from John. *Bitch, fucking slag, filthy slut, dirty whore* ... Tossing it into the bin and filling the kettle, she giggled. Now he knew what it was like, she reflected, recalling the day he'd announced that he was leaving her for another woman. Now the bastard knew how she'd felt when he'd dumped her for a slut.

Taking her coffee into the lounge, she gazed at the wet carpet and grinned. The evening had been most enjoyable, she mused, dragging the armchair back into place. Thinking about having two men, two cocks, she felt her clitoris swell and her juices of desire seep into the tight crotch of her knickers. She needed to masturbate, but she had work to do. Her web-design business was looking good now and the last thing she wanted was to neglect her work. She was about to fill a bowl with soapy water and clean the carpet when the doorbell rang. Sighing as she walked through the hall, she reckoned that John had come round to have another go at her.

'Paula,' she gasped in surprise as she opened the front door. 'No work today?'

'I have work every day,' the other girl replied, walking into the hall. 'I'm the boss, so I'm going in late.'

'Coffee?' Mandy asked her, leading her into the kitchen.

'No, I had one before I left home. Have you fixed anything up yet? With Gary and a friend, I mean.'

'Oh, er . . . no, no, I haven't.'

'Have you mentioned it to Gary?'

'Yes, and he . . . he doesn't think that any of his friends would be up for it. Blind dates are a thing of the past, Paula. Can't you bring one of your men friends along one evening?'

'I suppose so, but . . . I like the excitement of meeting someone new.'

'I'll ask Gary again, but I don't hold out much hope. Why don't we go out on the pull one night? Just the two of us, Paula.'

'I'd like that, but you're always so busy,' she sighed. 'What are you doing this evening?'

'Oh, er . . . I'm seeing David this evening. You know what it's like with several men on the go. I never seem to have a free evening.'

Paula cocked her head to one side and frowned. 'How many men *have* you got, Mandy?'

'I don't know,' she replied, laughing softly. 'I've lost count.'

'Could I come round one evening? When you're free, I mean.'

'Yes, yes, of course. We'll have a girlie evening and . . .'

'Talking of girlie evenings, have you ever had lesbian sex?'

'Well, I . . .' Mandy stammered.

'There's nothing like a change. Don't get me wrong, I'm not a lesbian. But I do enjoy a wet pussy now and then.'

'Yes, I have had lesbian relationships,' Mandy lied, hoping that Paula wasn't going to suggest that the two of them should have sex.

89

'I know a young lesbian. She's eighteen and really attractive. If you're into girls, you'll have to meet her.'

'Well, I ... as I said, I'm pretty busy most evenings.'

'You must meet this girl,' Paula persisted. 'She's tall and slim with long blonde hair and she is *so* horny. She shaves and her pussy is so smooth and tight and ...'

As Paula rambled on, Mandy couldn't imagine her indulging in lesbian sex. Were there no limits to the girl's sexual deviancy? Lesbian sex was something that Mandy would never get involved in. She'd known that some of the girls at school had played about with each other, indulged in mutual masturbation and even oral sex, but she'd been repulsed by the idea of licking another girl's pussy. Trying to push such images from her mind, she was pleased when Paula said that she had to go.

'Sorry it's only a fleeting visit,' she said. 'But I'd better get to the office and check up on the staff. Let me know when you're free.'

'Yes, I'll do that,' Mandy breathed, gazing at Paula's mouth and trying to imagine her licking a pussy. 'I must get on with some work. It's beginning to pile up and I don't like it when I get behind.'

'OK, I'll see you soon.'

Seeing Paula to the front door, Mandy wondered why she kept going on about a blind date. Perhaps it *was* just the excitement of meeting someone new, she reflected as she filled a bowl with hot soapy water and went into the lounge. As she cleaned the carpet, she began to wonder whether Paula was lying about her sexual conquests. She was successful in business, but she might not be so successful when it came to men. That would explain why she wanted Gary to set something up, Mandy reflected. As for her lesbianism ... Was Paula playing her own game of one-upmanship?

Mulling over the notion that Paula might have been dreaming up incredible stories of sexual conquests to show off somehow, Mandy wondered why such an attractive and vivacious woman didn't have men chasing after her. Paula looked good, she was successful, she had charisma ... Surely men chatted her up and asked her out? It seemed that she was into one-night stands, and there must be dozens of men who'd be happy to oblige. Reckoning that she'd got it wrong and Paula didn't have a shortage of men chasing her, Mandy thought that she'd been honest when she'd said that new relationships were exciting.

Having worked all day on a web-site design, only breaking off for lunch, Mandy was about to relax on the sofa when the doorbell rang. Walking through the hall, she opened the front door to find a teenage girl standing on the step. She was blonde and extremely attractive, and Mandy instinctively knew that she was Paula's young lesbian friend. Paula had a nerve, she thought angrily as she asked the girl what she wanted.

'I've brought some money round from Paula,' the girl replied. 'It's for the meal, or something. I'm Jackie.'

'Oh, er ... thanks,' Mandy said, taking the cash and gazing at the teenage beauty.

'Apart from the money, she told me that you were dying to meet me.'

'I'm sorry, but she's got it all wrong,' Mandy sighed. 'I don't even know you, Jackie. Why would I be dying to meet you?'

'Paula came into the office and said ...'

'Do you work for Paula?' Mandy asked her.

'Yes, I do.'

'I suppose she told you that I'm a lesbian?'

'She said that you were into girls.'

'You'd better come in,' Mandy said, inviting her over the threshold.

Leading Jackie into the lounge and indicating for her to sit on the sofa, Mandy thought the situation was strange. Why had Paula sent the girl round with the money? she wondered, eyeing the teenager's short skirt and long legs. This had nothing to do with the money for the meal. Paula could have brought the cash round at any time – there was no need to send a young lesbian. Jackie was an attractive teenager with long blonde hair and a sultry expression that was somehow sexually appealing. Her T-shirt was tight, the thin material faithfully following the firm mounds of her pert breasts. But what did she want? Lesbian sex?

'Tell me about Paula,' Mandy said, sitting in the armchair.

'There's not much to tell.'

'You work for her, so you must know something about her.'

'Look, if you're not interested in me—'

'I'm interested in Paula,' Mandy cut in. 'I've known her since we were at school together. Recently we met up again and . . . There's something about her that's been bothering me. I won't go into details, but something doesn't add up.'

'She can be strange at times,' Jackie said softly. Biting her lip, she hung her head. 'I told her that this wasn't a good idea. I didn't want to come here, but she insisted.'

'Why?'

'She wants me to get to know you. You see . . . she doesn't have any friends, men friends, and she thought that . . .'

'Hang on, hang on. We *are* talking about the same Paula, aren't we?' Mandy asked her.

'Yes, of course.'

'So, Paula has no men friends? I find that difficult to believe.'

'She's always *talking* about men, but she doesn't seem to have any relationships.'

'This is all falling into place,' Mandy muttered. 'I've been playing a game but all along Paula was the one who . . . Tell me more.'

'She said that you had several men on the go. She hasn't got a male friend and she thought . . . I shouldn't be telling you all this.'

'She's got a bloody nerve,' Mandy snorted. 'She's been making out that she has different men every night. She said that she has a string of men chasing after her.'

'She's always very busy at work and she doesn't really have the time to go out and meet people. She looks up to you, Mandy. She's always talking about you.'

'This is ironic,' Mandy sighed. 'All along, I've been looking up to her.'

'If she finds out that I've been talking to you like this, I'll be out of a job.'

'Don't worry, I won't say anything to her. I suppose, if anything, I feel sorry for her.'

Something was still bothering Mandy. Why send Jackie round with the money? Paula obviously wanted to meet Mandy's male friends, but why send Jackie round? Perhaps the young girl found it difficult to meet like-minded girls and hoped that Mandy would want sex with her. Eyeing again the girl's short skirt, her naked thighs, Mandy felt a quiver run through her young womb. She'd never met a lesbian before, and she began to wonder about Jackie's

93

young body, her firm breasts. *She shaves and her pussy is so smooth and tight* ... Recalling Paula's words, she knew that she had to take a grip on herself. Jackie was extremely attractive, but Mandy wasn't a lesbian.

'So, are you and Paula intimate friends?' she asked the girl.

'No, nothing like that. She knows my sexual preference and she thought you might like to meet me.'

'Without wanting to be rude, I am *not* a lesbian and I don't want to meet a lesbian. This doesn't make sense. If Paula wants to meet my male friends, why send you here? You said that she wanted you to get to know me. How will that help her meet my friends?'

'I don't know,' Jackie sighed. 'I suppose she thought that we might all become friends and, that way, she'd get to meet your male friends. She's very lonely, Mandy.'

'Successful, but lonely. It's sad really.'

'I've said too much,' Jackie murmured. 'I was supposed to come here and ... To be honest, I don't know *what* I was supposed to do. Paula comes up with these crazy ideas and confuses me. Last week she wanted me to go out with her so that she could meet a man. She thought that, with me there as bait, I might attract the men and she might get to meet someone.'

'God, she must be desperate. To use a young girl as bait ... As I said, everything fits into place now. The irony is that I only know two men. One is married and the other is old. Actually, I know three men. But the third one's a bastard. I certainly don't have any spare men hanging around.'

'Aren't you a lesbian, then?' Jackie asked dolefully.

'No, I . . . It's something I've never thought about. If you don't mind my asking, how did *you* become a

94

lesbian? I mean, how did you discover that you wanted girls rather than boys?'

As Jackie told her story of a friend sleeping over one night, how they'd ended up in the same bed and kissed and fondled, Mandy felt her clitoris swell and her juices of lust seep into the tight crotch of her knickers. The way the girl was talking about her friend's firm breasts and tight pussy, Mandy wondered whether she'd been missing out and should experience lesbian sex. She no longer had to play the game of one-upmanship with Paula, she reflected. But her curiosity was beginning to get the better of her. What would it be like to feel another girl's breasts, to slip her finger into another girl's wet vagina? Gazing at Jackie, she glimpsed the triangular patch of white material hugging her full sex lips as she moved about on the sofa. She'd never seen another girl's pussy, let alone . . .

'I'd better go,' Jackie said softly.

'Have you ever been with a boy?' Mandy asked her.

'I did try it once, but . . . It was awful. It just didn't feel right. So, you've never been with a girl?'

'No, I haven't. As I said, I've never even thought about it.'

'Maybe you *should* think about it, Mandy,' Jackie breathed huskily. 'You're very attractive.'

'No, I . . . I'm not that way inclined.'

'How do you know that?'

'Well, I . . . I just know. Besides, male and female fit together. Two females don't.'

'Don't they?'

'Well, no, of course they don't.'

'Paula said that I'd like you, and she was right.'

'I like you, Jackie. But not that way.'

'Only a girl knows how to pleasure another girl. You must have had men fumbling about between

95

your legs and been left wondering what it was all about?'

'Yes, I have. I suppose . . . now I use men for my own sexual satisfaction. The other day Paula said that, if a man doesn't make her come, she won't see him again. That's now my own philosophy.'

'Any man can make you come, Mandy. But I'm talking about *real* orgasms. It's an art, and one that I've perfected. There's far more to it than clit-rubbing and pussy-fingering. Have you ever been held on the verge of an orgasm until you're begging to come?'

'Well, I . . . I don't know.'

'As I said, it's an art. I can take a girl to the verge of an orgasm and hold her there until she's delirious, in a sexual frenzy. No man can do that.'

'I'm sure that *some* men know what to do.'

'Maybe. But you've never met one. And I doubt you ever will.'

Gazing wide-eyed at Jackie as she left the sofa and slipped her T-shirt over her head, Mandy stared at the firm mounds of her young breasts, her ripening nipples. Was this what Paula had planned? Jackie was a beautiful girl with perfect breasts but . . . What sort of girl would strip in front of a stranger? Was she a lesbian slut? What the hell was Paula's game?

Jackie ran her hands over her naked breasts and down to the smooth plateau of her stomach as if showing off her young body. She had a beautiful figure, Mandy thought, wondering what to say as the girl tugged her short skirt down her long legs and kicked the garment aside. Her long blonde hair cascading over her teenage breasts, she was stunningly attractive and incredibly sexually aware. The full lips of her pussy clearly defined by her tight knickers, she was also unbelievably alluring.

'Well?' Jackie breathed, smiling at Mandy. 'What do you think?'

'I ... I don't know what to say,' Mandy murmured. 'Apart from to ask you why you've stripped down to your knickers.'

'Because I think you should experiment.'

'Experiment? What do you mean?'

'Taste lesbian sex, Mandy. If you don't, you'll regret it for ever.'

'As attractive and beautiful as you are, *I*'m not a lesbian,' Mandy returned. 'I'm heterosexual. I always have been, and always will be.'

'You don't know until you try,' Jackie persisted.

Pulling her white cotton knickers down just enough to reveal the top of her hairless sex slit, she paused as if waiting for Mandy's reaction. Mandy tried to make out that she wasn't looking, but she felt her womb contract and her stomach somersault as she waited expectantly for the unveiling of the young girl's most private place. Easing the flimsy material down further, displaying the swell of her succulent pussy lips, Jackie allowed the garment to fall down her long legs and crumple around her feet. Kicking her shoes off along with her knickers, she took two paces forward and stood in front of Mandy with her feet parted.

'You may touch, if you want to,' she breathed softly.

'Jackie, I ...' Mandy began. 'I've already told you, I'm not a lesbian.'

'You don't have to be a lesbian to enjoy another girl's body,' Jackie retorted, grinning. 'You don't have to label yourself.'

'I'm *not* labelling myself. All I'm saying is ... Look, you don't even know me. To come here and strip off is ... Do you normally behave like this?'

'I've never behaved like this in my life. I've never met a girl as attractive and beautiful as you, Mandy.

Do you realise how wet you're making me? Feel me,
Mandy. Run your finger up and down my crack and
feel the wetness there.'

'No, I . . .'

'You've made my clit so hard. Why don't you feel
it?'

'Jackie, no.'

'You don't know me, and I don't know you. Your
parents and friends will never know about this, so
why not try it?'

Mandy bit her lip as she gazed at a globule of white
liquid seeping from the girl's tightly closed sex valley.
Her naked love-lips were full and puffy, she noticed
as her stomach again somersaulted. Full, hairless,
smooth, succulent, alluring . . . Tentatively reaching
out, she stroked the soft flesh of the girl's shaven
mons. Running her finger down to the puffiness of
Jackie's swollen outer labia, Mandy massaged the
globule of sex milk into her naked flesh. Jackie
quivered and breathed heavily as Mandy ran her
finger up and down her opening crevice. Parting her
feet wider, she stroked Mandy's long dark hair and
again invited her to feel the hardness of her clitoris.

Although Mandy knew that this was wrong, she
couldn't help herself as she slipped her fingertip into
the young lesbian's sex valley and moved up to the
hardness of her ripe clitoris. This was only experimenting, she thought as Jackie let out a rush of
breath. Experimenting, exploring, satisfying her curiosity . . . She wasn't a lesbian. And, as the girl had
said, no one would know anything about this.
Licking her red lips as she noticed a trickle of pussy
milk running down the girl's inner thigh, Mandy
thought about the tightness of Jackie's vaginal
sheath. She was young, fresh, and very wet. This was
perfectly harmless, she decided as she massaged the

gasping teenager's solid clitoris. No one would ever know what she'd done.

The temptation to move forward in the armchair and taste the hot milk flowing from Jackie's teenage pussy was overwhelming, but Mandy managed to restrain herself. Jackie took another step forward, placing her feet either side of Mandy's feet and jutting her hips forward. She was obviously offering the sexual centre of her young body to Mandy's pretty mouth, her tongue. Her heart racing, Mandy moved forward and perched her rounded buttocks on the edge of the chair. She was about to kiss the girl's swollen love-lips, but she raised her head and pressed her red lips against the smooth flesh of her stomach instead.

'You know what you want,' Jackie said softly. 'So why don't you do it?'

'I . . . I can't,' Mandy breathed. 'I'm not a . . .'

'No, you're not a lesbian. But you like sex. This is only sex, Mandy. There's nothing to be frightened about. It's not scary.'

It might not be scary, Mandy reflected. But it wasn't right to have such intimate physical contact with another girl. Again thinking that no one would know what she'd done, that she was simply experimenting and satisfying her curiosity, she parted the fleshy lips of Jackie's pussy and gazed at the intricate folds nestling within her creamy-wet valley of desire. Eyeing the open entrance to her wet vagina, she tentatively massaged the pink funnel of flesh surrounding her sex hole. This wasn't anything to do with lesbian sex, she tried to convince herself, slipping her finger into the girl's hot and very wet vagina. This was . . .

'God, yes,' Jackie gasped as Mandy's finger drove deep into the tight sheath of her hot cunt. 'Lick me, Mandy. Lick me and make me come.'

Still unable to bring herself to lick the teenage girl's pussy, Mandy slipped a second finger into her contracting vaginal duct and massaged her hot inner flesh. The girl swayed on her sagging legs, her breathing fast and shallow as she clung to Mandy's head for support. Mandy focused on her erect clitoris, the pink protrusion forced out from beneath its pink bonnet, and thought about sucking her there. An experience, she thought, torn between right and wrong. There was no game of one-upmanship now, but . . .

'Lick me,' Jackie breathed again. 'Just do it, Mandy.'

'I don't know,' Mandy began. 'I mean . . .'

'Try it, just this once.'

'Jackie, I'm not . . .'

'Please . . . I need to come. Please suck my clitty.'

This was only another step along the path of sexual experience, Mandy reflected. She'd been a prude before she'd bumped into Paula, and she was now coming out of her shell and learning about sex. But sex with another girl was wrong. No matter what Jackie said, it was wrong. *Only a girl knows how to pleasure another girl.* Mandy remembered the young lesbian's words. She was right – Mandy knew exactly how she liked her clitoris licked and sucked. Consequently, she knew how to pleasure another girl.

Sliding her fingers out of Jackie's tight sex sheath, Mandy leaned forward and tentatively ran her tongue up her open valley. Savouring her first taste of girl-juice, she closed her eyes and lapped up the hot milk flowing from the teenager's vaginal entrance. Her tongue bathed in the girl's lubricious pussy cream and she peeled her sex lips wide apart, pressing her wet lips hard against her open hole. She sucked

100

and the milky lubricant filled her mouth. She swallowed as she breathed in Jackie's girl-scent. Mandy knew that she could easily become hooked on the aphrodisiacal fluid, but she wasn't a lesbian.

Moving up Jackie's open sex valley to the solid protrusion of her clitoris and sweeping her wet tongue over its sensitive tip, Mandy vowed that she'd never do this again. It was nothing more than curiosity, she tried to convince herself as Jackie let out a low moan. Stretching the young girl's love lips apart to the extreme and pressing her mouth against the wet flesh surrounding her protruding clitoris, Mandy snaked her tongue around the sensitive budlette. Only a girl knows, she reflected, imagining how she'd like her own clitoris sucked and licked. No man could ever do this.

In her sexual frenzy, Jackie clutched Mandy's head, forcing her mouth harder against Jackie's solid clitoris. Nearing her climax, she placed one foot on the arm of the chair and parted her thighs wide to allow Mandy better access to her open vaginal crevice. Mandy sucked and slurped at her clitoris, her milky sex juices running down her chin as she took the girl closer to her orgasm. Jackie would want to reciprocate, she knew as she once more thrust two fingers deep into her rhythmically contracting sex duct. What would it be like to have another girl licking her pussy and sucking her clitoris to orgasm? she wondered. Was that what Mandy wanted?

David had known how to suck her to orgasm, but she'd come quickly. Could Jackie really hold her on the verge of orgasm until she begged to come? Mandy imagined herself sitting with her legs open, her bald pussy lips crudely displayed to the teenage lesbian. She couldn't bring herself to do it, she knew as she became acutely aware of her pussy-wet panties. To open the sexual centre of her young body to another girl would be embarrassing in the extreme.

Mouthing on Jackie's hard clitoris as the girl announced that she was close to her orgasm, Mandy felt her own clitoris swell and call for attention. She was desperate for an orgasm, and she began to wonder whether she should after all open her legs to Jackie. Sucking on the girl's pulsating clitoris, she imagined taking Jackie to her bed, their young bodies entwined in lesbian lust as they sucked each other's clitorises to orgasm. Jackie cried out as her climax erupted and orgasmic cream streamed over Mandy's thrusting fingers. Although she mentally affirmed to herself that she wasn't a lesbian, she knew that she'd invite Jackie round for another session of lesbian sex.

'Yes, yes,' Jackie cried, clinging to Mandy's head and grinding her open vulval flesh hard against her face. 'Don't stop. That's . . . that's perfect. God, yes, yes . . . Don't ever stop.'

This was another first, Mandy thought as Jackie gasped and writhed in the grip of her orgasm. From prude to bisexual nymphomaniac – this was another step along the path to her amazing transformation. As Jackie again cried out, her naked body shaking wildly as she rode the crest of her climax, Mandy pondered on the future. Her illicit act of lesbian sex would be for ever etched in her memory, and now she'd look at other girls in a different light. How would she look upon Paula now?

As Jackie began to drift down from her orgasm, Mandy thought about the next step in her transformation. Could she open her legs to another girl? she wondered anxiously. *Only a girl knows how to pleasure another girl.* That was obviously what Mandy wanted. This was a new concept in sex, she reflected as Jackie knelt on the floor at her feet. The girl's face was flushed, her pretty mouth grinning as she pulled Mandy's skirt up and tugged her panties down. Mandy reclined in the chair as her lesbian lover slipped her panties off her feet and parted her legs wide. She wanted to stop the girl, but she also wanted to experience a lesbian-induced orgasm. She knew that, if she pushed Jackie away now, she'd be left wondering for ever.

'It's all right,' Jackie breathed as she stroked the smooth flesh of Mandy's inner thighs and gazed longingly at the hairless lips of her pussy. 'Just relax, Mandy. Just relax.'

Closing her eyes, Mandy mused again about right and wrong. The feel of Jackie's hot breath on her inner thigh moving dangerously close to the opening valley of her vulva, she gazed through her half-closed eyelashes at the girl's long blonde hair. She tried to imagine that Gary was between her legs, but the softness of Jackie's lips as she kissed her pussy crack and the aroma of her perfume brought home the stark reality of the situation. As Jackie ran her wet tongue up and down Mandy's open sex-slit, she knew that there was no denying the truth. This was lesbian sex.

Jackie parted Mandy's sex lips wide, exposing her pink inner folds, her ripe clitoris, to her wet tongue. Mandy gasped, her young body writhing in the armchair, as the younger girl's tongue repeatedly swept over the sensitive tip of her clitoris. It was too late to turn back now, Mandy reflected as her milky juices of arousal decanted from the open entrance of her contracting vagina. Was she a fully fledged lesbian? Would she invite Jackie round again for lesbian sex?

Again vowing that no one would discover her illicit sex act with another girl, she wondered whether

Jackie would go blabbing her mouth off to Paula. Luckily, Paula didn't know Gary or David so word wouldn't get round in these quarters. Trying again to relax, Mandy pushed all thought of Paula from her mind. This was her first time with Jackie, and she didn't want distracting thoughts flooding her awareness. Lesbian sex, she thought dreamily as Jackie slipped two fingers deep into the wet heat of her spasming vaginal duct. Was it so wrong for two girls to enjoy each other's bodies? No one would know of her forbidden act.

'You're beautiful,' Jackie murmured as she licked Mandy's erect clitoris and fingered her tightening vaginal hole. 'I'm glad you shave.'

'Yes,' Mandy breathed, unsure what to say.

'You'd like to come now, wouldn't you?'

'Yes, I . . . I need to come.'

'A man would have taken you to your orgasm by now. It would have been over too quickly, Mandy. But I'm going to make you wait.'

As Mandy's solid clitoris began to pulsate in the beginning of her orgasm, Jackie moved down and kissed the smooth flesh of her inner thighs. Her neglected clitoris yearning for attention, Mandy felt her vaginal muscles tighten around the girl's fingers. She needed the relief of orgasm, she thought, recalling the girl's words. *I can take a girl to the verge of an orgasm and hold her there until she's delirious, in a sexual frenzy*. Her young womb contracting, Mandy arched her back as Jackie nibbled the smooth flesh of her outer labia. To be held on the verge of a climax was sexual torture, she thought as her arousal soared to frightening heights.

As her swollen clitoris was again sucked into Jackie's hot mouth, Mandy writhed and gasped as she thought that she'd at last be allowed her climax.

Her juices of lust flowing over the other girl's thrusting fingers, her clitoris teetering on the verge of erupting in orgasm, she dug her fingernails into the arms of the chair and begged Jackie not to stop. Withdrawing her fingers from Mandy's sex-drenched vagina and slipping her solid clitoris out of her wet mouth, Jackie moved down and sucked Mandy's milky juices from her gaping sex hole. Her painfully solid clitoris once more neglected, still on the brink of climax, she'd never experienced such a craving for sexual relief. Her hand finally running down over her stomach, her fingers massaging her clitoris, she was about to masturbate and reach her climax when Jackie grabbed her wrist.

'No,' the younger girl said firmly.

'Please . . .' Mandy whimpered. 'Please, I need to come.'

'You'll come when I say, and not before.'

'But . . .'

'The next time I visit you, I'll have to tie your hands,' Jackie threatened. 'Now, behave yourself.'

Again gripping the arms of the chair, Mandy watched as the girl ran her wet tongue over the puffy lips of her vulva. Her sex crack gaping wide open, her solid clitoris fully emerging from beneath its pink bonnet, she thought that her lesbian lover was going to make her wait for ever for her desperately needed orgasm. Again thrusting two fingers into Mandy's hot vagina, Jackie slipped another finger between the firm cheeks of her bottom and caressed the sensitive brown tissue surrounding her anus.

Mandy gasped as the girl's finger drove deep into the dank heat of her tightening rectal duct. Jackie certainly knew what she was doing, Mandy thought happily. But Mandy was desperate for an orgasm and writhed in her sexual frenzy as the other girl's fingers thrust repeatedly into her tight sex holes. Her clitoris begging for a wet tongue, her sex milk gushing from her bloated vagina, she became delirious and lay convulsing wildly in the armchair. But Jackie still wouldn't give her what she wanted. The girl deliberately teased Mandy's budlette, massaged the inner flesh of her wet vagina and hot rectum, but deliberately delayed bringing her solid clitty to climax. This really was sexual torture, Mandy thought as her young body shook and convulsed uncontrollably.

'For God's sake,' Mandy gasped. 'I need to come.'

'I know you do,' Jackie replied, giggling. 'You like my fingers in your hot little holes?'

'Yes, yes.'

'And you want me to suck your clitoris?'

'God, yes. Suck it now. Please . . .'

'You started off by saying that you weren't into lesbian sex, and now you're begging me to suck your clitoris.'

'Just *do it*, Jackie.'

Mandy let out a rush of breath as Jackie sucked her ballooning clitoris into her hot mouth and repeatedly swept her tongue over its sensitive tip. Her orgasm came quickly, her young body shaking fiercely as her hot pussy milk gushed over the girl's hand. Never had she known a climax of such amazing strength and duration. Gazing at the open valley of her vulva, her puffy pussy lips enveloping Jackie's pretty mouth, she clutched the girl's head and ground her open cuntal flesh hard against her face. Again and again, waves of lesbian-induced pleasure rocked her young body to the core as she listened to the slurping and sucking sounds of lesbian sex. Her pulsating clitoris pumping ripples of orgasm deep into her rhythmically contracting womb, her head lolling from side to side, her eyes rolling, she thought that she was going to pass out as her pleasure peaked.

'No more,' she managed to gasp. Jackie ignored her plea and continued to suck on her orgasming clitoris and piston her tight sex holes with her fingers. Again, Mandy begged the girl to stop, but she sucked and fingered her and sustained her amazing climax. 'My cunt,' Mandy breathed, her nostrils flaring, her eyes rolling. 'My beautiful cunt. God, no more.'

Finally drifting down from the most powerful orgasm she'd ever experienced, she lay trembling in the armchair as Jackie withdrew her wet fingers from her sated sex holes and slipped her deflating clitoris out of her hot mouth. Her mind blown away in the aftermath of her lesbian orgasm, her breathing fast and shallow, Mandy was unable to speak as Jackie asked her how she felt.

'There,' Jackie breathed. 'That's how a girl should be taken to orgasm.'

'Amazing,' Mandy gasped shakily. 'That was . . . God, that was amazing.'

'I thought you'd like it. No man will ever be able to do that for you. Only a girl knows . . .'

'How to pleasure another girl.'

'That's right. This is only the beginning of our relationship.' Climbing to her feet, Jackie grabbed her clothes. 'I can teach you so much more, Mandy. There's so much pleasure we can bring each other, so much we have to share.'

'I feel dizzy,' Mandy gasped. 'God, I feel . . .'

'Relax, and you'll soon feel better than ever. The longer a girl has to wait, the bigger her orgasm will be. You can try it when you masturbate. Take yourself to the edge of your climax, and hold yourself there for as long as you can. When you come, it will be fantastic.'

Finally opening her eyes and looking around the room, Mandy wondered where the younger girl had gone. As if waking from a dream, she wondered whether Jackie had been real. Looking down between her pussy-wet thighs at the gaping crack of her vulva, she realised that she'd soaked the armchair cushion with her juices of orgasm. Had Jackie been real? Or was she an apparition, an angel?

Hauling her trembling body out of the chair, she finally came to her senses and remembered that David was calling round that evening. Why hadn't he phoned? she wondered. Slipping her wet panties up her long legs and concealing the inflamed lips of her vagina, she flopped onto the sofa and lay with a cushion beneath her head. David should have phoned, she reflected. Had he given up on her? Had he called round and seen her though the lounge window? Drifting off into a deep sleep, Mandy didn't hear the phone ringing.

Six

Mandy woke on the sofa to find the sun streaming in through the lounge window. Her back aching, her thighs glued together with starched pussy milk, she clambered to her feet and glanced at her watch. Eight-thirty. Unable to believe that she'd slept for so long, she climbed the stairs and stepped into the shower. The events of the previous evening filtered into her mind as she washed the girl juice from her sex crack and inner thighs and she decided not to indulge in lesbian sex again. She was neglecting her web-design business and travelling along the road to what she believed would be her inevitable downfall.

'I don't want to become a bisexual whore,' she breathed as she went into her bedroom and brushed her long dark hair. 'One man,' she muttered as she dressed in a miniskirt and blouse. 'One man, one relationship.' David was the one, she mused as the phone rang. He was good company, he knew how to treat a girl and . . .

'It's me,' Paula announced as Mandy grabbed the bedside phone.

'Hello, me,' Mandy quipped. 'How are things?'

'Couldn't be better. I have a photo shoot this morning.'

'A photo shoot? What do you mean?'

'I'm into modelling. Didn't I tell you?'

'No, no, you didn't,' Mandy replied, wondering whether to believe her. 'So, you're a model?'

'I do a bit here and there. It's more of a hobby than anything else.'

'Sounds interesting,' Mandy said, stretching the phone lead as she tossed her hairbrush onto the dressing table. 'What sort of modelling is it?'

'Nude, of course. The money is excellent – not that I need the money.'

'No, I suppose not. By the way, I got the money from Jackie. Thanks for that.'

'Oh, yes. She's a little angel, don't you think?'

'She's an attractive girl, yes.'

'Did she come on to you?'

'No, of course not,' Mandy lied. 'All she did was give me the money.'

'Oh, I see. Didn't you fancy her?'

'No, not really. She's not my type. So, how are your men friends?'

'I went out last night with this really dishy man. God, Mandy, he was good in bed.'

'Take him to the wine bar this evening,' Mandy suggested. 'I'll bring Gary along and we'll make up a foursome.'

'OK, I'll do that,' Paula agreed, much to Mandy's surprise. 'About seven?'

'Seven will be fine. I'll ring Gary and tell him.'

'That's great. So, Jackie didn't stay for long?'

'She came in for a while and we chatted.'

'What about?'

'Well, nothing, really.'

'Mandy, are you keeping something from me?'

'No, of course not. Jackie and I chatted about this and that, and then she went.'

'Will you be seeing her again?'

'No – why should I? I mean, she only came round to give me the money. I have no reason to see her again.'

'No, I suppose not. OK, I'll see you this evening.'

'Don't be late, Paula. I'm looking forward to meeting your new man.'

'I won't be late. Bye.'

Mandy frowned as she replaced the receiver and sat on the edge of her bed. Either Paula was lying or Jackie had got it all wrong, she reckoned. Paula didn't seem to be short of men, and she certainly didn't come across as lonely. Paula was Jackie's boss, and it was unlikely that she'd tell the teenage girl about her private life. Jackie had somehow come to the wrong conclusion, Mandy reflected. She knew that Paula worked hard and probably thought that she didn't have time for socialising and meeting men.

Ringing Gary's office, Mandy bit her lip as she arranged to meet him at the wine bar. She'd decided to stick to one man, to David, but was now going to see Gary. Still, as far as she was aware, David hadn't contacted her. If he couldn't be bothered to ring her, then she wouldn't bother with him, she decided. Gary was over the moon and talked about going back to Mandy's place for coffee afterwards. It seemed that his wife would be out late, giving him a little freedom. Mandy agreed, and then went downstairs to check her emails.

'Shit,' she breathed, reading an email that had arrived the previous day. A representative from the large plastics company wanted to call round to see her that afternoon to discuss the web-site design. Mandy replied, giving her address and apologising for the delay in getting back to them. Within minutes, another email arrived. Jack Carforth, a company director, would be at Mandy's place at three o'clock.

111

'Shit,' Mandy muttered again. 'What shall I wear? What will he think of this dump?'

Having paced the lounge floor for several hours, Mandy almost jumped out of her skin when the doorbell rang. Opening the door, she gazed at the man and stammered as she invited him in. Jack Carforth was in his fifties and had greying hair, but he was not bad-looking. Leading him into the dining room, Mandy offered him a seat and asked him whether he'd like tea or coffee. Placing his briefcase on the desk, he said he wanted neither. Tall and wearing a suit, white shirt and tie, he looked rather foreboding. As he pulled his chair up to the desk, Mandy switched her computer on, hoping that she wasn't going to make a mess of the meeting.

'Relax,' he said, with a chuckle. 'Your hands are trembling.'

'I *am* a little nervous,' she confessed.

'Don't be. We've accepted your quote, and I'm only here to go through one or two things.' Opening his briefcase, Carforth showed Mandy some rough designs. 'This is the sort of thing we're after,' he said, placing a sheet of A4 on the desk. 'Company logo at the top, and then this blurb about the things we do, and the links to the other web pages down the side.'

'OK, that's fine,' Mandy said, studying the paper. 'I'll need a list of all the pages you want, and the content.'

'I've got each page drawn up,' he said, taking a wad of paper from his case. 'We've bought a domain name, and the FTP details are listed here. I know nothing about FTP or domains. That's your department.'

'No problem. Well, I can start on this straight away.'

'Good. Now that's over, I think I will have a coffee.'

'Er . . . I'll need to know the colour scheme and . . .'

'I'll leave that to you,' Carforth cut in. 'My fellow directors and I have some ideas, but we want to see what you come up with.'

'OK, I'll get the site up and running and you can check it out before we go live. Anything you're not happy with can be changed, of course.'

'We want to leave it all to you, Mandy. It's OK to call you Mandy?'

'Yes, of course.'

'Good. I'm Jack. Now, how about that coffee?'

Mandy brought up one or two points over coffee and was amazed when Jack pulled a chequebook from his briefcase and asked her how much she wanted up front. Agreeing to half the total cost, he wrote the cheque and indicated that he might have further work for her. The company was expanding, and another web site might be in the pipeline. Mandy was over the moon as she gazed at the cheque, but did her best not to show it. One thing was certain – with all this work to do, there'd be very little time for sex. During the day, at least.

Finally seeing him out, she closed the door and punched the air with her fist. 'Yes,' she cried. 'Yes, fucking yes.' This was a completely different ball game, she knew as she recalled the landscape gardener's web site. Gardeners, plumbers . . . This was a massive company with huge amounts of cash floating around. If they did want another web site, she'd be well on the way to success, she thought happily. And to have such a huge and respected company in her portfolio was bound to open other doors.

Too excited to eat, Mandy applied her make-up and brushed her long dark hair before leaving the flat and walking to the wine bar. What if Gary didn't turn up? she wondered anxiously. To spend the evening with Paula and her new man would be awkward without Gary there. Smiling as she walked into the bar and noticed Gary ordering a drink, she breathed a sigh of relief.

'I thought you might not turn up,' she said, joining him at the bar.

'I'll always turn up for you,' he said, chuckling. 'Vodka and tonic?'

'Please.'

'So, these friends of yours. Have you known them long?'

'I've known Paula since I was at school,' Mandy replied as he ordered her drink. 'I haven't met her boyfriend, though. If it gets boring, we can leave them here and go back to my place.'

'OK,' Gary said, taking the drinks from the bar and leading her to a table. 'I was wondering whether you'd set something up, like you did the other night.'

'Set something up?' she echoed, sitting next to him at the table.

'That bloke who came round and caught us . . .'

'Oh, no, no. It's nothing like that, I promise you.'

Mandy revealed her doubts about Paula and explained the game of one-upmanship she'd been playing. She liked the way that Gary listened intently, taking an interest rather than just nodding appropriately. It was a shame that he was married. There again, she didn't want to be tied down to one man. Her thoughts turning to David, she knew that she was confused. David was kind and considerate and . . .

'Hi,' Paula said as she breezed into the bar with a good-looking man in tow. 'This is Henry.'

'Hi, people,' Henry said, his face beaming as he gazed down the front of Mandy's loose-fitting blouse. 'Drinks all round?'

114

The introductions over, Henry went up to the bar and ordered the drinks as Paula sat opposite Gary. Henry seemed all right, Mandy thought. In his thirties with dark hair, he was wearing an open-neck blue shirt and dark trousers. He was probably loaded, Mandy decided as Paula chatted to Gary. Loaded, and good in bed. Placing the drinks on the table and sitting opposite Mandy, he stared again at her blouse and smiled.

'Paula's told me all about you,' he said.

'Nothing bad, I hope?' Mandy replied.

'I didn't tell him that you're bisexual,' Paula said, grinning at Mandy.

'Bisexual?' Gary echoed.

'Of course I'm not,' Mandy returned, forcing a giggle. Wishing she'd eaten before going out, she downed her second vodka and knew that the alcohol was going to her head. 'I'm only into cocks,' she said, immediately wishing that she hadn't.

'That's a shame,' Gary rejoined. 'I've always wanted to watch two girls getting it off together.'

The conversation, mainly dominated by Paula, centred on lesbian sex. Mandy was beyond caring as Gary bought the next round of drinks. It was nice to relax and let go for a change, she thought, throwing in the odd lewd remark. She knew that it was Henry's foot brushing her leg beneath the table. Winking at her, gazing at her blouse, he obviously fancied her. Mandy was flattered, but he was Paula's man and there was no way she'd get involved with him.

Paula left the table as her mobile phone rang. Wandering over to a quiet corner, her face set in a frown, she didn't seem at all happy. Reckoning that it was something to do with work, Mandy turned down Henry's offer of another drink. Dizzy on alcohol, she decided that it was time to go home.

Gary was ready to leave and, when Paula announced that she had to go and deal with some business, Henry offered to walk with her.

'No,' Paula murmured. 'I'll see you tomorrow. Sorry about this,' she said, smiling at Mandy. 'I'll ring you, OK?'

'OK,' Mandy said. 'We're about to go anyway.'

'Then there were three,' Gary said as Paula left the bar.

'It was nice meeting you both,' Henry said. 'I hope we can do this again soon.'

'Come back for coffee, if you like,' Mandy suggested.

'Well, if you're sure?'

'Of course I'm sure. That's OK, isn't it, Gary?'

'Yes, that's fine.'

Walking home with two men in tow, Mandy couldn't help thinking of the possibility that she might enjoy two cocks. Recalling Gary's comments when he'd been at her flat, she knew that he'd be up for it. But would Henry want to share a girl with another man? Reaching her flat, Mandy knew that her decision to stick with one man was a non-starter. The game of one-upmanship with Paula was over, but she'd been pondering for some time on the idea of two men using her. Deciding to play it by ear as Gary and Henry settled on the sofa, she made the coffees and joined them in the lounge.

'It's a shame Paula was called away,' she said, sitting in the armchair.

'I'm rather pleased,' Henry said, grinning at Mandy.

'Why's that?'

'Gary was just saying that it's great to be here with a beautiful young woman.'

'Was he, now?'

'I was saying that it would be fun to share you,' Gary said unashamedly, catching Mandy's eye and winking at her.

'Tell me more,' Mandy said. 'I'm intrigued.'

'Well, we thought that—'

'We thought that you might do a strip for us,' Henry cut in.

'Take all my clothes off in front of two men?' Mandy said, giggling as she felt her clitoris stir. 'That would be very naughty.'

'We like naughty girls,' Henry said.

Standing, Mandy unbuttoned her blouse and slipped the garment off her shoulders. This was what she'd been hoping for, she reflected as the men gazed longingly at the cups of her white bra. Was the game of one-upmanship with Paula over? Whether it was over or not, this was an opportunity not to be missed. Many times now she'd wondered about having two solid cocks to pleasure her. Two cocks, two tongues, four hands . . . No one would know, would they?

Unhooking her bra and allowing the cups to fall away from the mounds of her firm breasts, Mandy felt good as her audience gazed at her. She also felt that she had power over men. She was in control, she mused, running her hands over her rounded breasts. Not only was she well on the way to becoming a successful businesswoman, but she had what men wanted. She was in demand, at long last, she thought as she allowed her short skirt to fall down her legs. But what worried her was that she had no qualms about behaving like a common whore. Henry was Paula's boyfriend and Mandy should have felt guilty and ashamed but . . .

'Very nice,' Henry murmured, staring at the white material of her tight panties hugging her full sex lips.

117

'Don't stop there,' Gary said. 'I'm sure that Henry is eager to see your shaved pussy.'

'I hope you're only going to look,' Mandy said. 'I mean, I wouldn't want two men groping me.'

'We're perfect gentlemen,' Henry said, with a chuckle. 'Good grief, as if we'd grope you. We might do other things, but we wouldn't grope you.'

Sliding her panties down and kicking them aside along with her shoes, Mandy had never felt so aroused. She'd never really thought about her young body in the past. Now she realised that she had a good figure, beautifully rounded breasts, perfect sex lips ... She had what men wanted. And she knew how to use it. Paula was missing out, she thought, pleased that the other girl had been called away as the men gazed at her hairless vulva lips, her opening sex crack. It was ironic to think that Paula had wanted to meet Mandy's male friends, and now Mandy was standing naked in front of Paula's boyfriend.

Walking to the sofa and standing with her feet wide apart, she allowed the men to run their hands over her naked body. As their fingers toyed with her swollen pussy lips and encircled her erect nipples, she felt alive with sex. Her young womb contracting, her juices of lust streaming from her tight vaginal hole, she quivered as two fingers slipped deep into the wet sheath of her pussy. Yet another first, she thought dreamily as her clitoris swelled expectantly. She'd experienced lesbian sex with Jackie, and was now about to enjoy two cocks at once. Male hands reached behind her and clutched her firm buttocks, and she gasped as a fingertip teased the sensitive brown eye of her tight anus.

'Do what you like to me,' she said in her wanton abandonment. 'Use me.'

'I'd like to treat you like a slut,' Gary said.

'Yes,' she breathed as her vaginal muscles tightened around the intruding fingers. 'I *am* a slut. Do as you wish with me.'

Nothing mattered, Mandy thought as the fingers slipped out of her vaginal duct and the men left the sofa and almost tore their clothes off in their haste. No one would know of her debauchery. No one would know what she did in the privacy of her home. Besides, it was her life, her body, so what the hell? From prude to slut, she reflected as Gary knelt behind her and Henry knelt at her feet. One tongue running up and down her hairless pussy crack, another delving into the deep valley between her buttocks, she quivered and let out a rush of breath. This was sheer sexual bliss. Had she found her niche in life?

Her arse-globes held wide apart, a wet tongue lapping at the delicate flesh surrounding her anal hole, Mandy swayed on her sagging legs as her vaginal lips were stretched apart and her erect clitoris was sucked hard. Gary and Henry were her sex slaves, she thought as they attended her most intimate feminine needs. She'd have them round again and instruct them to pleasure her and take her to several multiple orgasms. What about Jackie? she thought as Gary lay on the floor on his back. Would she become Mandy's lesbian sex slave? One thing was for sure: Paula was missing out on the best sex ever.

Following Gary's orders and kneeling astride his hips, Mandy rested her weight on her hands and looked down at his grinning face as he eased the full length of his huge cock deep into her juice-drenched vaginal sheath. Henry knelt behind her and parted the rounded cheeks of her bottom. His bulbous knob stabbing at her well-salivated anal inlet, he let out a low moan of pleasure as his glans slipped past her defeated anal-sphincter muscles and entered the dank

119

heat of her tight rectum. Mandy gasped, her naked body shaking uncontrollably as his cock glided deep into her rectal duct and his knob came to rest in her bowels. Her sex holes bloated, stretched to capacity, she was amazed by the incredible sensations as her lovers began their slow fucking motions.

A dream come true, Mandy thought as her young body rocked with the crude double fucking. Listening to the squelching of her sex juices, the sound of flesh meeting flesh, she felt her pelvic cavity inflate and deflate as the two cock shafts synchronised their thrusting motions and repeatedly drove into her inflamed sheaths. Henry muttered dirty words as he shafted Mandy's tight anal duct, taking her arousal to amazing heights as Gary pinched and twisted her erect milk teats. *Tight-arsed slut, anal whore, cock-loving bitch . . .*

'I'm coming,' Mandy breathed, her solid clitoris massaged by Gary's pussy-wet shaft. 'God, yes, I'm coming.' Her orgasm erupting within the swollen bulb of her sensitive clitoris, her sex holes tightening, gripping the thrusting penises, she cried out in the grip of her illicit climax. Quite involuntarily, she let out a gush of hot urine as her muscles spasmed. Gary thrust his cock into her contracting vagina harder and faster as the hot liquid ran over his bouncing balls. He asked her to pee on him again, obviously loving the sensation. Still in the grip of her orgasm, Mandy managed to squirt once more, her hot piss raining down over Gary's cock and balls as he announced that he was coming.

'Yes,' Henry gasped, his creamy spunk jetting deep into Mandy's bowels and lubricating his pistoning cock.

'You beautiful little slut,' Gary cried, his sperm issuing from his throbbing knob and flooding her inflamed vaginal cavern.

Again and again, Mandy cried out as her orgasm peaked, rocking her abused body to the core. This was real sex, she thought dreamily as a river of spunk flowed down her inner thighs. Imagining John walking into the room and witnessing her double fucking, Mandy knew that this was her way of life now. Her climax once more peaking, she knew that she could never be faithful to one man, not even to David. With the money beginning to roll in and men to pleasure her, she'd want for nothing. Collapsing on top of Gary as her climax finally waned, she turned her thoughts to Jackie.

What would the girl say if she could see Mandy now? But Jackie would never discover the shocking truth. Jackie, David, Paula . . . no one would discover Mandy's secret and most sordid life. As the phone rang and the deflating cocks slipped out of her inflamed sex ducts, she wondered whether it was David calling. It was too late, she reflected. She was now hooked on the double penetration of the tight holes between her slender thighs. She might see David again, she mused as she rolled off Gary's trembling body and lay on her back on the floor. But David couldn't turn the clock back. Mandy was now a fully fledged slut and she would never return to her old way of life.

'You're incredible,' Henry gasped, gazing at the fresh sperm oozing from Mandy's gaping sex holes. 'I've never known anyone like you.'

'I reckon she's unique,' Gary said. 'I wish my wife was like you, Mandy.'

'I don't think I'd make a very good wife,' Mandy said, giggling as she propped herself up on her elbows and focused on the spunk streaming from her yawning vaginal valley. 'I wouldn't be a faithful wife, I know that. Mind you, I'm a pretty good slut.'

121

'You're a *fantastic* slut,' said Henry, praising her again.

'How do I compare with Paula?'

'A million times better.'

'Good, I'm pleased to hear that.'

'And you're a million times better than my wife,' Gary rejoined.

'You two are pretty good. Is there any chance of doing it again?'

'Well, I think I could manage it,' Henry replied, running his hand up and down his stiffening shaft.

'And me,' Gary said, his cock rising from his wet balls and standing to attention. 'We'll swap this time. You do her pussy, Henry, and I'll do her bum.'

Taking her position over Henry as he lay on his back, Mandy grinned as his solid cock slid deep into her sperm-laden vaginal canal. Gary knelt behind her, his bulbous knob sliding into her spunk-lubricated rectal sheath with ease. This time, Mandy did the work, the two men remaining still as she rocked back and forth, shafting her tight holes on the two granite-hard penises. The sound of squelching sperm mingling with gasps of pleasure, she let out a yelp as Gary slapped the naked orbs of her firm bottom. Again and again, he spanked her rounded buttocks, sending her arousal sky-high as she gasped and whimpered in her decadent act. Her sperm-flooded sex sheaths inflamed, rhythmically contracting and gripping the solid cocks, she squeezed her muscles and showered Henry's balls with her hot urine.

Mandy imagined three men using her young body as the men gasped and neared their second orgasms. Three cocks, she thought, her solid clitoris massaged by Henry's thrusting shaft. One rock-hard cock repeatedly driving into her wet vagina, another pistoning her rectal cylinder, and a third bloating her gobbling mouth. The ultimate act of decadence, she thought as the birth of her orgasm stirred deep within her contracting womb. Three cocks fucking her young body, using and abusing her . . .

'Yes,' Henry cried, his sperm jetting from his throbbing knob and flooding Mandy's inflamed vaginal throat. 'Tight-cunted whore. God, you're fucking tight.'

'Dirty little slut,' Gary breathed as his knob swelled and pumped its orgasmic cream deep into the very core of her young body. 'Arse-fucking slag.'

'Fuck me senseless,' Mandy gasped as they rocked their hips. 'Fuck me until I scream.'

'Cum-loving slut, piss-whore, filthy-cunted little tart . . .'

Listening to their crude words as they once more flooded her sex sheaths with their creamy sperm, Mandy let out a cry as her own orgasm erupted within the pulsating nub of her solid clitoris. Gary repeatedly spanked her glowing buttocks as he rocked his hips and shafted her burning rectal tube. Her long black hair cascading over her sex-flushed face, her eyes rolling, she again imagined a third cock bloating her mouth, the throbbing knob pumping its orgasmic liquid down her throat as her vagina and rectum flooded with fresh spunk. Paula had nothing on her now, she thought as Gary continued to spank the glowing cheeks of her stinging bottom. Mandy had left Paula in the dust.

'Christ,' Gary breathed as he slipped his spent penis out of Mandy's sperm-bubbling rectum. 'She's fucking incredible.'

'We'll definitely do this again,' Henry gasped as Mandy rolled off his naked body and crumpled on the floor beside him.

'Which did you prefer, Henry?' Gary asked the man. 'Her arse or her cunt?'

Sitting up and resting his back against the wall, Henry grinned. 'To be honest, her cunt is almost as tight as her arse,' he replied.

'A double fucking constricts both holes,' Gary said with a chuckle. 'But I think her arse feels tighter.'

'Do you reckon we could both get our cocks into her tight little cunt?'

'I've seen pictures like that,' Gary replied. 'The next time we're here, we'll give it a go.'

'Or two cocks up her bum?'

'Bloody hell, Henry, now that *is* an idea.'

Mandy loved the way the men talked about her as if she wasn't there. Discussing her arse and her cunt, planning what they'd do to her the next time they were at her flat ... Their crude words exciting her, she'd have liked to have taken their cocks into her tight holes again. But she was exhausted and she doubted that they'd be able to manage a third time. As they talked about bondage and whipping, she knew that her next session with the men was going to take her further along the road to her complete and utter debauchery. Watching them dress, she curled up into a ball on the floor as sperm oozed from the inflamed holes between her thighs. The experience had left her exhausted, but also craving more crude sex. The experience had plunged her deeper into the pit of depravity.

Mandy said nothing as the men thanked her. Gary asked her whether she was all right, and she managed a smile. Her naked body still shaking in the aftermath of her double fucking, she listened as they left the room and the front door finally closed. Her dream had come true, she mused. But now she had another dream. Three cocks shafting her tight holes, filling her young body with creamy sperm. Four cocks? she wondered, hauling her sagging body up as the phone rang.

'Hi, Mandy,' David said as she pressed the receiver to her ear. 'I rang last night, and this evening, but . . .'

'Sorry,' she breathed. 'I . . . I've not been feeling too well. I went to bed early last night.'

'God, I'm sorry. Have I woken you?'

'No, no, I was just dozing. I didn't hear the phone last night. I must have been sleeping.'

'Is there anything I can do for you? I could come round and . . .'

'No, no, I'll be OK. I think it was a tummy bug.'

'Well, if you're sure? Oh, by the way, I was talking to your dad earlier.'

'Oh?'

'He's having a barbecue tomorrow evening for your mum's birthday.'

'God, yes, her birthday. I'd forgotten all about that.'

'He's invited me and he'll obviously ask you along. It'll be like the old days, Mandy. Of course, we won't be able to have a kiss and a cuddle, but . . .'

'I suppose I ought to see them,' Mandy sighed. 'Especially as it's Mum's birthday.'

'You don't sound very keen.'

'It's just that . . . I'm not sure what's happening tomorrow evening.'

'Oh, I see.'

'David, what are your plans? I mean, where do you see us going?'

'Plans, for us? Well, I know that I'm a lot older than you, but . . . I want to look after you, Mandy. You're in your flat alone every evening, you don't seem to get out and meet people or have a social life . . .'

'I do have *some* friends.'

'Yes, but . . . as you said, you've not had a proper relationship for two years. I'm old, so I don't expect you to . . . what I mean is . . . God, I'm making a mess of this.'

'I know what you mean. At least, I think I do. My life is complicated at the moment.'

'Complicated? Do you mean your work?'

'No . . . well, there is that. I'm not the sort of girl you think I am, David.'

'I know exactly what sort of girl you are, Mandy. Good God, I've known you for years. You're sweet, innocent . . . and you need looking after.'

'Yes, well . . . Look, I'll go to the barbecue. It'll be nice to see Mum and Dad – and you, of course.'

'OK, that's great.'

'I should be feeling a lot better by then. Thanks for ringing, David.'

'If there's anything worrying you, you will tell me?'

'Yes, yes, of course.'

'OK, you have a good night's sleep and I'll see you at the barbecue.'

Sighing as she hung up, Mandy climbed the stairs to her bedroom. She liked David and, had he come along before Gary, she'd have enjoyed a long-term relationship with him. But now that Gary was on the scene, and Henry and Jackie . . . She could never be faithful to one man, she knew as she slipped beneath her quilt. Her fingers delving between the fleshy lips of her pussy, she massaged her swelling clitoris and quivered as the heavenly sensations transmitted deep into her contracting womb. If only David was there now, she thought dreamily as her vaginal muscles tightened. If only *any* man was there in her bed.

Her thoughts now constantly centred on crude sex, and she wondered how many more men she'd meet, how many cocks would drive deep into her young vagina and splatter her cervix with fresh sperm. Feeling wicked, and sexually alive, she reached to the

126

bedside drawer and pulled out her torch. The plastic shaft was long, thick and hard, and she knew that it would make an ideal phallus. Parting the inflamed lips of her vulva, she eased the end of the torch into her sperm-flooded sex duct and let out a gasp.

As she drove the plastic shaft in and out of her tightening vagina, the rounded end battering her ripe cervix, Mandy parted her slender legs to the extreme and again massaged the sensitive nub of her erect clitoris. 'My cunt,' she breathed in her decadence. 'God, my beautiful cunt.'

Her crude words sending her into a sexual frenzy, she repeatedly rammed the plastic torch deep into her tight sex duct. Imagining the men's cocks shafting her, fucking the tight holes between her thighs, she pictured a third cock bloating her mouth, the purple knob driving to the back of her throat. Three cocks, four, five . . . How many cocks could her young body take? she wondered.

Leaving the torch in place, Mandy grabbed a plastic pen from the bedside table and slipped the rounded end into her tight anal hole. Never had she abused her young body like this, and she realised just how much pleasure she'd missed over the years. Holding the torch and the pen, repeatedly driving the two phalluses into her spunk-laden sex sheaths, she whimpered incoherent words of crude lust as she massaged her swollen clitoris.

'I'm coming,' Mandy breathed as her clitoris pulsated. 'God, I'm coming.' Her orgasm erupting, shaking her perspiring body, she screamed in the grip of her self-induced pleasure. Her anal muscles gripping the thrusting pen, her vagina spewing out its fresh girl-milk, her clitoris pulsating fiercely, she tossed her head from side to side and screamed again as her pleasure peaked and shook her to the core.

Wishing that Gary and Henry were there, she imagined sucking on their cocks, their knobs double fucking her mouth and pumping creamy spunk down her throat. Gary, Henry, David . . . Three men, three cocks fucking her young body and pumping her full of male cream. Her orgasm finally melting, she lay convulsing and gasping in her bed. At last, she thought dreamily. At last, she'd discovered the delights of her naked body. She'd discovered sex, deviant sex, and couldn't give it up. Wishing again that David had asked her out before she'd become a slut, she slipped the plastic phalluses out of her burning sex ducts and closed her eyes. Wondering when she'd see Jackie again, she was desperate for more crude sex. David, Gary, Henry, Jackie . . . Who would be next on her list of sexual conquests?

Seven

After breakfast, Mandy sat at her computer and tried to get on with some work. *You're sweet, innocent . . . and you need looking after*. David's words haunted her, played on her mind, as she cleared the way to begin work on the large web site. Spreading the sheets of A4 paper out on the desk, she reclined in her swivel chair and sighed. She had two choices, she decided. She could either forget her sordid life and enjoy a proper relationship with David, or . . . But she knew in her heart that she couldn't deny herself the amazing pleasure of two cocks shafting her tight sex holes.

'What the hell's happened to me?' she whispered, recalling her life before Paula. She'd been isolated and lonely with no sex life, not even enjoying masturbation, but she hadn't had to endure this confusion. The game of one-upmanship with Paula had been fun at times, but it was no longer a game. Her debauched fantasies of crude sex had now become reality. Recalling her father's words, she bit her lip and grimaced. *Be careful what it is you want, because you just might get it*. She *had* wanted to be like Paula, she reflected. She'd wanted to be bubbly, earn decent money and have several men on the go and . . . But now?

Mandy thought about her life before Paula as she wandered into the lounge. She'd had a routine, the shopping, her work, cleaning the flat . . . If she hadn't met Paula at the bus stop that fateful day, things wouldn't have changed, she reflected as the phone rang. Flopping into the armchair and grabbing the receiver, she was pleased to hear her mother's voice. Trying to sound pleased about the barbecue, she didn't let on that she already knew about it.

'It'll be nice to see you,' her mother said. 'We don't see much of you any more. Why don't you come over more often?'

'I hadn't forgotten about your birthday, Mum,' Mandy said. 'It's just that I've been really busy. My work is taking off at last. I'm beginning to earn some decent money.'

'That *is* good news, Mandy. You've put so much effort into it, you deserve to have some success. By the way, David will be coming this evening.'

'Oh, that's nice. I haven't seen him for . . . for a long time.'

'Between you and me, I think he must have a young lady in his life.'

'What makes you think that?'

'He seems different – happy and . . . Let's just say it's a woman's instinct. How about you? Do you have a young man, yet?'

'No, no,' Mandy lied. 'I'm too busy with work to bother with men. Look, I'll see you later, Mum. I have a lot to do today.'

'OK, dear. Why don't you stay for the night?'

'Yes, I might do that. I'll see you later.'

Working on the web site until mid-afternoon, Mandy finally switched her computer off and went up to her bedroom. Deciding to take Jack Carforth's cheque to the bank on the way, and buy a card and

130

a present for her mother, she dressed in a knee-length skirt and white blouse. It would be nice to be away from the flat for the night, she mused as she closed the front door behind her. And away from the telephone. Wondering whether Henry had spoken to Paula since last night, she hoped he wouldn't say that he'd gone back to Mandy's place. It was odd that Paula hadn't phoned, she thought. There again, she was probably busy at work.

'Mandy,' her mother said, her face beaming as she opened the front door. 'Come in, come in. David's in the garden with your father.'

'Thanks,' Mandy said softly, kissing the woman's cheek and following her into the kitchen. 'It's good to see you, Mum. Happy birthday. Here's your card and present.'

'Oh, thank you. It's nice to see you, dear. By the way, I was right about David.'

'Oh?'

'He *has* got a young lady. And you'll never guess. She's only your age.'

'Oh, I see. That's rather young, isn't it?'

'That's what I thought. But if they're happy . . .'

'Mum, what would you say if I went out with a man of David's age?'

'I don't know. He'd be old enough to be your father, but . . . Happiness comes first, Mandy. If you found a man of David's age, and you were happy, then I'd be happy for you.'

Biting her lip as her mother poured her a glass of white wine, Mandy wondered what David had said about his so-called young lady. He wasn't stupid, she thought as she sipped her wine. He wouldn't have said anything about Mandy. Following her mother into the garden, she hugged her father and then smiled at David. This was going to be difficult, she knew as he took her hand and kissed her cheek.

'It's great to see you,' David said, pulling out a patio chair and gesturing for her to sit down. 'So, what have you been up to?'

'She's been working and earning money,' her mother said proudly as David sat opposite Mandy. 'She's doing very well, aren't you, dear?'

'Yes – yes I am.'

'I always knew you'd do well,' her father said, standing by the barbecue and prodding the sausages with a fork. 'She's a hard worker, David. She'll go far.'

'Yes, indeed,' David said, gazing into Mandy's dark eyes. 'You're into web-site design, aren't you?'

'Yes, that's right,' Mandy breathed, her stomach somersaulting as he reached across the table and squeezed her hand. 'All work and no play, though, I'm afraid.'

Sipping his beer as her parents went into the kitchen, he leant forward across the table. 'I've really missed you,' he whispered.

'I've missed you, David. What did you tell my parents about your young lady?'

'Oh, your mother guessed,' he said with a chuckle. 'Don't worry, I didn't give the game away.' Lowering his head and gazing into his glass of beer, he squeezed her hand again. 'Mandy, if ever we . . . I mean, if we get serious about each other, what would your parents say?'

'Well, I . . . I don't know.'

'I feel that I have an obstacle course in front of me,' David sighed. 'Firstly, there's my age. I'm old enough to be your father. I don't really know how you feel about me, and then there's your parents to worry about.'

132

'You're thinking too far ahead, David. Let's just see what happens, OK?'

'OK. I'm sorry. It's just that I haven't been able to stop thinking about you. What we did down by the river was . . .'

'More beer, David?' Mandy's father asked as he stepped onto the patio.

'Oh, er . . . yes, thanks.'

'Are you staying the night, Mandy?'

'I think so, Dad.'

'In that case, finish your wine and I'll top you up.'

Downing her drink and watching her father refill her glass, Mandy couldn't work out her feelings for David. Unlike Gary, he obviously wanted a lot more than a quick fuck, she reflected. Asking her father to leave the wine bottle on the table, she thought that getting tipsy might bring out her true feelings. David was a lovely man, she thought, gulping down her drink as he smiled at her. His age didn't come into it and she wasn't too worried about her parents, so what was the problem?

Refilling her glass, Mandy knew what the problem was. Her love of sex with different men, the amazing pleasure she'd derived from having two cocks ramming deep into her sex sheaths, her incredible experience with Jackie, her insatiable clitoris . . . David had money, a lovely house, he was kind and considerate, he was good in bed . . . What more could a girl want? Two cocks, she reflected. Three cocks, spunk flooding her mouth, her vagina, her tight rectum and . . .

'I wouldn't cramp your style,' David said, breaking her reverie as if he'd been reading her thoughts.

'What do you mean?' she asked him.

'You're young, Mandy,' he whispered as her father hovered by the barbecue. 'You'll want friends of your own age and you'll want to do things and go places

133

where an old man like me wouldn't fit in. I understand that so, should you decide that you want to be with me, I won't stop you from living your life.'

'The thing is . . .' she began, sighing as her mother placed a plate of garlic bread on the table. 'I'm going to take a look around the garden,' she said, smiling at her mother.

'I'll go with you,' David said, leaving the table as Mandy wandered across the lawn.

Making out that she was looking at the flowers as her mother said how nice it would be if she rented her flat out and moved back home, she felt more confused than ever. Why couldn't David have come along before she'd met Paula? she wondered as he stood by her side. Why couldn't he have come along before she'd opened her pussy lips to Jackie, Gary and Henry? David wanted a serious relationship with her, her mother wanted her to move back home . . . Maybe the barbecue wasn't such a good idea, she mused, walking to the end of the garden.

'Are you all right?' David asked her, joining her behind the hedge.

'I'm confused,' she replied honestly.

'It's me, isn't it? I'm sorry, Mandy. I should have kept my big mouth shut.'

'No, no, it's not just you. Mum wants me to move back, I'm really busy with my work and . . .'

'Is there someone else? Look, if there is . . . What I'm trying to say is that I wouldn't mind.'

'You wouldn't mind?' she said in surprise, frowning at him.

'As I said, I wouldn't cramp your style.'

'I'm not saying that there is anyone else but, if there was, you wouldn't mind? You wouldn't mind if I went out with another man?'

'I'm in love with you, Mandy. I'll do whatever it takes to be with you.'

'That would be awful for you, David. Knowing that I was out with some man, knowing that I was sleeping with another man . . .'

'If you came home to me afterwards, I wouldn't mind.'

'It wouldn't work, David. It would tear you apart.'

'I'd live in the hope that, one day, you'd want only me.'

David didn't know what he was saying, Mandy thought as he placed his hands on her shoulders and gazed into her wide eyes. If he knew that she'd been out with another man, fucking another man, he couldn't welcome her home as if nothing had happened. If he knew that her pussy was brimming with another man's spunk, it just wouldn't work. Besides, she wouldn't want a relationship like that. What would he think if he knew about Jackie? she wondered as he leant forward and kissed her full lips. What would he think if he knew that she'd enjoyed lesbian sex with a teenage girl?

Unzipping his trousers, Mandy pulled out David's flaccid penis and retracted his foreskin as their tongues entwined. He breathed heavily through his nose as she rubbed her thumb over the silky-smooth surface of his swelling knob. He must have thought this was a sign of her acceptance, she thought dreamily as her clitoris swelled and her juices of lust seeped into the tight crotch of her panties. In reality, it was nothing more than a sign of her increasing thirst for sex.

Wanking his solid cock, she wanted to show David that she was a slut. She wasn't the sweet little girl who used to live next door, the innocent little virgin who'd enjoyed his company at her parents' barbecues. She'd grown up, gone out into the big bad world – and opened her tight cunt to other men and a girl and discovered crude sex. Sex with two men, sex with a teenage girl and . . . She couldn't give up her new-found life. Lifting her skirt and pulling the front of her panties down, she held his cock tight and increased her wanking rhythm.

'Come in my knickers,' she breathed huskily, pressing his bulbous knob against her hairless sex slit. 'I want you to spunk in my knickers, David.'

'Mandy, I . . . Why?'

'I want to feel your spunk against my cunt. I want to feel my spunked knickers against my cunt all evening.'

As his fresh sperm jetted from his throbbing knob and ran down the creamy valley of her vulva, he threw his head back and moaned softly. If this didn't give him a better picture of the sort of girl she was, then nothing would, Mandy thought. Talking about his spunk running down her cunt crack, she held him close and continued to wank his solid shaft until he began to crumple. Finally staggering back, he watched as she pulled her panties up and allowed the thin cotton material to soak up the product of his orgasm.

'God,' David breathed. 'That was amazing.'

'My knickers are wet and sticky,' Mandy whispered as her father called that the food was ready.

'I didn't realise that you liked . . . well, that sort of thing.'

'You'd be surprised by the things I like,' she said, giggling.

'Go on, surprise me.'

'We'd better go and eat.'

'Yes, yes, of course.' Walking back to the patio, David took Mandy's hand. 'What sort of things are you into?' he asked her.

'Water sports,' she whispered. 'Come on, the food smells good.'

David frowned at her as they walked to the table where each of them took a plate. Mandy knew that she'd shocked him, but she wanted him to realise that she wasn't the innocent little girl he once knew. Her panties glued to her hairless pussy lips by his drying sperm, she helped herself to a burger and a sausage and retook her seat at the table. Her father started chatting to David, going on about the weather and the possibility of rain, but David obviously wasn't listening. Taking a bread roll from the table, Mandy smiled as David sat opposite her.

'This looks good,' she said, sandwiching her burger between the two halves of the roll.

'Yes, yes, it does,' David breathed. 'Mandy, have you ever . . . what you were talking about just now, have you done it?'

'Of course,' she replied, grinning at him. 'With another girl.'

'What?' he gasped.

'With another girl,' she repeated, taking a bite from her burger.

'God, I . . . I had no idea that you . . .' His words tailing off as Mandy's mother brought out a bowl of salad, he took a gulp of beer. 'This is lovely,' he said, smiling at the woman. 'I'm really hungry.'

'I've told you before that you don't eat properly,' Mandy's mother said. 'Living alone like you do, I'll bet you survive on takeaways.'

'I'm a pretty good cook,' he replied as she laughed.

'You need a good woman to look after you, David.'

Mandy's father chuckled. 'Are you making him an offer?' he said as he prodded the barbecue coals with a stick.

'You have a good woman, don't you, David?' Mandy's mother said. 'You'll have to bring her round so we can meet her.'

137

'Mum,' Mandy sighed. 'David isn't your son.'

'You never know,' David said. 'My young lady might move in with me one day.'

'Really?' Mandy breathed, smiling at him. 'What's she like?'

'She's extremely attractive. She's a lot younger than me, but we get on very well.'

'Are you in love with her?'

'Yes, very much.'

'And is she in love with you?'

'I think so, yes.'

'So, what does she look like? Is her hair long or—'

'Stop questioning the poor man,' Mandy's mother cut in. 'I'm sure we'll all get to meet her in time.'

'She's got long dark hair,' David murmured, gazing into Mandy's eyes. 'She's the most beautiful girl I've ever met. But there is one problem.'

'Oh?' Mandy whispered, cocking her head to one side as her mother went back into the kitchen. 'What's that?'

'She can be very naughty,' he said softly.

Asking herself what David might have thought of her lewd confession, Mandy began to wonder whether she should have said anything. Downing another glass of wine with her food, she also wondered whether David had believed her. He might have thought that she was joking. But he had to know that the girl he was in love with wasn't a sweet little thing any more. When her parents joined them at the table, Mandy wondered what her mother would really think if she knew the truth. Would the woman be happy to think that Mandy was screwing David?

As the wine flowed and the sun began to sink behind the trees, Mandy knew that she needed some time alone with David. They needed to talk and . . .

No, she thought. *She* needed to talk. She needed to sort out her feelings, decide on what sort of life she wanted. If she could just forget about David, things would be a lot easier, she mused. But she couldn't forget about him. The way he cared for her, the way they'd made love by the river ... She was going to have to sort her feelings out, and her life.

'I'm getting chilly,' her mother said. 'I think I'll go in.'

'And me,' her father murmured, leaving the table. 'Help yourself to beer, David. There's plenty more in the fridge.'

'I will, thanks,' David replied. Waiting until her parents had gone into the house, he smiled at Mandy. 'I've enjoyed this evening,' he said.

'It's not over yet, David.'

'You're not rushing off, then?'

'Not if I'm staying here for the night. David, what I said earlier about another girl ...'

'It's your life, Mandy. I wouldn't try to change you, I can promise you that.'

'Don't you want to know the sordid details?'

'Only if you want to tell me.'

'Actually, I didn't do that with another girl. I mean, I had sex with her, but I didn't do that.'

'Oh, right. Well, er ...'

'I'm not a lesbian, David. I was experimenting, sexually, with another girl. Does that shock you?'

'Nothing shocks me,' he said, chuckling as he went to the fridge and grabbed another beer. Retaking his seat, he reached across the table and held Mandy's hand. 'Whatever you've done in the past is your business,' he said gently. 'We all have a past.'

'This girl ...' she began. 'She's not past, she's present.'

'Oh, well . . . have you known her long?'

'David, I wouldn't want or expect you to put up with me and the way I behave.'

'But, Mandy . . .'

'David, listen to me. Recently, I've discovered myself. I have to admit that my discovery is confusing, but it's also exciting.'

'I'm not with you.'

'I've been putting it about. I've been having sex with different men, and a girl.'

'Yes, well . . . you're young, Mandy. You're enjoying life, and there's nothing wrong with that.'

'I'm a slut, David.'

'Of course you're not. As I said, you're young and . . .'

'David, I am a slut.'

'I don't care what you are, I'm in love with you. You can fuck ten different men every day, that wouldn't change the way I feel about you.'

'You're either madly in love, or just plain mad.'

'Both, I reckon. Tell me something. Do you love me? No, no, I'll rephrase that. Do you think you might love me in the future?'

'I love you now,' she confessed. 'I love you now, but I can't change the way I am. Now it's my turn to rephrase. I don't want to change the way I am.'

Mandy felt selfish and guilty as David squeezed her hand again. But she knew that she had to be honest with him. The last thing she wanted to do was hurt him. If he later discovered that she'd been cheating on him, screwing other men and sleeping with a teenage girl behind his back, he'd be devastated. Pouring another glass of wine, she decided not to stay at her parents' house that night. She needed time and space to think, and to get on with her work first thing in the morning.

'You could sell your flat,' David said.

'Sell it? why?'

'Move in with me. I have a big house so you could have your own office and . . .'

'Hang on, David. We've only been out together once. I really don't think . . .'

'Mandy, we've known each other for years. I think we can dispense with courting.'

'No, no . . . I need time to think, David. Besides, what would my parents say?'

'We'll talk to them, explain that we're in love.'

'I don't know that I'd want to live next door to them.' Gulping down her wine, she stood up. 'I think I'll walk home,' she said. 'I want to be up early tomorrow and get some work done.'

'Oh, well . . . Would you like me to walk you home?'

'No, it's not far. Look, we'll talk about this again.'

'Ring me tomorrow.'

'Yes, yes, I will. I've enjoyed the evening. Thanks, David, it's been lovely.'

'I suppose I'll get back, then. Are you sure you won't stay?'

'I can't. I have too much work to do and I want to make an early start.'

'OK, I'll talk to you tomorrow.'

Before leaving, Mandy explained to her parents that she wanted an early start in the morning and had decided not to stay the night. Her mother was disappointed, but Mandy promised to call round more often. Walking home, she couldn't stop thinking about David's proposition. It seemed that nothing would put him off. Sex with different men, water sports, lesbian sex . . . Nothing would change his mind about her, she knew as she reached her flat.

Sighing as she found Jackie sitting on the step, she asked her what she was doing.

'I've been waiting for you,' Jackie replied.

'How long have you been here?' Mandy asked her as she climbed to her feet.

'About two hours. I need to talk to you.'

'It's rather late, Jackie.'

'Yes, I know.'

'I suppose you'd better come in.'

Leading the girl through to the kitchen, Mandy filled the kettle and took two cups from the shelf. Asking Jackie what she wanted to talk about, Mandy tried not to think about lesbian sex as she gazed at the firm orbs of the other girl's teenage breasts just visible through the opening of her white blouse. Did she want sex? she wondered, recalling the hairless lips of her teenage pussy. Pouring the coffee, she felt her clitoris swell, her juices of arousal soak into her sperm-starched panties.

'I just wanted to spend some time with you,' Jackie finally said.

'It's rather late,' Mandy sighed. 'Perhaps we could arrange an evening.'

'Yes, I'd like that.'

'What do you really want, Jackie? To wait outside for two hours . . .'

'I just wanted to be with you. Would you let me stay here with you for the night?'

'What? Well, I . . . I don't know, Jackie.'

'I'll be good. You know how good I am, so let's go to your bed and love each other.'

'Jackie, I . . . I have problems at the moment,' Mandy sighed. 'I'm trying to decide whether to . . . I've spent the evening with a man and I'm not sure about my feelings for him. No, that's not right. I know how I feel, but I'm trying to . . .'

'How does that affect us?' Jackie cut in, tossing her long blonde hair over her shoulder.

'Us? Jackie, we're not an item.'

'Exactly. So whether you're with this man or not doesn't affect us.'

'It affects *me*, Jackie. It affects me, the way I think and the things I do.'

Mandy glanced up at the wall clock as she sipped her coffee. Jackie's offer about going to bed was tempting, but she didn't want to get too involved with the girl. Jackie would turn up again and again, she'd want nights of lesbian passion and sex and ... Confused, Mandy knew that she was going to have to sort herself out. She had work to do, serious work on the web site, and she couldn't cope with a flood of conflicting emotions.

Finishing her coffee as Jackie unbuttoned the front of her blouse, Mandy gazed at the girl's bared breasts, her elongated nipples. Wishing that she'd never met her and enjoyed lesbian sex with her, she knew that she couldn't fight her inner desires. Her clitoris calling for attention, her juices of desire seeping between the hairless lips of her vulva, she finally gave in and told Jackie that she could stay for the night.

'Just this once,' she said. 'I don't want you turning up on my doorstep as and when you feel like it.'

'OK,' Jackie breathed excitedly, pulling on the brown teats of her firm breasts. 'Shall we go to bed, then?'

Leading the girl upstairs, Mandy knew that she was making a mistake. *Only a girl knows how to pleasure another girl.* Jackie undressed quickly, unveiling the beauty of her teenage body and slipping beneath the quilt. Mandy sighed as she stripped and hung her clothes over the back of the chair by the dressing table. This wasn't what Mandy wanted but, as she slipped into the bed beside Jackie and huddled close to the warmth of her young body, she once more felt her clitoris call for attention.

'This is nice,' Jackie breathed, wasting no time as she moved down the bed and settled between Mandy's open legs. 'Mmm, you taste beautiful.'

'It's sperm,' Mandy said as the girl licked each of her swollen pussy lips in turn. 'You like the taste, then?'

'It's different. Yes, I do like it.'

'Perhaps you should find yourself a man.'

'No, I don't think so. I only want you, Mandy. The man you were with, did you enjoy making love with him?'

'I . . . we didn't make love. He came in my panties.'

'And you liked it?'

'Yes – yes, I did.'

'He won't make you as happy as I can. Relax, and I'll make you very happy.'

Closing her eyes as Jackie slipped her tongue between the fleshy pads of her outer lips, Mandy let out a rush of breath. She could feel the girl's long blonde hair tickling her inner thighs, cascading over the smooth plateau of her stomach as she repeatedly ran her wet tongue up and down the full length of her sperm-sticky vaginal crevice. This seemed so natural, Mandy thought dreamily as her juices of lust flowed in rivers from her opening vaginal hole. Jackie was so warm, sensuous, loving . . . But Mandy still couldn't decide what it was that she wanted. Did she want a male, a female, or several men?

As Jackie opened Mandy's pussy lips wide and slipped her tongue deep into the older girl's tight sex sheath, Mandy had never felt so comfortable and relaxed. Perhaps she *should* be with another girl, she nused as Jackie reached up and tweaked her erect nipples. Looking up at the ceiling, she thought that it could be a man between her splayed thighs, licking deep inside her wet vagina. But no. There was something very different about a girl. There was something special about Jackie.

'Do a little pee for me,' Jackie breathed through a mouthful of vaginal flesh.

'What?' Mandy gasped. 'You want me to . . .'

'Yes, just a little bit. Give me a little dribble.'

Squeezing her muscles, Mandy couldn't believe what she was about to do. She'd joked with David about enjoying water sports with another girl, but she'd never dreamed that she'd do it. This was another first, she thought as she felt the hot liquid dribble between her inner lips. Jackie lapped up the golden liquid and breathed heavily through her nose as she drank. Sucking and slurping, the teenage girl moved down and licked the sensitive brown tissue surrounding Mandy's wet anus.

'God, yes,' Mandy whimpered, lifting her firm buttocks clear of the bed to give her lesbian lover better access to her private hole. 'Push your tongue inside,' she breathed. 'Push it in as far as you can.'

Complying, Jackie licked deep inside Mandy's rectal sheath. Again, Mandy released a dribble of golden liquid as her clitoris pulsated and her vagina spasmed. Lost in her lesbian arousal, she raised her buttocks further and opened her legs to the extreme as Jackie tongued her rectal duct. Moving up to her gaping vaginal entrance and licking her there, she repeatedly ran her tongue over both holes. Jackie gasped as her tongue swept over the delicate tissue of her anus and then up to her dripping sex hole. Never had she felt so aroused, she thought as she released a further stream of hot liquid. Begging for more, Jackie slurped and drank as the golden rain showered her pretty face and flooded her open mouth.

'Don't stop,' she gasped as she drank.

'I need to come,' Mandy said shakily. 'Jackie . . . make me come.'

'Don't be naughty,' the girl retorted. 'You know very well that you're not allowed to come yet.'

'Please . . . for God's sake.'

'I'll spank you if you're bad.'

'Yes, yes – spank me hard.'

Lost in her arousal, Mandy whimpered and writhed on the bed as Jackie spanked her wet buttocks. The loud slaps resounded around the room, mingling with Jackie's slurping and sucking, and Mandy felt that she was drifting on clouds of lesbian lust as her young body shook uncontrollably. Their lesbian act couldn't have been more intimate, she thought, as Jackie halted the spanking and drove a finger deep into Mandy's tight rectum. Forcing another finger in alongside the first, the other girl stretched Mandy's anal inlet open to capacity and began her crude thrusting.

Mandy cried out, her eyes rolling, her breathing fast and shallow, as her naked body writhed on the bed and another gush of hot liquid rained over her lover's face. Finally sucking Mandy's swollen clitoris into her hot mouth, Jackie repeatedly thrust her fingers deep into both of her sex ducts and took her closer to her desperately needed sexual climax. Teetering on the verge of her orgasm, Mandy grabbed Jackie's head and ground her open vaginal flesh hard against her wet face as her climax finally erupted within the pulsating bulb of her swollen clitoris.

Crying out in the grip of the most powerful climax she'd ever experienced, Mandy gyrated her hips, forcing her pulsing sex bud into the girl's mouth as her pussy milk gushed and flowed in torrents over her thrusting fingers. Again and again, waves of orgasm crashed through her quivering body as she rode the crest of her lesbian-induced climax and writhed uncontrollably on her bed. Another gush of hot liquid showered Jackie's face as she gobbled and sucked between Mandy's parted sex lips and continued to piston her tight holes with her fingers. Mandy could hear the lesbian girl slurping, sucking and drinking, as she sustained her incredible climax.

This was amazing, Mandy mused in her sexual delirium as her orgasm peaked and shook her naked body to the core. David couldn't do this, she reflected. David, Gary, Henry . . . Only a girl knows how to pleasure another girl. Her sex holes inflamed, her pussy milk flowing in rivers, her clitoris finally began to deflate as her orgasm began to fade. Gasping for breath, writhing on the wet bed, she knew that she'd see Jackie again. Whether she wanted it or not, this was going to be a long-term relationship.

'Are you all right?' Jackie asked her as she appeared from beneath the quilt and lay by Mandy's side. Whimpering, dazed, Mandy was unable to speak. 'That was a good one, wasn't it?' Jackie said, giggling. Locking her wet lips to Mandy's mouth in a passionate kiss, she squeezed the firm mounds of her breasts and pinched her ripe nipples. 'You're beautiful,' she breathed, moving down and sucking Mandy's erect milk teat into her hot mouth. 'I'll always love you and make you come, Mandy. Always.'

Finally coming to her senses, Mandy lay quivering on her bed as her lover bit gently on each milk teat. Jackie certainly was amazing, she thought dreamily as the girl's fingers thrust deep into her sex-drenched vaginal sheath and massaged her hot inner flesh. She was also insatiable. Feeling dazed after her incredible orgasm, Mandy moaned softly as her lover stirred the cream within her tightening vagina. Writhing, gasping, she wondered about the future as her sensitive clitoris swelled again and demanded attention.

Lesbian sex with Jackie was beautiful and felt so natural, but images of rock-hard cocks loomed in her conflicted mind. Her thoughts also turned to David as Jackie massaged her hot vaginal flesh and induced her lubricating milk to flow in torrents. She'd have to see him again, if only to tell him that it was over between them. Could she do that? she asked herself. David had made his plans, said that he wouldn't cramp Mandy's life, would allow her to go out with other men and . . . Confused as never before, Mandy wondered what Jackie was doing as she slipped her fingers out of her wet sex sheath. Turning her head to face her, she smiled.

'Are you asleep?' she asked her.

'Just about,' Jackie breathed softly, her eyes closing. 'Remember this night, Mandy. Remember the sex, the feelings . . .'

'I will,' Mandy said. 'How could I ever forget?'

Mandy kissed her pussy-wet cheek and rested her head on the pillow beside her lesbian lover. It had been an interesting evening, she thought, recalling David's cock sperming in her panties. She had to decide what she was going to do with her life, she knew as she closed her eyes. She'd see Jackie again, she was sure of that. But what about David?

Eight

Mandy woke to find Jackie sleeping beside her. The events of the previous evening filtering into her mind as sleep left her, she slipped her hand between the girl's legs and massaged the hairless lips of her vulva. The valley of her pussy was creamy-wet and hot and Mandy imagined licking her there. Her battle between right and wrong was becoming insignificant. Sex was sex, she mused. With a man, with another girl, sex was sex, so why not enjoy it?

Moving down, she parted the girl's long legs and lay on her stomach with her head between Jackie's firm thighs. Breathing in the scent of her pussy, she planted a kiss on the puffy lips of her teenage vulva. Her tongue delving into her valley of desire, she tasted her slick wetness. Jackie stirred and stretched her limbs as Mandy repeatedly swept her tongue over the solid bulb of her clitoris. This seemed so natural, Mandy thought again as she parted the teenage girl's fleshy outer labia and sucked her ripe clitoris into her hot mouth.

Jackie stirred again and let out a soft moan of pleasure as Mandy repeatedly swept her tongue over the sensitive tip of her erect clitoris. The taste of the girl's open pussy, the heady fragrance, the heat and wetness ... Mandy moved down her yawning sex valley and slipped her tongue into the damp warmth of her open hole and licked the creamy walls of her young vagina. Again breathing in the girl's sex-scent, she felt her own clitoris stir, her juices of desire flow from her neglected vagina.

Lapping fervently at Jackie's vaginal entrance, drinking her lubricious offering, Mandy jumped when a gush of hot liquid flooded her mouth. Initially shocked, she moved back and grimaced as the tangy flavour woke her taste buds. Watching as the other girl squirted a little more liquid, she pressed her full lips over Jackie's hole and allowed her mouth to flood with the golden nectar. Breathing heavily through her nose, she swallowed hard. Jackie writhed on the bed, clutching Mandy's head and forcing her to drink from her young body. Another first, Mandy thought, savouring the golden juice. Had Paula done this? she wondered as she drank.

The golden flow ceased and Mandy positioned her naked body on top of Jackie, with her open vaginal slit hovering over her pretty face. Lowering her head, Mandy ran her tongue up and down her lesbian lover's wet valley of desire, repeatedly licking her clitoris and lapping up her creamy juices. Jackie reciprocated, sucking on Mandy's solid clitoris and tonguing her cream-dripping sex hole. Writhing on the bed, their naked bodies entwined in lesbian lust, the girls slurped and lapped between each other's thighs until they were both on the verge of orgasm.

Releasing her own golden shower, Mandy sucked hard on the other girl's swollen clitoris as they shuddered and writhed in their girl-lust. Their orgasms erupting, they sucked out each other's pleasure as their faces were splashed and drenched with golden rain. Mandy had never experienced sex like this. Locked in the sixty-nine position, they drank from each other's bodies as they squirmed in the grip of their powerful orgasms.

Mandy had never imagined that she'd be having any sex at all in her lonely bed, let alone sex with another girl. Until recently, her bed had been used purely for sleeping. She hadn't even allowed her fingers to part her fleshy pussy lips and massage her clitoris to orgasm, until she'd met Paula. Once more draining her bladder as her orgasm peaked, the golden nectar raining down over her lesbian lover's flushed face, Mandy forced her mouth harder against Jackie's gaping vaginal hole and sucked out the cocktail of cream and hot liquid. Lost in her girl-loving, her naked body shaking uncontrollably, she now knew that she could never be without Jackie.

As her orgasm finally began to fade, Mandy wondered what it would be like to live with the girl. They'd be good together, she thought as she collapsed on her female lover's naked body and gasped for breath. They'd love every night, drink from each other, enjoy massive orgasms and . . . Coming to her senses in the aftermath of her orgasm, Mandy thought of David. He wanted her to move into his house. She could never live with anyone, she decided, clambering off Jackie's sex-wet body and resting her head on the pillow.

'It won't work,' she thought aloud.

'What won't?' Jackie asked her.

'Er . . . nothing. Jackie, that was beautiful.'

'It was wonderful,' the girl sighed. 'I'd love to fill your hot pussy with a banana and eat it out of you. Do you have a banana?'

'Yes . . . no, I mean. Look, I have work to do. God, I haven't been shopping for ages.'

'I'll do the shopping for you.'

'Don't you have work today?'

'Yes, but I'll do it in my lunch hour. When I get back this evening, I'll cook you a nice meal. What would you like? How about . . .'

'Hang on, hang on,' Mandy interrupted the girl. 'When you get back this evening?'

'Here, when I get back here with the shopping.'

'Jackie, I . . . I'm going out this evening.'

'That's OK. I'll be here when you get back and we'll love each other again and . . .'

As Jackie told her about her plans, Mandy stared at the ceiling and tried to think straight. Jackie couldn't just move in, she mused anxiously. It would be handy if the girl did the shopping, but . . . As the phone rang, she leapt out of bed, slipped into her dressing gown and went downstairs to the lounge. It would have been easier to have grabbed the bedside phone, but she didn't want Jackie listening to her conversation. If it was David, she wanted to talk in private.

'It's me,' Paula said as Mandy pressed the receiver to her ear.

'Hello, me,' Mandy sighed.

'Sorry, did I wake you?'

'No, no. I was in the shower.'

'I rang last night but you must have been out. So, how are things?'

'Fine,' Mandy breathed, hearing Jackie go into the bathroom. 'And you?'

'I'm OK. I was wondering what you thought of Henry?'

'Yes, he's . . . he's a nice man,' Mandy replied, feeling guilty.

'Sorry I had to rush off the other night. Anyway, I thought we'd do a foursome again.'

'With Henry?'

'Yes, of course. You and Gary and Henry and me.'

'Oh, well . . . yes – yes, that would be nice.'

'Are you all right, Mandy? Only, you sound worried or something.'

'I'm fine, honestly. It's just that I have a mountain of work to do and it's playing on my mind.'

'Did you have a late night? Were you a naughty girl?'

'I was a naughty girl, yes. I had lesbian sex last night and I'm shattered.'

'Lesbian sex? Anyone I know, such as Jackie?'

'Who? Oh, no, no.'

'Tell me more.'

'We're both into water sports,' Mandy said triumphantly, realising that she was still playing the game of one-upmanship.

'Wow, really? That's something I've never done.'

'Haven't you?' Mandy asked her in surprise. 'You don't know what you're missing.'

'Well, there *are* limits.'

'I didn't think you had limits, Paula.'

'And I thought you were a shy little thing. You've got a string of men, and now you play water sports with another girl. Have you always been like this?'

'Only since I met . . . I mean, since I met the girl several years ago. I suppose I've always been over-sexed.' Dreaming up a story, Mandy was loving the game. 'Do you remember Bryony from school?'

'Er . . . no, I don't think so.'

'Never mind. Anyway, I'd better—'

'What happened with this Bryony?'

'I've been seeing her on and off since we left school. She's a right little nymphomaniac. I thought you'd had lesbian sex, Paula?'

'Yes, yes, I have. This Bryony, would it be possible for me to meet her?'

'Well, I'm not sure. Look, I can't talk now. I have so much work on at the moment. If I don't get started, it will never be finished.'

'Oh, right. By the way, I thought Gary was nice.'

'Yes, he is. And he's loaded.'

'Really?'

'It's funny, Paula. When we met up, you told me about your men and your gardener and the cleaning woman. I didn't like to say too much at the time, but . . . I haven't done the housework or washing and ironing for years. My lesbian friend does all that for me.'

'You *are* doing well. I thought you had a man to do your shopping?'

'Bryony does it now. The trouble is, I have too many sexual partners. I'm like you, in that respect. I have men on the go everywhere.'

'They can be a pain,' Paula sighed. 'Henry is my main man at the moment. He's damned good in bed and he has a cock to die for. It's so big, Mandy. I'm telling you, it would rip you open.'

'I didn't think his . . . well, you're a lucky girl. Has he got money, though?'

'He's absolutely loaded. I'd better get on with some work, Mandy. I'll ring you later and we'll fix something up.'

'OK, great. Bye.'

Hanging up, Mandy grinned. Paula had never been into water sports? she mused triumphantly. Mandy was now well ahead in the game of one-upmanship, and she hadn't had to lie about lesbian sex and water sports. But where was her deviant lifestyle getting her? Her thoughts turned to Henry – she hadn't reckoned his cock was that big. He was big *enough*, but nothing like Paula had suggested. Why was she lying? Mandy wondered as she made two cups of coffee. There was something about Paula that didn't add up, but she couldn't put her finger on it. Henry was her man, or he had been. Perhaps she was just exaggerating about his cock.

'I'll make a mental shopping list,' Jackie said as she bounded down the stairs after a shower. Her long blonde hair cascaded over her white blouse and she looked stunning. 'I'll do the shopping in my lunch hour and see you when I get in from work.'

'Oh, right,' Mandy said, wondering what to say. 'I've made you a coffee.'

'I'll buy a rubber sheet for the bed,' Jackie said, giggling as she sat at the kitchen table.

'Jackie . . .' Mandy began. 'It's nice of you to do the shopping. The thing is—'

'I have money,' the girl cut in. 'My father gives me an allowance. I only work to keep him happy. He's got more money than you could ever imagine.'

'Really?' Mandy said, her interest rising.

'He bought me a house and a car. I'm an only child, so he spoils me rotten. Mum left years ago, so Dad only has me. You'll have to come round to my house.'

'Yes, I'd like that. How old is your dad?'

'He's thirty-six. You must meet him. We'll have to go to his house – I'm sure you'll like him.'

'I'm sure I will.'

'It's strange, really. He has all that money, and no woman in his life. So, what would you like to eat this evening? Apart from my pussy, I mean.'

'Anything, I'm not bothered,' Mandy replied nonchalantly. 'Does your dad know that you're a lesbian?'

'Yes, and he's fine about it.' Leaving the table and opening the fridge, she sighed. 'Milk, cheese, eggs, butter . . . looks like you're low on everything.'

'Yes, I should have been shopping days ago but I've been so busy.'

'That's OK, you have me to do it now.' Jackie downed her coffee and kissed Mandy's cheek. 'OK, I'd better go. I have to walk home and get my car. I didn't use it last night in case I wanted a drink. I'll see you later.'

'Yes, right.'

'What time are you going out?'

'I'm . . . I'm not sure,' Mandy sighed. 'I'll be here when you get home. When you get back, I mean.'

'OK, keep your pussy warm and wet for me. Bye.'

Thirty-six years old, single, loaded, and with a horny lesbian daughter, Mandy thought. 'Before you go . . .' she called, following Jackie to the front door. 'How about taking me to meet your dad this evening?'

'OK, he'd like that.'

'Right, well . . . I'll see you later, then.'

Wandering back into the kitchen as Jackie closed the front door, Mandy sipped her coffee and made her plans. *Thirty-six years old, single, loaded . . .* She imagined having a sexual relationship with both father and daughter and grinned. The evening was going to be interesting, she thought, taking her coffee into the dining room and switching her computer on. Very interesting.

After working all day on the web site, Mandy had a shower and dressed in a red miniskirt, stockings, and white blouse. Pacing the lounge floor, wondering what time Jackie would return, she was becoming impatient. If Gary turned up, things could be very awkward, she mused anxiously. She didn't want anyone else to meet Jackie. The girl was her secret, and she was determined to keep it that way. She grabbed the ringing phone and felt her stomach churn as David asked her out for the evening.

'I can't,' she breathed. 'I'm sorry, David. I'm . . . I'm seeing a client about a web site this evening.'

'OK, not to worry. Work must come first. How about tomorrow?'

'Yes, yes – that should be fine.'

'You obviously got home safely last night. Did you sleep well? Did you dream about me?'

'I went straight to sleep. I never dream.'

'I had the most amazing dream about you, Mandy. We were in this huge bed and—'

'There's the doorbell,' Mandy cut in. 'It'll be my client.'

'Yes, I heard the bell. OK, I'll see you tomorrow.'

'OK, bye.'

Letting Jackie in, Mandy helped her to lug several carrier bags of shopping into the kitchen. This had saved a lot of time, she thought as she put the food away. Time, and money. Looking forward to meeting Jackie's father, she suggested that they should leave straight away and eat later. Jackie was happy with that. Clutching Mandy's head, she kissed her full lips and slipped her tongue into her mouth. Mandy felt her stomach somersault, her clitoris swell and her pussy milk seep into her tight panties as she returned the passionate kiss.

'I want you,' Jackie breathed.

'Later,' Mandy said, pulling away. 'Let's go and see your dad first.'

'OK, my car's outside.'

Mandy grabbed her handbag and left the flat, eyeing Jackie's short skirt as she followed her down the path to the street. She had beautiful long legs, she thought. Shapely thighs, trim, firm buttocks ... Trying not to think about lesbian sex, she pondered on meeting the girl's father. Feeling anxious, she recalled taking John round to meet her parents. It had all been rather awkward, she reflected, wondering what he was doing now. Wallowing in self-pity?

'Wow,' Mandy breathed as they reached Jackie's car. 'A Mercedes?'

'As I said, Dad bought it for me.'

'That's a coincidence,' Mandy murmured, sitting next to Jackie and closing the door. 'Paula has one just like this.'

'Did she tell you that?' Jackie asked her as she drove off.

'I've been in it. She gave me a lift and—'

'That was this car,' Jackie cut in as she turned onto the main road. '*My* car.'

'What?'

'She borrows it sometimes, to do her shopping. She doesn't have a car so . . .'

'But I thought she was loaded?'

'She earns good money, but she's not loaded.'

'Hang on, Jackie. Paula is your boss, isn't she?'

'Yes, she runs the office I work in.'

'She doesn't own the company?'

'Own it? God, no. Did she tell you . . . ?'

'No, no, she didn't say anything. I just assumed that she . . . I obviously got the wrong end of the stick. Who would have thought that I'd be in the very same car with you?'

'I'm happy that you're with me, Mandy. You do know that I'm in love with you, don't you?'

'Yes, I had gathered that,' Mandy replied with a giggle. 'I must admit that I . . . well, I have feelings for you.'

'Wet feelings?' Jackie asked, laughing as she turned onto a long driveway and pulled up outside a Victorian mansion. 'Pussy-wet feelings?'

'Very pussy-wet. This is a lovely car, Jackie.'

'I don't use it that often. I walk to work, unless it looks like rain. Don't you have a car?'

'No, I can't afford one,' Mandy sighed.

'You can use mine whenever you want to. OK, here we are. This is Dad's place.'

Leaving the car, Mandy gazed at the stone steps leading up to a huge oak door. The man was obviously rich, she thought, following Jackie up the steps. Jackie took a key from her bag, opened the door and invited Mandy in. The hall was the size of her lounge, Mandy observed, feeling anxious again as Jackie called out for her father. Following the girl into a massive room, Mandy looked at the antique furniture. A grandfather clock ticking in the corner, a leather Chesterfield by a huge open fireplace ... The man was obviously very rich.

'This is Mandy,' she said as a good-looking man entered the room. 'Mandy, this is Nick, my dad.'

'I'm pleased to meet you,' Mandy said, shaking the man's hand.

'You're a sweet little thing,' he said, chuckling as he looked her up and down.

'Don't start, Dad,' Jackie said. 'I'm sorry, but he has an eye for the girls.'

'Rather like you, Jackie,' he retorted, chuckling again. 'Er ... are you two ... I mean, are you together?'

'I think so, Dad. You'd better ask Mandy.'

'Yes, we are,' Mandy said softly.

'I'm pleased to hear it. I hope the relationship lasts a long time, Mandy. It'll be nice to have a cute little thing like you calling round.'

'Dad, stop it,' Jackie sighed. 'Sorry, Mandy. He's just a dirty old man. Perfectly harmless, but very dirty.'

'It's a funny set-up, Mandy,' Jackie's father said, winking at her. 'Jackie and I are both into girls.'

'It's certainly different,' Mandy murmured.

'Right, let's all sit down and have a cosy chat. Jackie, why haven't you been round to see me?'

Mandy gazed around the room again as Jackie talked to her father. Surrounded by all this luxury, she speculated why Paula had lied to her. Her old school friend didn't even own a car, let alone a new Mercedes. She didn't own the company, and Mandy began to wonder whether she had two houses. It was a shame that she'd had to lie, she thought dolefully. There again, in the beginning Mandy had lied. The game of one-upmanship was being played on both sides, she reflected. Of course, had she not bumped into Paula, she'd never have met Gary or David or ... Gazing at Jackie, she realised that she'd have never met the girl if it hadn't been for Paula.

Mandy's thoughts were still confused, but she was beginning to understand how much Jackie meant to her. She'd only been with the girl for a couple of days, and yet ... Was this love? Jackie's father obviously had no problems about his daughter's lesbian relationship, but Mandy knew that her own parents wouldn't be so understanding. Her father would probably disown her, she reckoned. And her mother would be devastated. But it was early days yet.

'You've only known each other for a couple of days?' Jackie's father said. 'Well, I hope you stay together.'

'We will,' Mandy said. 'For always.'

'Are you moving in with Jackie?'

'Well, I—'

'We haven't made any plans yet, Dad,' Jackie cut in. 'Mandy has her own flat, so . . .'

'It seems daft to live separately. Why not move in together?'

'We probably will, Nick,' Mandy breathed. 'You don't mind me calling you Nick?'

'Well, it's better than Marjorie,' he returned, chuckling. 'Rent your flat out and move in with Jackie.'

'I suppose the rent would pay the mortgage.'

'Mortgage? God, you don't want a mortgage.'

'I have no choice, I'm afraid.'

'If you two are serious about each other, I'll . . . Give it a couple of months and, if things are working out, I'll pay the mortgage off for you.'

'No,' Mandy gasped. 'I couldn't let you . . .'

'Of course you could – don't be so silly.'

Stunned, Mandy returned Jackie's smile as the girl talked to her father about her house. The situation was running away with her. She'd only met Jackie twice and . . . But there was definitely something about the girl. It wasn't only sex, she knew as gazed into her lover's blue eyes. Her stomach somersaulting, she wondered again whether she was in love. That was the last thing she'd expected, or needed – especially with another girl.

Her plans to seduce Jackie's father seemed so wrong now. He was a lovely man, and he was loaded, but his daughter . . . What the hell did she feel for Jackie? Was it possible to fall in love with someone of her own sex? Thinking once more about what her parents would say, she reckoned that they need never know. She could introduce Jackie as a friend, and they wouldn't have a clue that they were enjoying lesbian sex together. Maybe things would work out, she thought as Jackie offered to show her around the house.

Following the girl up the huge staircase, she wondered what Paula would think of the mansion. She'd grab Nick, and his money, she knew that much. Why had Paula lied to her? she asked herself again as Jackie led her into a large bedroom. The car, owning the company, two houses . . . Why the hell did she have to lie about everything? It wasn't as if Mandy was rich and successful, so why should Paula make out she was some kind of high-flying businesswoman?

161

'This was my bedroom,' Jackie said, sitting on the edge of the bed. 'It still is, I suppose.'

'Wow, it's lovely,' Mandy said softly, gazing around the luxurious room. 'This is a different world. My flat is so small and . . .'

'But it's your home. Money isn't everything, Mandy.'

'Try telling Paula that.'

'There's something wrong with Paula,' Jackie sighed. 'She's a lovely girl, but there's something very wrong with her. When she suggested that I should meet you . . . I think she was trying to get me to find out about you.'

'Find what out?'

'How well you're doing with your business, how much money you have, that sort of thing. She also wanted to meet your male friends.'

'The whole thing was a game,' Mandy confessed. 'She said that she owned her own company and two houses and the car . . . I suppose I made out that I was doing very well just to keep up with her.'

'Will you tell her that you know the truth?'

'No, I won't say anything. I like her and we get on very well. Why ruin it by exposing her as a liar?'

'Well, I won't say anything to her. After all, she is my boss. The last thing I want is trouble in the office.'

'Why do you work, Jackie? You said something about your dad wanting you to work.'

'That's right. He believes that, although I have a never-ending supply of money, I need work experience. Life experience, he calls it. He doesn't want me to become a stuck-up little rich kid. I don't want that, either. Come and sit next to me.'

Joining the girl on the bed, Mandy closed her eyes as they locked their lips in a passionate kiss. Jackie's hand wandered over Mandy's young body, squeezing

the pert mounds of her breasts, toying with her erect
nipples though her blouse. Trembling, breathing
heavily, Mandy clung to the other girl, breathing in
her perfume as she parted her slender thighs and
allowed her to slip her hand up her short skirt. Their
tongues entwined, Jackie pressed her fingertips into
the warm swell of Mandy's tight panties and massaged her there.

'What about your dad?' Mandy asked, slipping her
tongue out of Jackie's wet mouth.

'It's all right, he won't disturb us.'

'But . . .'

'He would never just walk into my bedroom – trust
me.'

Opening Mandy's blouse and easing her firm
breasts out of her bra, Jackie leaned forward and
sucked on each milk teat in turn. Mandy gasped, her
head thrown back as her lesbian lover suckled at her
breasts like a baby. The girl's teeth sank gently into
the dark disc of her areolae, and Mandy clung to her
head and whimpered as the sensations permeated the
taut mound of her mammary sphere. The girl's hand
pulled her panties aside, her finger delved deep into
her moistening vaginal duct, and she lost herself in
her lesbian arousal.

She'd never felt like this before, Mandy reflected as
her clitoris swelled. She'd thought that she'd been in
love with John, but now she realised that it hadn't
been love at all. Was this love with Jackie? she
wondered dreamily. Or was this purely lust? Whatever it was, she decided to enjoy her new relationship.

'I want to lick you,' Jackie breathed, slipping her
finger out of Mandy's tight pussy and kneeling on the
floor. 'I want to drink from your pussy.'

Reclining on the bed, Mandy sighed as the girl
slipped her knickers off. 'God, yes,' she gasped as

Jackie ran her wet tongue up and down her opening vaginal crevice. 'Lick deep inside me.'

Gazing up at the high ceiling, Mandy once more let out a gasp as Jackie's tongue slipped deep into her juice-bubbling vaginal hole. Pressing her lips hard against the pink funnel of flesh surrounding the entrance to her wet sex sheath, Jackie sucked out her juices of desire. Mandy listened to the slurping, the gulping, as the girl drank from the sexual centre of her quivering body. She needed the relief of orgasm, but she knew that she'd be forced to wait until she writhed and begged. No man could do this, she reflected as Jackie's nose massaged the solid bulb of her ripe clitoris. *Only a girl knows . . .*

'You know what I want,' Jackie breathed.

'What?' Mandy murmured.

'I'm thirsty, Mandy. Give me a drink.'

'But . . . what about the bed? It'll get wet and your dad . . .'

'I won't waste one drop, I promise you.'

Squeezing her muscles, Mandy released a dribble of golden liquid. Listening to Jackie repeatedly swallowing hard, she realised that, only a few weeks previously, she'd have thought the act was disgusting. But then she'd met Paula and her life had changed. Now she was heavily into any and every possible lesbian sex act. What would David think of her? She flexed her vaginal muscles again as Jackie sucked hard. More to the point, what the hell would her parents think?

Her clitoris grew solid in its arousal and Mandy begged her lover for her orgasm. With the girl's father downstairs, they had very little time, and Jackie moved up her vaginal valley and sucked her ripe clitoris into her wet mouth. Mandy's orgasm came quickly. Writhing on the bed, stifling her gasps of lesbian pleasure, she grabbed Jackie's head and forced her mouth hard against the pink flesh surrounding the base of her pulsating clitoris.

Mandy rode the crest of her climax as Jackie mouthed and licked on her orgasming clitoris and sustained her amazing pleasure. Mandy involuntarily let out another gush of hot liquid, soaking her lover's face as she cried out in the grip of her lesbian climax. Again and again, waves of pure sexual bliss crashed through her trembling body, reaching every nerve ending, tightening every muscle. Her mind was made up, she decided in her sexual frenzy. She was in love with Jackie, and she'd stay with her.

'God,' she breathed shakily as her climax began to fade. 'That was . . . that was amazing.'

'I'm soaked,' Jackie said, chuckling. 'It's all down my blouse.'

'I can't get up,' Mandy said. 'I feel like I'm floating.'

'You stay there and recover, and I'll go downstairs. Join me when you're ready.'

As the door closed, Mandy managed to haul her trembling body up. Swaying on her sagging legs, she slipped her panties back on and brushed her dark hair away from her flushed face with her fingers. Jackie certainly knew how to please a girl, she thought happily as she looked around the room. Imagining Jackie growing up in the huge house, slipping into the bed each night, she thought about the future.

Making her way downstairs, Mandy decided that the next step would be to see Jackie's house. They couldn't share her own flat as it was far too small but, if Jackie's place was big enough, they'd set up home together. About to wander into the lounge, she stopped by the door as she heard the girl talking to her father.

'Yes, I am in love with Mandy,' she said.

'That's good,' her father said. 'I want you to be happy and, I must say, I've not seen you this happy in ages. Will Mandy be moving in with you?'

'I hope so. I don't want to push her, but I think she'll move in.'

'That *is* good news. How long are you staying? Only I need to talk to you about money.'

'That's up to Mandy. I think we're going back to her place and . . .'

'I'll walk home,' Mandy said, entering the room. 'If you two need to talk, I'll walk back.'

'Take my car,' Jackie said, grabbing the keys from her bag.

'Are you sure?' Mandy asked the girl as she took the keys. 'How will you get back?'

'I'll borrow Dad's car.'

'Oh, will you?' her father said, with a chuckle.

'Actually, if it's all right with you, Mandy . . . I might stay here tonight. I need to chat to Dad about things, so I'll come round to your place tomorrow.'

'OK, that's fine.'

'Now, you listen to me, Mandy,' her father said. 'I want you to be happy. You're a lovely girl, and I want you and Jackie to be very happy together.'

'We will be,' Mandy said, smiling at him.

'OK, you go home – I hope we meet again very soon.'

Kissing Jackie's cheek, Mandy smiled. 'You'll be seeing a lot more of me,' she said, leaving the room. 'See you tomorrow, Jackie.'

'OK, bye.'

As she drove home, Mandy hoped that she'd see Paula in the street when she passed the wine bar. No such luck, she realised. It would have been fun to blow the horn and wave. Finally pulling up outside her flat, she locked the car and walked into the small hallway. After Nick's huge house, the flat seemed so poky and dull, she thought as she filled the kettle for coffee. She was going to check her emails, but she had other things on her mind as she sat in the lounge.

Gary, David, Henry, Jackie . . . Sipping her coffee, Mandy thought about the people in her life. The temptation to move in with Jackie was overwhelming, but could she stay faithful to the girl? Jackie would want her to make a commitment, and she'd never agree to Mandy screwing several men on the side. The time had come to decide. Nick's offer to pay off her mortgage obviously came into the equation, but she didn't want to be swayed by money.

'What do I really want?' she sighed. 'What the hell do I *really* want?' As the phone rang, she remembered that she'd arranged to see David. God, she thought, realising that he was waiting for a decision. Ignoring the phone, she sighed. Her life had become a complete mess. Although she had feelings for David, she wished that she'd never bumped into him and agreed to go out for a drink. Gary was a great guy and an amazing lover. His life wasn't complicated. He didn't put pressure on her or want anything more than sex. Even though Gary was married, he was able to get out and enjoy sex on the side. If only David was more like Gary. David was in love with her, that was the problem.

Nine

Mandy sighed as she kicked the quilt aside and climbed out of bed. She still hadn't reached a decision, and she was beginning to think that she'd better not arrange anything with Jackie for a while. Fortunately, Jackie wasn't pushing her, so there was no hurry. After a shower and breakfast, Mandy was about to get down to work when the phone rang. Her heart missing a beat, her stomach somersaulting, she hoped that it was Jackie.

'Hi, sexy,' Gary said. 'How about having a little fun today?'

'This evening, you mean?' Mandy asked him.

'No, during the day. I have a friend who wants to meet you.'

'He wants to meet me? Why?'

'Why do you think?'

'Oh, I see. Look, I'm working today and . . .'

'You can take an hour off, surely,' he persisted. 'I thought you enjoyed having two cocks?'

'Yes, yes I do,' she murmured pensively. 'It's just that . . . I have to work something out. I need to make a decision.'

'What about?'

'The future. This friend of yours . . . what's he like?'

'He's young, only eighteen. Do you fancy three cocks?'

'Three? Well, I don't know.'

'Come on, Mandy. I know you'd enjoy three hard cocks. I have two friends, if you're interested.'

'Actually, that might help me to decide,' she thought aloud. 'OK, bring your friends round.'

'Good girl, I knew you'd be up for it. Say, half an hour?'

'Yes, yes – I'll be ready.'

'Great. I'll see you soon.'

Mandy replaced the receiver and paced the lounge floor, deep in thought. She knew that, unless she experienced three men, three cocks, she'd be forever wondering what it would be like. If she did decide to commit herself to Jackie, then she wanted to be one hundred per cent certain that she was doing the right thing. And she wanted to be sure that she wouldn't stray and cheat on the girl. Three cocks, she mused excitedly. A dream come true?

Gazing out of the lounge window, Mandy felt her clitoris stir and her juices of desire seep into the tight crotch of her cotton panties. Trying to push thoughts of Jackie out of her mind, she wondered what David was doing. She imagined living with him and couldn't see how he'd be happy for her to enjoy three cocks. Recalling his words, she knew that it wouldn't work. *You can fuck ten different men every day, that wouldn't change the way I feel about you.* There was no way he could sit at home waiting for her, knowing that she was being screwed by three men. Besides, it wouldn't be fair.

Answering the door, she gazed at Gary. 'Hi,' she said, eyeing the two young men standing behind him. 'Come in.'

'This is Rod,' he said, stepping into the hall. 'And this is Tony.'

169

'Pleased to meet you,' Mandy breathed, feeling a little embarrassed as she led them into the lounge. 'Er . . . I suppose I'd better . . .'

'Take your clothes off?' Gary said, winking at her. 'Yes, I . . .'

'We'll sit down and watch the strip show.'

As her audience watched from the sofa, Mandy felt like a common stripper. This was purely a sexual thing, she reminded herself as she unbuttoned her blouse. There was no need for guilt or embarrassment. This was also a means to an end, a way to decide what it was she really wanted. She didn't look upon the young men as lovers. They were simply people with cocks to be used for her own gratification. They weren't particularly good-looking, but that didn't matter.

Slipping her blouse off her shoulders, she unhooked her bra and allowed the cups to fall away from the firm mounds of her young breasts. The men gazed longingly at them, licking their lips as they focused on her elongating nipples. A feeling of power gripped her as she realised that she could have any man eating out of her hand. This was what Paula had boasted about, she reflected as she slipped her skirt down her long legs and kicked it across the room. A string of men in tow, every sexual experience imaginable, sex with girls . . . But Paula had been lying.

Wearing only her panties, Mandy ran her hands over her breasts and tweaked her ripe nipples. The men watched, waiting in anticipation for her to slip her panties down and reveal the most private part of her young body. Teasing her audience, Mandy pulled the front of her panties down just enough to expose the top of her hairless slit. Her arousal rising fast, her sex juices soaking into the crotch of the tight material, she felt her clitoris swell as she imagined

170

three hard cocks driving into her holes. Paula would love to be in this situation, she thought as she turned and ran her hands over the firm orbs of her bottom. Had the girl ever actually had sex? she wondered. Was her entire life a lie? Henry had said that he fucked her, so . . .

'Now *that*'s an arse waiting to be fucked,' one of the young men said.

'You won't believe how tight her little bumhole is,' Gary said, chuckling.

As the men murmured dirty comments to each other, Mandy turned and faced them. They'd waited long enough, she decided. Tugging her panties down and allowing them to crumple around her feet, she proudly displayed the hairless crack of her young vulva to their wide eyes. Her outer lips puffing up, her inner labia emerging from her tight slit, she stood with her feet wide apart and allowed her audience to take a good look at her femininity.

'Beautiful,' one of the young men breathed. 'God, how I love shaved pussies.'

'And me,' the other said.

'You're happy with Mandy, then?' Gary asked them.

'Yes,' they murmured in unison, unable to take their eyes off her sex crack.

Standing in front of one of the young men, Mandy jutted her hips forward and ordered him to lick her crack. Complying eagerly, he pushed his wet tongue into her creamy sex valley and tasted her hot vaginal milk. Realising again the incredible power she had over men, she knew simultaneously that Jackie was the only one who could lick and suck her clitoris to those amazingly powerful orgasms. The young man licking between the hairless lips of her pussy was doing very well, but he didn't have the oral expertise that Jackie had.

Moving to the other young man and instructing him to lick her opening crack, Mandy watched as he slipped his tongue between her puffy love lips and tasted her there. Her clitoris now solid in arousal, her sex juices streaming from her vaginal entrance, she smiled at Gary as he winked at her. All three cocks would be hard and ready to penetrate her love holes, she knew as the young man drove his tongue deep into the heat of her cream-dripping vagina. Three cocks – a dream come true.

Stepping back and positioning herself on all fours in the centre of the room, Mandy ordered the three men to strip and join her on the floor. They removed their clothes hurriedly, their huge cocks waving from side to side as they looked down at her young body. Mandy asked them to lick the brown ring of her anus, take turns to wet her there in readiness for their cocks. Gary was obviously the boss: he knelt behind her, parted her firm buttocks and began lapping at her anal inlet as the others waited their turn.

'You taste lovely,' Gary breathed as he repeatedly ran his wet tongue over the delicate brown tissue surrounding her anal inlet. 'I could tongue your arse all day long.'

'What about the boys?' Mandy asked him, gasping as he yanked her rounded buttocks further apart. 'You must share me, Gary.'

'I know,' he sighed. 'But I could still lick you all day.'

'OK, now the next one,' Mandy said. 'And remember, only lick my bum. I'm saving my cunt for later.'

As one of the lads changed places with Gary and began his anal licking, Mandy let out a rush of breath. This was like having three sex slaves at her beck and call, she thought happily. She could feel his hot breath, his saliva running down the gaping valley of her vagina. Her young body quivering, she rested her head on the floor as he slipped his wet tongue deep into her tight rectal duct and tasted her there. David would never put up with her debauched behaviour, she knew as her clitoris swelled painfully. At his age, he'd like the idea of a young girl living with him and might think that he'd be able to put up with anything. But it wouldn't be fair on him.

Her thoughts turning again to Jackie, Mandy wondered whether *she* would put up with her infidelity. Would she turn a blind eye to Mandy's debased sex sessions with three men? Mandy still had to decide what it was that she really wanted. A loving relationship with David, a lesbian relationship with Jackie, or a life of debauched sex with anyone and everyone? This session with three men would help her to decide, she mused as the second young man knelt behind her and licked the brown ring of her sensitive anus.

Ordering Gary to kneel in front of her, she sucked his purple plum into her wet mouth and rolled her tongue over its silky-smooth surface. His knob was beautifully salty, and she hoped that his heavy balls were full. She then ordered one of the young men to take up the same position and push *his* cock into her mouth. Obeying, he took Gary's place, slipped his cock-head into her open mouth and let out a gasp. This was sheer bliss, Mandy thought dreamily as she tasted his salty knob. A tongue delved deep into her hot rectal duct and her naked body quivered uncontrollably as she mouthed on the young man's swollen knob before ordering the last man to kneel in front of her.

Sucking on the third knob, breathing in the aphrodisiacal scent of the youth's pubic curls, Mandy ordered Gary to slip his cock into her cream-dripping vagina. He complied, driving his solid shaft deep into her hot sex sheath as she suckled on the swollen knob bloating her sperm-thirsty mouth. Following her instructions, Gary slipped his cock out of her pussy and knelt in front of her as one of the young men pushed his rock-hard cock deep into her contracting pussy. Tasting her own juices of arousal as she sucked on Gary's cock, she looked up and instructed her slaves to sink their cocks into her wet pussy in turn and then allow her to suck her cream from their bulbous knobs. They moved around her naked body, each driving his cock into her tight vagina before offering their juice-dripping knobs to her open mouth.

Having sucked her hot cream from each cock several times, Mandy finally ordered one of the young men to position himself beneath her. Gazing down at his grinning face as he lay on the floor, she gasped as his cock-shaft drove deep into her yearning vaginal duct. Again giving her orders, she felt her young womb contract as Gary pressed his bulbous knob hard against her well-salivated anus. His solid penis slipped into her tight anal duct and his knob journeyed along her rectum to the dank heat of her bowels as she opened her mouth and sucked on the third erect cock.

As the men rocked their hips, fucking her wet holes, she imagined John walking in and witnessing her debased behaviour. This was the ultimate in degradation, she reflected happily. Her three holes fucked by three rock-hard cocks, this was the ultimate act of whoredom. The sound of gasping and squelching resounding around the room, the noise of flesh slapping against flesh filling her ears, she closed her eyes as hands kneaded the firm mounds of her breasts.

'Treat me like a common slut,' Mandy breathed, momentarily slipping the swollen knob out of her mouth. 'Treat me like a filthy whore.'

'You're a tight-cunted little slag,' the man beneath her said as she sucked again on the ballooning knob hovering before her flushed face.

'A filthy little bitch,' Gary rejoined, repeatedly ramming his purple knob deep into the wet heat of her bowels.

'Suck out my spunk, you dirty little tart,' the man in front of her growled as he rammed his solid knob to the back of her throat.

Mandy lost herself in her arousal as the three cocks fucked her sex holes and the men delivered their running commentary. Their crude words exciting her, their hands running over her trembling body, she knew that she was about to enjoy the first orgasm of this session as her womb rhythmically contracted and the sensitive bulb of her solid clitoris swelled. Her pleasure building, her pussy milk spewing from her bloated sex sheath, she swivelled her hips and forced the nub of her pulsating clitoris hard against the erect cock shafting her tight vaginal duct.

Her orgasm erupting, her abused body shaking uncontrollably, Mandy drank the creamy spunk from the throbbing knob bloating her mouth as her vagina and rectum flooded with sperm. The men gasped and mouthed their crude comments as they pumped her naked body full of their orgasmic cream. This was the ultimate act of wantonness, she thought. What would her parents say if they were to discover the sordid truth about their sweet little girl? she wondered. They'd disown her, she knew as she repeatedly swallowed hard.

But no one *would* learn of her despicable behaviour, she thought as the holes between her splayed thighs overflowed and spurted hot spunk over the men's balls. No one would discover the wanton acts of debased sex that she committed in the privacy of her own home. She couldn't do this in David's house, she thought as she sucked the last of the spunk from the knob filling her mouth. And she didn't want to have to sneak men into Jackie's house when the girl was out. She didn't want to lie and deceive, or have to go out somewhere to enjoy her decadent sex sessions. Living alone in her flat was her only option, she mused as the three cocks deflated and finally slipped out of her spunked sex holes.

'That was good,' she gasped. 'But not good enough. You all came too quickly.'

'Sorry,' Gary said. 'But there was such a build-up that I don't think any of us could hold back.'

'All change places and this time make it last longer,' Mandy instructed her sex slaves. 'This time, fuck me until I'm dry and sore.'

Swapping places, the men toyed with their cocks, stiffening them in readiness to penetrate her sex holes again. The man behind her finally drove his solid organ deep into the tight sheath of her rectum while Mandy sucked on the knob hovering in front of her face as the third member drove deep into the restricted duct of her vagina. Gobbling and sucking on one bulbous glans, she could feel the other two knobs pressing together through the thin membrane dividing her sex ducts. This was real sex, she thought as the men rocked their hips and fucked her trembling body. This was the height of decadence.

The squelching sounds of crude sex were louder this time. Each thrusting cock was lubricated by another man's creamy spunk and Mandy breathed heavily through her nose as her nipples were pulled and pinched. Fingernails biting into the sensitive flesh

176

of her rounded buttocks, her vaginal lips pulled wide apart by unseen hands, she rocked her young body back and forth to meet the thrusting cocks. Her pelvic cavity repeatedly inflating and deflating, the man kneeling before her ramming his knob to the back of her spunked throat, she hoped that her slaves would be able to stiffen their cocks for the third time and once more swap places and shaft her young body. All three holes fucked by all three cocks, she mused in the grip of her debauchery as her anal ring rolled back and forth along the veined shaft fucking her tight rectum. Fucked nine times by three cocks, Mandy thought. The ultimate act of wanton whoredom.

The men lasted a lot longer this time. Her tight vagina becoming dry and inflamed, her rectal tube burning, Mandy once more rocked back and forth to meet the thrusting cocks. Again and again her rectal sheath expanded, opening to capacity as the pistoning organ drove deep into the very core of her young body. Sinking her teeth gently into the veined shaft bloating her pretty mouth, she snaked her tongue around the rim of the bulbous knob. The men gasped and Mandy again felt hands groping the firm mounds of her breasts, kneading the rounded cheeks of her bottom and stretching the lips of her vulva wide apart.

The man kneeling behind her was the first to reach his orgasm. His creamy sperm lubricating the burning duct of her tight rectum, he held her hips tight and repeatedly rammed the full length of his solid penis deep into the core of her trembling body. The man beneath her gasped and announced his imminent coming, and Mandy felt the gush of his sperm fill her contracting vagina as her mouth flooded with spunk. Rocking back and forth like a rag doll, her long black hair cascading over her sex-flushed face, she moaned through her nose as the men drained their balls for the second time.

Mandy gasped for breath as one deflating knob left her spunk-flooded mouth. The two other male shafts left the fiery holes between her spunk-dripping thighs, making loud sucking sounds. She licked her sperm-glossed lips and ordered the men to stiffen their cocks and swap places again. They each had to manage one more fucking, she thought as sperm oozed from the inflamed hole of her anal eye. For her dream to come true, they had to stiffen their cocks and pump her holes full of spunk one more time.

A solid cock slipped into her gasping mouth and she savoured the bitter-sweet taste of her rectum on it as she swept her tongue over the swollen knob. Her eyes rolled as a man clambered beneath her naked body and drove his solid organ deep into her sperm-drenched vagina. She sucked hard on the knob filling her aching mouth and waited expectantly for the third cock to penetrate her fiery anal duct.

Mandy knew that, whatever choice she made for the future, she had at least experienced three cocks. But, as a swollen knob slipped past her defeated anal sphincter muscles and sent delightful quivers through her young pelvis, she was sure that she wouldn't have the will-power to deny herself the pleasure of further multiple fuckings. Staying faithful to Jackie would be impossible. The solid shaft drove deep into her rectum, impaling her completely, and she knew that she'd have to tell Jackie the truth. She'd be unable to say goodbye to her male lovers.

'Her arse is swamped with spunk,' the young man behind her said, chuckling as he began his anal-fucking motions. 'It's spurting all over me.'

'I've never known such a dirty slut,' the other young man said. 'I could understand if she was a prostitute and was making us pay for this. But to do this because she loves it, she must be a nymphomaniac.'

'I don't care what the slut is, as long as she opens her dirty little cunt and also takes it up her arse.'

'And in her mouth. She's a filthy little whore, and whores are made to be fucked. The next time we come here, I'm going to . . .'

Listening to their crude banter, Mandy wondered whether to give up her web-site business and earn money by selling her young body for crude sex. Wondering how much she'd make from a session like this, her reverie was broken as a hand landed across one of her buttocks with a deafening slap. She didn't want a gruelling spanking and she tried to move her head back and slip the cock out of her mouth to protest, but her head was held tight. Again and again the hand spanked her glowing buttock so hard that she squeezed her eyes shut and moaned through her nose.

'Not too hard,' Gary said as loud slaps resounded around the room.

'The harder, the better,' the young man retorted. 'Sluts like her need a damned good thrashing.'

Spunk jetting from the throbbing knob and flooding her mouth, Mandy involuntarily released a gush of urine as the merciless spanking continued. Laughter filled the room as Mandy's golden liquid splashed over the men's bouncing balls. Her buttock stinging like hell, she opened her eyes wide as the man behind her yanked his rock-hard cock out of her burning rectum and tried to force it into her vagina alongside the first cock. She'd tear open, she was sure as the bulbous knob was forced into her stretched sex

179

cavern. As the shaft drove deep into her aching vaginal duct alongside the first cock, she couldn't believe that her tight sheath had opened wide enough to accommodate two huge penises.

Her solid clitoris was forced out from beneath its pinken hood and another gush of urine sprayed from her small pee-hole. This was degradation beyond belief, Mandy thought as the men found a pace for their thrusting rhythm. The two swollen knobs repeatedly battering her ripe cervix, sperm flowing from the restricted sheath of her rectum, she moaned again through her nose as two fingers drove deep into her tight anal duct. There was no way she could halt the abuse of her naked body, she knew as the man fucking her aching mouth held her head tight. Her right buttock still stinging, she grimaced as a hand now repeatedly spanked the previously unblemished skin of her other bum cheek.

Her nipples painfully pinched and twisted, a third finger forcing its way into her hot rectum, Mandy thought that the men had lost control of their actions. She no longer had power over her slaves, she reflected anxiously as her vaginal cavern stretched painfully to accommodate the huge cocks. Was this the life she wanted? she asked herself. Three men using and abusing her young body . . . Now she was a slave to the men.

Her mouth again flooding with creamy sperm, she repeatedly swallowed hard as the thrusting cocks pumped their sex fluid into the yawning fleshy cavern of her aching vagina. Her naked body was awash with the products of male orgasm and she breathed heavily through her nose as the men drained their balls. Their cocks finally began to deflate and the male shafts slipped out of Mandy's inflamed sex holes as she keeled over and lay on her back. She knew that she couldn't take any more.

'Talk about tight,' she heard a distant voice say through the mist of her blown mind.

'The slut took a double cunt-fucking,' someone breathed.

'Next time we'll give her a double arse-fucking.'

Delirious in the aftermath of her gruelling ordeal, Mandy was oblivious to her surroundings as the men dressed. A crumpled heap of female flesh, she lay on the floor trembling uncontrollably as sperm oozed from the abused holes between her splayed thighs. She didn't hear the men leave the flat. Unsure whether she'd been sleeping or not, she finally hauled her naked body up and flopped into the armchair. The phone rang.

'It's me,' Paula said. 'How are things?'

'Oh, er . . . hi,' Mandy stammered. 'I'm . . . I'm fine.'

'Are you sure? You sound different.'

'I've had three men here this evening. Needless to say, I'm worn out.'

'Three men? God, Mandy. Where do you find all these men?'

'It was Gary and two teenage friends of his. God, what a session.'

'I wish I'd been there. Why didn't you invite me round? If you're having an orgy, I'd . . .'

'I didn't know until the last minute. Anyway, I thought you had more than enough men on the go?'

'Yes, yes, that's right. But I'd have loved to have joined in.'

'Next time, maybe.'

'I'm phoning because I have the day off. I thought I might come round for a chat over coffee.'

'Yes, that's fine. Just give me half an hour to shower and dress.'

'Great, I'll see you soon.'

Replacing the receiver, Mandy looked down at the inflamed lips of her hairless pussy, the deluge of sperm flowing from the aching sheath of her inflamed vagina. She'd beaten Paula hands down, she thought as she climbed the stairs to the bathroom. Paula was nothing more than an office worker with no car and no money. It was a great shame that the girl had lied, she thought as she stepped into the shower and washed the spunk from her young body. They'd been friends at school, and that friendship could have continued if she hadn't . . . They might as well remain friends, Mandy decided.

After her shower, Mandy dressed in a miniskirt and T-shirt, went downstairs and filled the kettle. There was no need to let Paula know that her lies had been discovered. There was no point in causing a rift between them. Answering the door and leading the girl into the kitchen, Mandy poured the coffee and sat opposite her at the table. Paula looked tired, she thought as she asked her what she'd been up to. More late nights? Or too many nights home alone, drinking wine?

'Nothing much,' Paula said softly. 'I've just been working hard, as usual.'

'I must come and see where you work,' Mandy said, smiling at her. 'You'll have to show me round the place.'

'Yes, I . . . I'm pretty busy what with board meetings and . . . The car outside . . . Has Jackie been here?'

'What car?' Mandy murmured, forgetting that the Mercedes was parked outside.

'I thought I saw Jackie's car in the street. I must have been mistaken.'

'She hasn't been here, Paula. Talking of Jackie, what's she like? I mean, does she have her own flat or—'

'She's never said much about her private life,' Paula cut in. 'She never mentions her home or family. I have asked about it, but she just clams up. Maybe she's hiding something.'

'Has she talked about being a lesbian? I remember you saying that you'd had sex with her.'

'Yes, we ... we did have a fling. Why all these questions about Jackie?'

'I'm intrigued, Paula. I'm mean, it's not every day you meet a real-life lesbian.'

'She's a funny girl, keeps herself to herself. I think she must have money because her car ... It's only an old car, but ...'

'I thought I saw her driving a Mercedes the other day,' Mandy said, waiting for the other girl's reaction.

'Yes, she ... she borrows my car on the odd occasion.'

'I'd like to meet her again. I only saw her once, when she brought the money round, but she seemed nice. You'll have to take us out in your Mercedes one evening. We could all go to that pub down by the river.'

'You don't want to bother with Jackie,' Paula said, forcing a giggle.

'But you were the one who wanted me to meet her.'

'Yes, well ... I just thought that you might enjoy a little lesbian sex with her. She has a lovely body but, to be honest, she's boring.'

'I think I'll meet her again anyway,' Mandy persisted. 'She was only here for a few minutes, so I don't know what she's like. She did seem quite chatty. I think I'll call into your office and see her.'

'No, no ... she's leaving at the end of this week. Going abroad, I think. Let's not talk about her. Tell me about these three guys.'

'There's nothing to tell, really,' Mandy said, concealing a grin. 'Three guys, three cocks ... Nothing to write home about. Going back to Jackie ...'

'God, not again,' Paula sighed.

'Lesbian sex intrigues me. I'd like to ... well, I'd like to try it.'

'Well, *I*'m here,' Paula said, with a giggle. 'I'm game for anything.'

Wishing she'd kept her mouth shut, Mandy thought that Paula must have been joking. She didn't *really* want lesbian sex, did she? But perhaps Paula was a lesbian? She didn't seem to have much luck with men, and she'd talked about Jackie in the past, so ... Mandy tried to imagine what it would be like to feel Paula's tongue lapping at her wet vaginal entrance. It would certainly bring a new aspect to their friendship. The trouble with Paula was that she'd told so many lies that Mandy didn't know what to believe any more. Deciding to call her bluff, she grinned.

'OK,' she said, finishing her coffee and leaving the table. 'Come into the lounge and teach me about lesbian sex.'

'What, now?' Paula breathed, her eyes wide.

'Yes, why not? I've just had a shower and my pussy is smooth and bald, so come and play with me.'

'Well, I ...'

'Come on, Paula. We've both had lesbian sex before. You're the one with real experience, so teach me.'

Paula followed Mandy into the lounge, her expression pained as she glanced at her watch. She wasn't going to get out of this, Mandy thought. She'd lied about everything, and she was probably lying about having had lesbian sex. Now she was going to have to prove herself. Mandy didn't particularly want the other girl licking between her thighs, but she looked upon it as a moment of truth. Slipping her panties down, she sat in the armchair with her legs open and her skirt pulled up over her stomach.

'Well?' she breathed, smiling at Paula. 'That's what you're into, isn't it?'

'I don't have a great deal of time,' the girl murmured, staring wide-eyed at Mandy's shaved outer lips, her tightly closed sex crack.

'If I remember correctly, you said that you enjoy a wet pussy now and then. Do you remember saying that when you were here?'

'Yes, yes, I do. It's just that . . .'

'Give me a quick licking, Paula. Just for five minutes, OK?'

As the girl knelt in fron to her, Mandy moved forward in the armchair and positioned her firm buttocks over the edge of the cushion. Paula had tripped over her own lies, she mused. Owning a successful business, a new Mercedes, having a string of men chasing after her, and then saying that she enjoyed a wet pussy now and then . . . she'd got herself into a corner, and she couldn't back out.

Parting the fleshy lips of her vulva and exposing her creamy-wet sex hole, Mandy felt no shame or embarrassment. She was used to sex now, crude sex with both men and a girl. Exposing the most private part of her young body, she felt her arousal heighten, her juices of lesbian desire flowing from her open hole. Paula's eyes were wide, her mouth hanging open, as she gazed at Mandy's blatantly displayed pussy. There was no way out of this, Mandy thought again. If the girl was going to retain any credibility, she was going to have to commit the lesbian sex act.

Paula moved forward, her eyes squeezed shut as she planted a kiss on Mandy's hairless mons. Poking her tongue out and tentatively licking the swollen outer lips of Mandy's vagina, she mumbled something about the time. Mandy's arousal was running high, though, and she ignored Paula's comment. Holding Paula's head and forcing her mouth hard against her own open sex flesh, Mandy let out a gasp of pleasure. Paula licked the pinken folds of Mandy's inner lips, her tongue delving into her tight vaginal sheath as Mandy writhed and gasped in the armchair.

This was definitely Paula's first taste of lesbian sex, Mandy thought as she gazed at the girl's closed eyes. Why did she have to tell so many lies? Swivelling her hips and aligning the swollen bud of her clitoris with Paula's wet mouth, she ordered her to suck. Paula complied, pressing her lips against the wet flesh surrounding Mandy's clitoris and sucking hard. She wouldn't have to lie about licking a girl's pussy now, Mandy reflected as her clitoris swelled in the girl's hot mouth.

'Suck my clit hard,' Mandy breathed as she neared her orgasm. 'And finger my tight little cunt.' Her crude words sent her arousal soaring and she gripped the arms of the chair as her reluctant lesbian lover thrust two fingers deep into her contracting vagina and repeatedly swept her wet tongue over the swollen tip of her sensitive clitoris. 'More fingers,' Mandy gasped, arching her back as the birth of her orgasm stirred deep within her young womb. 'I'm coming. Finger-fuck my cunt harder. I'm . . . I'm coming.'

Her pleasure erupting, her young body shaking uncontrollably, Mandy had never dreamed that she'd be licked and sucked to orgasm by her old school friend. The day Paula had pulled up at the bus stop and given her a lift, she'd never have believed that her life was about to change so dramatically. Her pussy milk spewing over the girl's hand as she repeatedly rammed her fingers deep into her spasming vagina, Mandy writhed and whimpered in the grip of her lesbian-induced climax. Her lower stomach rising and falling jerkily, her eyes rolling, her thighs twitching, she cried out as her orgasm peaked and rocked her young body to its core.

Her pleasure finally began to fade and she looked down at Paula, the girl's full red lips pressed hard against the pink flesh surrounding Mandy's deflating clitoris. Had she enjoyed it? she wondered dreamily as Paula's fingers left her vaginal sheath with a sucking sound. Paula raised her head and licked her lips as she gazed at the sheer pleasure evident on Mandy's flushed face. Paula was good, Mandy thought. But not as good as Jackie.

'That was heaven,' Mandy breathed softly as the other girl rose to her feet and wiped her mouth on the back of her hand. 'Did you enjoy it?'

'Yes,' Paula murmured, forcing a smile.

'We must do it again. Come round this evening, and I'll suck your clit to an orgasm so intense that you'll pass out.'

'I . . . I can't this evening. I'm . . . I'm seeing Henry.'

'Tomorrow, then,' Mandy persisted.

'Yes, maybe. Look, I have to go. I'll ring you, OK?'

'Yes, ring me and we'll arrange a lesbian sex evening.'

'I have to go,' Paula repeated.

As Paula left, Mandy hauled her quivering body out of the chair and slipped her panties back on. Three cocks, she thought as she went into the dining room and sat at her computer. Three cocks, and then sex with another girl. It had been an interesting day so far. But now she had work to do. She could feel her clitoris swelling again, her juices of desire oozing between her inner lips, and she knew that she had to stop thinking about sex. Hoping that Jackie wouldn't come round before the evening, Mandy set to work on the web site.

Ten

Jackie turned up at six o'clock, beaming as she flung her arms around Mandy and kissed her full lips passionately. Mandy breathed in the girl's perfume and absorbed the warmth of her teenage body as they embraced. She still hadn't come to a decision, she reflected, her heart racing as Jackie's wet tongue slipped deep into her mouth. Tasting her saliva, she closed her eyes and wondered about the future for the umpteenth time. She was going to have to decide one way or the other, she knew as their lips finally separated.

'Come to my house,' Jackie said, her blue eyes sparkling lustfully.

'What, now?' Mandy asked her.

'Yes, now. I had a long chat with my dad last night.'

'Oh? Is everything all right?'

'Yes, yes. You work from home, right?'

'Yes.'

'Dad got some men round to my house today. They've made a . . . Come with me now, and I'll show you.'

Taking the car keys from the hall table and passing them to Jackie, Mandy grabbed her bag and followed the girl through the front door. It seemed that Jackie and her father were making plans for the future, but Mandy didn't want to be pressurised or pushed into something that she might regret later. She'd had a good day working on the web site and the job would be finished well ahead of schedule. The last thing she wanted was to jeopardise her business.

Sitting next to Jackie in the Mercedes, Mandy thought again about David. He was going to be hurt, she knew. He was going to feel the pain and desolation she'd felt when John had left her for a slut. David was getting on in years, and the chances of him finding a young girl were remote. The last thing Mandy wanted to do was hurt him, but she knew that he'd feel the pain of love lost at some stage.

Taking the car up a long drive and pulling up outside a large detached house, Jackie switched the engine off and climbed out. Mandy followed her to the front door, trying to take in the sheer size of the vast front garden. It was incredible to think that a girl of eighteen should own such a property, she thought as she followed Jackie into the large hall. She must have a gardener, a housekeeper and . . .

'This way,' Jackie said, bounding up the large staircase. 'I'll show you the surprise.'

'God,' Mandy gasped as she followed the girl into a large room and looked around her. 'It's amazing. But why a plush office like this?'

'It's *your* office,' Jackie replied. 'There's the computer, the telephone, and there's a TV and hi-fi . . .'

'My office?' Mandy breathed.

'If you decide to move in with me you'll need somewhere to work. Dad had it all fitted out today. What do you think?'

'Well, it's amazing,' Mandy breathed, sitting in the executive swivel chair at the desk. 'It must have cost a fortune.'

'Dad only has the best. Everything is new, from the carpet to the desk and ... Do you like it? Will you be able to work here?'

'God, yes. Pens, paper, a coffee pot ... You've thought of everything.'

'If there's anything else you need, just let me know.'

'Jackie, I ... I don't know what to say.'

'Don't say anything. There's no rush, so take your time and let me know when you've come to a decision. Now, come and take a look at our bedroom. Sorry, *my* bedroom. It won't be ours until you ... Come and take a look.'

Following the girl out of the room and along the huge landing, Mandy knew that her decision should be based on Jackie as a person, not on the money she had. Her decision also depended on the lifestyle she wanted. Three men, three cocks, sex with Henry, David and ... Or, a life of lesbian sex with Jackie. Lesbian sex, and love? Jackie was beautiful, but Mandy had only just met her and didn't really know her.

'The bed,' Jackie announced proudly, waving her hand at the king-size double bed.

'Wow, it's big enough for four people,' Mandy gasped.

'I was going to talk to you about that.'

'What, four people in one bed?'

Jackie sat in the armchair by the window and smiled. 'I know that you've had men friends,' she began as Mandy sat on the edge of the bed. 'And you might still need men for certain things. I'm a lesbian, through and through, and I don't want or need men. Apart from my dad, that is. I love him very much and ... The point is, what do you want?'

'I don't know,' Mandy sighed. 'That's the trouble, I just don't know.'

'OK, here's the deal, as my dad would say. When you move in . . . *if* you move in with me, and you feel that you need a fling with a man, then go ahead.'

'But . . . Jackie, I couldn't do that to you. I couldn't cheat on you.'

'Don't look on it as cheating. Anyway, it won't be cheating if you tell me that you're going to meet a man. Look, I don't want you to commit yourself and then regret it later and destroy my life by leaving me.'

'But I couldn't . . .'

'I've given this a lot of thought, Mandy. How about a cooling-off period? A sort of probation period where, say, after a month or two, you decide one way or the other. After all, you don't even know whether you'll like living with me, let alone still want men.'

'I don't want a month,' Mandy said. 'I don't want a probation period. Just give me twenty-four hours.'

'Is that all?'

'Yes, that's all. I've had two long-term relationships, and they both ended in tears. I've recently been asked by a man who's old enough to be my father to move in with him and become his partner.'

'Oh, I . . . I didn't realise.'

'I've known him all my life. However, I'm not moving in with him because I don't love him.'

'So I'm top of the list?' Jackie asked her expectantly.

'I've been seeing three men – all three together, if you see what I mean?'

'I'm bottom of the list.'

'But I don't want to carry on like that.'

'Top of the list, again.'

'Earlier today, I had sex with Paula.'

'Back to the bottom.'

'Stop it, Jackie. It's not funny.'

'Sorry. So, how long have you had a thing with Paula?'

'I haven't, apart from today. I've been trying to decide, Jackie. I've fucked three men at once, had sex with Paula and . . .'

'So, after all this sex with different men and a woman, have you decided?'

'If I move in with you, I'll be one hundred per cent faithful to you. I've been cheated on in the past, and it hurts. I would never cheat on you. Also, I wouldn't want your dad to pay off my mortgage. I'd rent the flat out and pay it that way.'

'OK.'

'Plus I'd pay my way with the bills and food and things.'

'That's easy because dad pays all the bills, apart from the food.'

'I wouldn't want you giving me money.'

'OK.'

'And I wouldn't want . . .'

'We've covered the things you wouldn't want. Is there anything that you *would* want?'

'Love.'

'You've got that, Mandy. You have all my love, for ever. Shall we go down to the kitchen and cook something? I don't know about you but I'm starving.'

'Yes, that's a good idea.'

Mandy followed Jackie downstairs to the huge kitchen and looked around her. Everything was new and very expensive, she thought, sitting at the pine table. It would be a luxury to live in Jackie's dream home, but . . . In a way, she wished that she hadn't seen the house. The thought of living there was beginning to influence her thinking. Trying to push all thoughts of luxury and money from her mind, she gazed at Jackie. Her long blonde hair shining in the light, her small breasts clearly outlined by her tight blouse, she was a stunning girl. Mandy eyed her long legs, her short skirt, and pictured the hairless lips of her teenage pussy. If she moved in with the girl, she knew that her parents would never understand. A lesbian daughter? Her father would disown her.

'You look deep in thought,' Jackie said.

'Oh, er . . . yes, I was thinking about food.'

'Do you like curry?'

'Yes, very much.'

'I make my own,' Jackie said proudly, opening the freezer. 'I make a huge batch and then freeze it.'

'Don't you get lonely living in this big house?'

'Yes, sometimes. I'm at work all day but the evenings can be dull.'

'Take me to bed,' Mandy said, leaving the table and moving to the door.

'Aren't you hungry?'

'Yes, for your pussy. Come on, we'll have the curry later.'

Slipping out of her clothes in the bedroom, Mandy watched Jackie undress. Her body was perfect, she observed excitedly. The hairless lips of her pussy were perfectly formed, symmetrical and full with a deep dividing crack. The gentle rise of her lower stomach was smooth and inviting, her breasts were small but hard and pointed with beautifully elongated nipples. Mandy began to feel jealous as she gazed at the huge bed and wondered how many other girls Jackie had made love with.

'I don't know anything about you,' she said, slipping beneath the quilt with the girl. 'How many relationships have you had?'

'Only a few,' she replied, snuggling up against Mandy's naked body. 'One was serious, but it didn't last long.'

'Did you love her?'

'I thought I did, but I was wrong. I was living at home with Dad, so we didn't live together.'

'So, why didn't it last?' Mandy ventured to ask her.

'She only wanted my money. Unlike you, all she thought about was money.'

'Jackie . . . has anyone else been in this bed with you?'

'No one's been into my house, let alone the bed.'

Mandy closed her eyes as Jackie disappeared beneath the quilt and sucked her ripe nipple into her hot mouth. Arching her back, she let out a sigh as the girl ran a finger up and down the opening valley of her pussy. This wasn't just sex, Mandy thought dreamily as she breathed in the scent of Jackie's young body. Her solid clitoris responding to the girl's massaging finger, she knew that there was more to their relationship than sex. Was it love?

As Jackie moved down and licked the swollen lips of her hairless pussy, Mandy felt the girl's fingers delve deep into the wet heat of her contracting vaginal sheath. Massaging her inner flesh, Jackie ran her tongue over the sensitive tip of Mandy's solid clitoris. Mandy gasped, arching her back again as her young womb contracted and her pussy milk spewed from her tight vagina. This was sheer sexual bliss, she thought happily. Lesbian sex, lesbian lust . . . lesbian love?

Still in two minds as to whether to move in with Jackie, Mandy recalled the three solid cocks driving into her sex holes. Jackie was gentle in her feminine loving, but Mandy had enjoyed the rough masculinity of the men. Could she survive without the colder, harsher side of sex? Two cocks forced into her tight vagina, the naked-buttock spanking . . . Could she deny herself the pleasure of crude sex for ever?

'I want to spank you,' Jackie said, her pretty face emerging from beneath the quilt. 'I don't know whether you're into—'

'Yes, I am,' Mandy cut in, rolling over onto her stomach and jutting her naked buttocks up. 'You must have been reading my mind.'

'Your bum is all red,' the girl breathed, running her fingertips over the firm mound of Mandy's bottom.

'Yes, I . . . The men spanked me.'

'In that case, I'd better spank you for being a naughty little girl,' Jackie said, giggling as she ran her fingertips over the crimsoned flesh of Mandy's naked bottom.

The slap of Jackie's hand across her naked buttocks echoed around the room and Mandy squeezed her eyes shut and buried her face in the pillow. Again and again, the girl slapped her stinging buttocks as Mandy writhed on the bed and gasped into the pillow. Mandy knew that she was coming closer to making her mind up as the gruelling spanking continued. She was becoming used to the harder side of sex, and knew now that she couldn't live without spanking. If Jackie spanked her regularly . . . Wondering what the girl was doing as she opened the bedside table drawer, Mandy wondered whether she had a vibrator. Paula had said that she used a vibrator, but Paula told lies.

Gasping as Jackie massaged cold cream into the deep valley between her stinging buttocks, Mandy breathed out hard. She'd never had her naked body so expertly attended, she reflected happily as she relaxed and enjoyed the sensual massage. Feeling warm and cosy with her teenage lover, she relaxed completely and imagined waking every morning to a massage – and several massive orgasms. Life with Jackie would be good, she decided.

A hard, cold object pressed against the well-greased eye of her anus and Mandy squeezed her eyes shut. The huge shaft entered her tight rectal duct, slowly driving deep into the very core of her naked body, stretching her open to capacity, and she began to quiver uncontrollably. Sinking her teeth into the pillow as the huge object drove deep into the dank heat of her bowels, she thought that she'd split open. Never had she experienced such pleasure from the tight duct of her rectum. Even the men's cocks hadn't been this big and if this was the sort of thing Jackie had planned for her she wouldn't need the men.

'Is that nice?' Jackie asked her as she twisted the huge phallus.

'Yes, yes,' Mandy breathed.

'OK, I'll turn the control up a little bit. How's that feel?'

'God, it's beautiful,' Mandy gasped into the pillow as amazing vibrations permeated deep into her bowels.

'Full power will be too much for you, but I'll turn it up a little higher in a minute.'

Mandy breathed heavily into the pillow as Jackie left the huge vibrator in place and spanked her naked buttocks again. She could feel her juices of arousal streaming from her neglected vagina, her clitoris swelling painfully as the vibrations deep within her bowels mingled with the stinging pain in her buttocks. The spanking stopped and Mandy listened as Jackie again took something from the drawer.

'God, no,' Mandy gasped as the girl drove another huge vibrator deep into the restricted sheath of her young vagina. 'Jackie. I'll . . . I'll split open.'

'Of course you won't,' the girl replied, giggling. 'But you will have the biggest orgasm ever. I'll turn the first one up a little higher, like that. And I'll set this one about there. So, how does that feel?'

'Like heaven,' Mandy breathed. 'God, I think I'm about to come.'

'In that case, I'll lower the settings. You're not going to come for a long time.' Taking something else from the drawer, Jackie giggled again. 'You'll reach the point where you're desperate for your orgasm so, to stop you rubbing your clit and bringing yourself off, I'll do this.'

Pulling Mandy's hands behind her back, Jackie cuffed her wrists and pushed the vibrators fully home. Mandy writhed on the bed, sinking her teeth into the pillow again as the vibrations transmitted deep into her rhythmically contracting womb. Her erect clitoris forced out from beneath its pink bonnet, pressing hard against the vibrating shaft, she was sure that she'd soon reach her orgasm. But Jackie once more adjusted the control, turning it down to its lowest setting.

The mild vibrations playing on her solid clitoris, her vaginal muscles gripping the huge shaft, Mandy closed her eyes again and relaxed as Jackie ran her fingertips up and down her inner thighs. No man could bring her such amazing pleasure, she mused dreamily, thinking again that moving in with Jackie was a good idea. Raising her head as the other girl tugged the pillow from beneath her, she watched as she sat with her legs wide and rested her back against the headboard. Mandy gazed wide-eyed at the bald lips of Jackie's young pussy, her gaping sex crack, as she parted her legs wider.

'Give me a licking,' Jackie breathed. 'Suck out my milk and drink it all up.'

'I need to come,' Mandy said, kissing the swollen lips of the girl's vulva.

'You won't be coming for a long time yet. Now, be a good little girl and lick my pussy.'

Slipping her tongue into her lover's open sex hole, Mandy savoured the taste of her lubricious cream. Jackie gasped, moving forward a little and forcing her open vaginal flesh hard against Mandy's mouth. The vibrators buzzed softly, playing deep within her tight sex sheaths, and Mandy felt the birth of her orgasm stir within her young womb. She was about to come, she was sure as her clitoris swelled and began to pulsate. Jackie had been wrong, she reflected, drinking the hot milk from her lover's teenage vagina. She wasn't going to have to wait for her orgasm.

The vibrator pressed against her swollen clitoris sending beautiful sensations deep into her pelvis, and Mandy felt her orgasm building. But then it faded. The vibrations were mild, holding her on the verge of her climax and not allowing her the relief she craved. Sucking Jackie's solid clitoris into her wet mouth and running her tongue over its sensitive tip, she felt again her climax building. This was sexual torture, she thought. Her hands cuffed behind her back, there was no way she could massage her yearning clitoris.

'Please,' she begged, her dark eyes looking up expectantly at her girl lover. 'Please, let me come.'

'All in good time,' Jackie breathed. 'Keep sucking and licking me and, if you're a good little girl, I might allow you to come.'

Again sucking the solid nub of Jackie's erect clitoris into her hot mouth, Mandy knew that she couldn't endure the sexual torture for much longer as the vibrators buzzed softly within her young sex ducts. Her hands cuffed, all she could do was wait until her lesbian lover allowed her the pleasure that she craved. Her vaginal muscles spasming, gripping the massive phallus stretching her sex sheath, her anal sphincter muscles aching, her tethered body convulsed wildly as she teetered on the verge of her orgasm.

Ignoring Mandy's pleas for orgasm, Jackie held her head tight and ground her own open vaginal flesh hard against the older girl's mouth as her own orgasm welled from the depths of her teenage womb. Her pussy milk spewed over Mandy's flushed face as she cried out and her clitoris erupted, sending shock waves of pure sexual bliss through her quivering body. Mandy sucked hard on her pulsating clitoris, breathing heavily through her nose as her chin was splattered with the girl's copious pussy milk. Her young body rigid, desperate for sexual relief, she sucked out the last ripples of sex from Jackie's pulsating sex bud and looked up at the girl once more.

Gasping, Jackie pulled the swollen lips of her vulva wide apart and grinned at Mandy. 'Press your mouth against my pussy hole,' she ordered her.

'I need to come,' Mandy whimpered futilely. 'Please . . .'

'First, you must drink,' Jackie cut in. 'Press your open mouth over my hole, and I'll give you a drink.'

Complying, Mandy pressed her parted lips hard against the pink funnel of flesh surrounding Jackie's gaping vaginal entrance and waited expectantly. She could hear Jackie gasping, feel her vaginal entrance tightening as she squeezed her muscles. A dribble of hot liquid issued from her small pee-hole and trickled into Mandy's mouth as she let out another gasp. A small jet gushed into Mandy's mouth and filled her cheeks. She swallowed hard.

The jet became a steady flow and Mandy swallowed repeatedly, drinking the golden liquid from the sexual centre of her lesbian lover's naked body as the younger girl gasped and writhed. The liquid gushed in torrents and she almost choked as her mouth overflowed. But Jackie held her head tight, forcing her lips hard against her open hole as she drained her bladder. Finally breaking free, Mandy gasped for breath and coughed and spluttered.

'I couldn't breathe,' she complained.

'You did very well,' Jackie praised her. 'You can have another drink later.'

'God, I need to come now,' Mandy gasped as her clitoris swelled painfully against the buzzing vibrator. 'Please, I need to . . .'

'Clean my pussy first,' Jackie ordered her. 'Lap up my cream and pee and clean me thoroughly, and then I'll allow you to come.'

Mandy lapped at the girl's dripping vaginal hole, sucking out the sex juice and golden liquid and cleansing her there. Licking Jackie's hairless vaginal lips, Mandy finished the job and hoped that she'd be allowed her pleasure now. Jackie finally moved away and placed the pillow beneath Mandy's head before turning the controls on the vibrators up. Mandy gasped again, her muscles tightening, her tethered body becoming rigid as her clitoris immediately exploded in orgasm.

Writhing and gasping uncontrollably on the bed, Mandy let out a scream as Jackie again spanked the crimsoned flesh of her rounded buttocks and added to her incredible pleasure. Again and again, waves of orgasmic bliss crashed through her tethered body, tightening every muscle and reaching every nerve ending. Her orgasm crescendoing, her vaginal milk spewing from her bloated sex sheath, she sank her teeth into the pillow as Jackie thrashed her bare bottom harder.

Her climax running on, Mandy thought that she'd never come down from her pleasure peak as Jackie continued to spank her glowing buttocks. The vibrators buzzing within her contracting sex ducts, her pussy milk squirting over her inner thighs, she involuntarily let out a gush of golden liquid as she whimpered into the pillow. Finally halting the gruelling thrashing, Jackie grabbed the plastic shafts of the vibrators and repeatedly yanked them out of Mandy's inflamed holes and drove them back deep into her writhing body.

'No more,' Mandy managed to gasp as she lifted her head off the pillow. 'Jackie, please . . . I can't take any more.'

'You've been a good little girl,' Jackie praised her, finally switching the vibrators off. 'I'll allow you to rest for a while before making you come again.'

'No, no . . . I can't come again,' Mandy breathed. 'I'm exhausted.'

'All right, but you'll have another orgasm later.'

'Take them out now. Take the vibrators out before I tear open.'

Slipping the plastic shafts out of Mandy's burning sex ducts, Jackie placed them in the bedside drawer and rolled Mandy over onto her back. Her hands still cuffed, the weight of her naked body resting on her arms, Mandy quivered as the younger girl scooped out her orgasmic cream and offered her dripping fingers to her mouth. Ordering her to suck up her own juices, Jackie pushed her fingers into Mandy's pretty mouth and then scooped out more cream from her vaginal sheath.

'Drink it all up,' she said, smiling as Mandy sucked on her wet fingers. 'You're my little baby, and I have to give you your milk.'

'Release my hands now,' Mandy said, rolling onto her side.

'All right, but I'll cuff you again later.' Releasing the cuffs, Jackie grinned. 'There, now you can rest for a while. You're my baby girl and I have to look after you. Sleep now, and I'll come back later.'

Pulling the quilt over Mandy's naked body, Jackie left the room and closed the door. Mandy closed her eyes, breathing deeply as her young body calmed down after her amazing orgasm. The bed was comfortable, she thought dreamily. Warm, cosy, comfortable . . . Life with Jackie would be heavenly, she thought. A beautiful house, a beautiful teenage girl, lesbian love, spanking and . . . Mandy knew that she'd have to tell her parents at some stage. She couldn't pretend that Jackie was nothing more than a friend for too long. Her parents would eventually become suspicious and start asking awkward questions.

Debating whether she should tell David the truth, she wondered what he'd say. He wouldn't go running to her parents, she was sure of that. Knowing David, he'd probably say that she didn't know what she was doing, that her lesbian relationship was nothing more than youthful curiosity, and he'd wait for her to come to her senses and move in with him. There was no way she could live with a man old enough to be her father, and certainly not next door to her parents. Mandy would still be a young woman when David was drawing his pension and preferred to sit by the fire in his slippers and . . . No, David would never be like that, she thought as she drifted off to sleep.

Waking with a start, Mandy looked around the bedroom and wondered where she was. Was it morning? As sleep left her, she recalled her incredible orgasm. Where was Jackie? Glancing at her watch, she held her hand to her mouth. Nine o'clock – she must have slept for hours. She leapt off the bed, dressed and made her way downstairs where she found Jackie in the lounge.

'I have to get home,' she breathed. 'I must have slept for . . .'

'Stay the night,' Jackie said. 'You don't have to go home.'

'No, I . . .'

'We haven't eaten yet. Would you like some curry?'

'No, Jackie. I have things to do and . . . I have to go.'

'Will I see you tomorrow?' the younger girl asked expectantly as she stood in front of Mandy. 'You could come here, or I could go to your place.'

'Yes, maybe. I mean . . .'

'It's all right, I realise that you have to sort things out. As I said before, I won't push you – I don't want to rush you.'

'I'll let you know one way or the other tomorrow, I promise.'

'I'll be awake all night,' Jackie sighed. 'Mandy, if it's going to be bad news . . . well, I'd rather know now.'

'No, no . . . Look, just give me until tomorrow.'

'All right. Do you want to take the car?'

'I think I'll walk home. To be honest, I need the fresh air.'

Kissing Mandy's mouth, Jackie held her close. 'I'll be waiting to hear from you,' she said softly.

'Yes, yes, of course. Thanks for . . . well, you know.'

'You go home and do some thinking. Call me tomorrow, OK?'

'OK, Jackie. Thanks.'

Leaving the house, Mandy realised that she now had Jackie hanging on as well as David. At least she was in demand, she thought as she headed home. As her panties soaked up her pussy milk, she couldn't stop thinking about Jackie and the amazing sex she'd had with the teenage girl. Thinking again about her parents, what they'd say if they discovered that their daughter was a lesbian, she decided to call in and see them. It was getting late, but they'd still be up and about. David would also be up and about, she thought as she walked past his house.

'Mandy,' her mother said, beaming as she opened the front door. 'What a lovely surprise.'

'I was just passing,' Mandy said, following the woman into the lounge. 'I thought I'd come and see you.'

'You've only just missed David,' her father said, wandering into the lounge. 'We've been having a beer and a chat in the garden.'

'David? Oh, right.'

'Are you feeling all right?' her mother asked her. 'Only you look worried.'

'I'm confused,' Mandy confessed, sitting on the sofa.

'I'll leave you two to chat,' her father said, leaving the room.

Her mother sat next to her and frowned. 'What is it, Mandy?' she asked her.

'I have to make a decision, Mum. I've fallen in love and . . .'

'I thought as much,' the woman interrupted her, smiling. 'What's he like? Tell me all about him.'

'It's a she, Mum.'

'She? I don't understand. What do you mean?'

'It's a girl. I'm in love with a girl.'

'Oh, I . . . I see. How long have you known her? I mean, are you sure that you're in love and it's not just a crush?'

'It's not a crush. I haven't known her for very long, but I do know that I'm in love with her. I had to tell

you, Mum. I've been worrying and thinking and . . .
What will Dad say?'

'You leave your father to me. Look, all I want is
for you to be happy. To be honest, I'd rather see you
settle down with a young man. There'll be no
children, of course.'

'God, I hadn't thought of that,' Mandy sighed.

'There again, you might not have had children with
a man so . . . Let me go and talk to your father. You
stay here.'

'OK, Mum, thanks.'

Mandy shook her head as the woman left the
room. Was this a good idea? It might have been best
to say nothing, but Mandy didn't want to have to
hide anything from her parents. She didn't want to
have to live a lie, the way Paula had. Twisting her
long dark hair nervously around her slender fingers,
she felt her heart banging hard against her chest as
she waited for her father to walk into the room.
Would he go mad? Would he disown her? This was a
terrible situation, she thought as she breathed slowly
and deeply and tried to calm herself.

'So,' her father said, walking into the room with
her mother in tow. 'You're in love?'

'Yes, Dad,' Mandy murmured, her dark eyes
looking up at him.

'What's this girl like? How old is she?'

'She's amazing, Dad. She's beautiful and good
company and . . . she's eighteen.'

'Rather young, isn't she?'

'Well . . .'

'I hope she's not the butch type with shaved hair
and . . .'

'She has long blonde hair and she's extremely
feminine.'

'When do we get to meet her?'

'Well . . . whenever, I suppose. I mean, I haven't actually decided because . . . I wanted your opinion.'

'Mandy, love is a very rare thing. Most people never find love and, if you're sure that you love this girl, then we're happy for you.'

'Really?' Mandy said, grinning.

'We'd both rather see you with a young man but . . . What's her name?'

'Jackie.'

'OK. What do her parents think?'

'There's only her dad. Her mum ran off years ago and . . . her dad is fine about it. She has her own house and . . .'

'So will you bring her round to meet us?'

'Yes, of course.'

'I have to say that this has come as rather a shock, Mandy. We were hoping that you and David . . . Well, we thought that . . .'

'David has obviously spoken to you.'

'No – no, he hasn't. We could see the way you two were together at the barbecue. When he said that his girlfriend was young and had long dark hair . . . You were holding hands and gazing at each other, so it was pretty obvious.'

'David wants me, but . . . I don't love him, Dad. It's as simple as that.'

'From a man old enough to be your father, you've gone to a young girl of eighteen?'

'I already knew Jackie. I was torn, in two minds.'

'And now you're sure?'

'Very sure.'

'All right. Well, I hope you'll be happy.'

'I know I will.'

'Why don't you stay here for the night?' her mother asked her.

'No, I . . . I think I'll go back to the flat. Thanks

anyway, Mum.' Leaving the sofa, Mandy kissed her mother's cheek and then hugged her father. 'I'll see you both soon,' she said, walking to the front door.

Leaving the house, Mandy felt as if a weight had been lifted from her shoulders. But, strangely, she was still in two minds about moving in with Jackie. Her parents had accepted the way she was, Jackie's father was happy . . . This was a big step, she thought as she walked back to her flat. She knew that she was going to have to let Jackie know one way or the other tomorrow. She couldn't keep the girl waiting any longer. David was still waiting too, she reflected anxiously. What would he say when she turned him down for a girl?

Eleven

As she tidied and cleaned her flat, Mandy thought about the future. She had to come to a decision, she thought for the umpteenth time. The time she'd spent with Jackie had been amazing, and she wanted more, but . . . She sighed as the doorbell rang and wandered through the hall, checking her long dark hair in the mirror on the way. She should have contacted David, she reflected. She'd left him wondering, hoping, and that wasn't fair.

'Oh, Paula,' she said, opening the door wide. 'Come in.'

'I was just passing,' Paula said, walking into the hall. 'I thought I'd call round and . . . and have a chat.'

'Oh, right. Er . . . would you like some coffee?'

'No, I'm fine, thanks. Mandy, the things we did . . .'

'Ah, you want more,' Mandy said, giggling.

'No – no, I don't,' the girl replied firmly. 'I lied about having lesbian relationships in the past. I'm not that way inclined at all.'

Mandy frowned. 'So you didn't enjoy it?' she asked her.

'No, it's not for me.'

'Why did you lie, Paula? I don't understand.'

'Oh, I don't know. To be honest, I have big problems.'

'Come and sit down,' Mandy said, leading her into the lounge. 'I think you'd better tell me about it.'

Wondering whether the girl was about to admit to lying about everything, Mandy sat in the armchair as Paula settled on the sofa. Paula's make-up was impeccable, her miniskirt and blouse immaculate, but she looked tired, her expression pained. Fiddling nervously with her long blonde hair, she was obviously very worried about something, and Mandy wondered whether Henry had told her that he'd been to the flat and had sex with Mandy. To steal her friend's man wasn't a good thing, she reflected. But why had Paula lied about enjoying lesbian sex? Why make up crazy stories like that? There again, Mandy too had dreamed up crazy stories of debauched sex.

'I have to move out of my house,' Paula sighed.

'But why? It's your place, so . . . Are you selling it?'

'It's a long story. I need a place to rent. I have to move out tomorrow.'

'God, Paula. I don't understand . . . Where will you go?'

'I don't know. It'll take a while to find a place, and then I'll need references and . . . I don't know what I'm going to do.'

'What about all your men friends? Surely one of them can put you up until you find a place?'

'I don't . . . No, no, I can't do that. I was wondering whether you could put me up?'

'Well, I . . .'

'I know that it's a lot to ask. But I'm at my wits' end.'

'Paula, with all your money, why not go into a hotel for a while?'

'No, you don't understand. I have money, yes. But it's all tied up at the moment.'

'What about your other house? The big house that you rent out, I mean.'

'I . . . I can't throw the people out, can I? Can you put me up or not?'

'This has come as a shock,' Mandy sighed, reckoning that Paula had been thrown out of her house because she hadn't paid the rent. Paula didn't have any money, nor did she own property, but she was Mandy's friend. 'Would you be interested in renting this place?' Mandy asked her.

'Yes, but . . . Are you moving out?'

'Yes, I am. It's taken me a long time to decide, but I'm moving out tomorrow.'

'That's brilliant, Mandy. You've bought a house, then? You said that you were looking for a place.'

'I haven't exactly . . . Yes, I've bought a house.'

'You must be doing really well.'

'Not as well as you,' Mandy said, smiling at her friend.

'Yes, well . . . Will you be leaving the furniture?'

'Yes, of course. If you recall, I said that I'd only bought this old stuff as I was going to rent the place out.'

'Yes, I remember you saying. Well, this is amazing. Who would have thought that I'd end up renting your flat?'

'What about your house? What's happening there?'

'I'll be renting it out soon,' Paula replied awkwardly. 'It's a long story and . . . I have to have some work done on the place. The roof is leaking and . . .'

'This is great,' Mandy cut in to save the girl from having to come up with more lies. Feeling impish, she grinned. 'At least you still have your new Mercedes,' she said.

'Yes – yes, I have.'

'And all your men friends?'

'Yes, they're still hanging around. Mandy, I don't have any cash for a deposit. I'll be able to pay the rent, so don't worry about that.'

'I don't need a deposit,' Mandy said. 'I'll work out the rent and get my solicitor to draw up a contract. Like you, I'm a businesswoman and I like to do things properly.'

'You're a successful businesswoman,' Paula sighed, hanging her head.

'So are you. God, you own a huge company and . . . Anyway, I have a few things to do.'

'Yes, me too. I'll bring my things round tomorrow morning, if that's OK?'

'Do you need a hand?'

'No, no, I'll be fine. Thanks, Mandy, I really appreciate this.'

'That's what friends are for. I'll give you the key tomorrow and you can sign the contract and . . . God, what a turnaround.'

'Where is your new house? I'll have to come and have a look once you've settled in.'

'Yes, I'll . . . I'll let you know.'

'OK, I must go. By the way, I'd rather people didn't know that I'm renting your place.'

'People?'

'Well, Jackie . . . There again, you never see her.'

'If I do see her, I won't say anything. Don't worry, Paula.'

'Thanks, Mandy.'

'No problem. I'll see you in the morning.'

As she walked Paula to the front door, Mandy couldn't believe her luck. The flat rented out to her best friend, she was now free to . . . Realising that she'd made her decision, she bit her lip as she wandered into the dining room and sat at her computer. She couldn't change her mind and let

212

Paula down, she reflected. Now she was going to have to move in with Jackie. Unless she went back home to her parents, she mused. Or she could move in with David and . . . God, no.

'Hello,' she said, answering the phone.

'Hi, Mandy,' Jackie breathed huskily. 'Have you recovered from our night of passion?'

'Yes, I have,' Mandy replied, with a giggle. 'You wore me out.'

'So, have you given any thought to—'

'I've just found a tenant for my flat,' Mandy cut in.

'You're going to move in with me?'

'Well . . . I haven't quite decided. I mean . . .'

'It's OK, take your time,' Jackie said softly.

'I have a couple of things to do before deciding.'

'I'm at work, so I can't chat for long. Paula hasn't turned up yet.'

'She's been round here. She left ten minutes ago.'

'She'll be here soon, then. Did you say anything about us?'

'No – no, I didn't. Jackie, I don't want her to know about us.'

'Neither do I, so don't worry. So, when will I see you?'

'Tomorrow, I think. I might ring you later, if that's OK?'

'I'd love you to ring me later, Mandy. I must go, bye.'

Mandy replaced the receiver and knew that she had to get on with her work. The web site was going well, but she didn't want to get behind schedule. If she did move in with Jackie, she wanted to earn her own money and be self-sufficient rather than rely on the girl to survive. At least the rent from the flat would pay her mortgage, she reflected happily. Her thoughts turned to David – she felt bad about him. She should have contacted him and . . . Grabbing the phone, she called him.

'I thought you'd disappeared from the face of the earth,' he said.

'Sorry, David. I've been so busy that I haven't had a free moment. So, how are you?'

'I'm fine. I rang several times last night. I thought we were going to meet and . . .'

'Sorry, I was . . . I had to go out.'

'I'm still waiting for you to decide,' he said quietly. 'Is that why you're calling? Have you come to a decision?' he asked her expectantly.

'No, I . . . I need to see you. We need to talk.'

'OK, where and when?'

'This evening. Let's go to the river pub.'

'I'll pick you up at seven.'

'Yes, that's fine.'

'You won't let me down, will you?'

'I'll be waiting for you at seven. I promise you, David.'

'Great.'

Hanging up, Mandy knew that she had to meet David. He'd been good to her, and she couldn't dump him over the phone. This might be her last day of freedom, she mused as she switched the computer on and got down to work. She was going to have to let Gary know that she was moving out, but she'd worry about that later. Reading an email from a potential client, she realised that her work was piling up. Business before pleasure, she mused, replying to the email.

David arrived at seven o'clock wearing a white shirt, blue jeans, and a huge grin. As she sat beside him and he drove to the pub, Mandy reckoned that he'd assumed that she was going to move in with him. He didn't stop smiling and chatting about the future until they'd reached the pub. Locking the car, he suggested a walk along the river bank to their special spot, and Mandy knew that he wanted sex.

This wasn't going to be easy, she thought as they sat on the short grass and gazed at the river. She had to tell him that she wouldn't be moving in with him, but she didn't want to hurt him. Hoping that they could still be friends, she wondered whether to dream up some story or other about moving away. But she didn't want to live a lie. Her parents knew the truth, so it was only fair to tell David.

'I'm going away,' she said softly, immediately wishing that she hadn't.

'But ... where to?' he asked her, his dark eyes frowning.

'I haven't told Mum and Dad yet. I'm going to rent my flat to a friend, and I'm going to stay with a girl I know.'

'What, locally?'

'About twenty miles away. I'm moving tomorrow.'

'I see,' he sighed. 'So you've decided against living with me?'

'For the time being, yes. I want to get my business off the ground, David.'

'You could have your own office at my place.'

'No, no ... Living next door to Mum and Dad would cause complications. I need a year out, just to work on the business and ...'

'I can wait a year,' he cut in, smiling at her. 'I'll wait as long as it takes.'

'David ... It might be never.'

'Then I'll live in hope.'

'You're making this very difficult for me.'

'I know, and I'm sorry. I should have realised that a young and beautiful girl like you wouldn't want to be with an old man like me. Enjoy your life, Mandy.

You never know, the day might come when you change your mind. When you've lived and loved and cried ... well, as I said, I'll live in hope. So, how about that drink?'

'How about making love first?'

'Mandy, I . . .'

'Don't you want me?'

'Yes, that's the trouble.'

'Then take me.'

Reclining on the grass, Mandy closed her eyes as David unbuttoned her blouse and exposed her naked breasts. Her nipples rising in the relative cool of the evening air, standing up from the dark discs of her areolae, she let out a sigh of pleasure as he leaned over and sucked each ripe milk teat in turn. He was a lovely man, Mandy thought as her arousal soared. But thoughts of Jackie haunted her. The girl would be at home, wondering whether Mandy was going to move in with her. Had she phoned? Mandy wondered as David's hand slid beneath her short skirt and his fingers pulled her wet panties to one side. Perhaps she'd gone to the flat looking for Mandy?

As David slipped a finger deep into her tight vaginal sheath, Mandy arched her back and gasped. No man was a match for Jackie's expertise, she thought dreamily as her clitoris swelled and her juices of arousal flowed. She could feel David's hardness pressing into her hip as he massaged her inner flesh and sucked on her sensitive nipple. Then again, Jackie's vibrators had been incredible but were no substitute for a solid cock. To feel a man's cock driving deep into the wet heat of her tight vagina, his spunk bathing her cervix and flooding her sex sheath . . .

'You're beautiful,' David murmured, slipping her wet nipple out of his hot mouth.

'And you're amazing,' she breathed.

'We'd be good together, Mandy.'

'Don't talk,' she sighed. 'Just love me.'

Although she hadn't yet moved in with Jackie, Mandy felt guilty. On the grass by the river with a man's fingers deep inside her young pussy, it was as if she was cheating on the girl. What was Jackie doing? she wondered again as David moved down and kissed the smooth flesh of her inner thighs. Was she sitting in her luxury home making her lesbian plans for the future? Was she hoping, dreaming?

As David slipped her panties down and pulled them off her feet, Mandy parted her legs to the extreme. Offering him the sexual centre of her young body, she lay beneath the evening sun with her eyes closed. His tongue ran up and down her opening valley of desire, sweeping over the sensitive tip of her erect clitoris, and he again drove two fingers deep into her yearning love sheath. Mandy could feel her vaginal muscles tightening, gripping his fingers as he repeatedly thrust into her tight sex sheath.

Her arousal reaching frightening heights, her pussy milk lubricating David's pistoning fingers, Mandy let out a whimper as her clitoris responded to his sweeping tongue. What would Paula do when she moved into the flat? she wondered as David took her closer to her orgasm. The girl didn't have a string of male lovers, she had no money, no car . . . She was desperate for sex, Mandy thought as her young body began to tremble. She needed a man and . . . Wondering whether Gary and his friends would call at the flat and give Paula what she wanted, Mandy thought that things might work out well for everyone. Apart from David, that was.

David wouldn't give up, Mandy knew as he sucked her erect clitoris into his hot mouth and drove at least four fingers into her spasming vaginal sheath. Perhaps he'd get on well with Paula? she mused dreamily as her young womb contracted and climax approached. But Mandy couldn't worry about Paula. The girl was going to have to sort her own life out. As for David . . . Mandy had her own problems, her own decisions and life to sort out and she couldn't start worrying about other people.

Her clitoris erupting in orgasm, she arched her back, dug her fingernails into the soft grass and whimpered in the grip of her amazing pleasure. She needed David's hard cock thrusting deep into her dripping vagina, she thought as her thighs twitched and her eyes rolled. To feel his solid cock driving deep into her tight sex duct, his sperm gushing and bathing her ripe cervix . . . That was something Jackie could never give her.

Her orgasm peaking, shaking her young body to the core, she wrapped her legs around David's head and forced his mouth hard against her pulsating clitoris. He was a nice man, she thought as he continued to suck on her orgasming clitoris and piston her vaginal duct. He was *too* nice, that was the problem. Had he treated her like a slut, had he used and abused her naked body for his own sexual pleasure . . . He'd never get into peeing and spanking, she reflected as her climax began to fade. David was too loving and caring to commit such beautifully degrading and humiliating acts. He needed a decent woman, she thought as he slipped his fingers out of her sated vagina and sat back on his heels.

'I love you, Mandy,' he said, smiling at her.

'I know you do,' she breathed shakily, propping herself up on her elbows. 'That's the trouble, David.'

'How do you mean?'

'You're too nice.'

'You want me to be nasty?' he asked her, chuckling.

'No, not nasty. Well, I suppose . . . I don't know what I mean.'

'I'll do anything, Mandy. Just tell me how you want me to be, and I'll do my best to please you.'

'No, no . . . I don't want you to please me. I want you to please yourself. Tell me what your fantasies are. What would you really like to do to a girl?'

'Well, I don't really know. I like what we do together.'

'Let's play a game.' Standing up and pulling her panties on, Mandy grinned. 'You chase me into the woods and—'

'Chase you?' he cut in, frowning at her.

'Right, this is the game. You don't know me. I'm walking along by the river and you see me go into the woods. You feel horny and you imagine my tight little cunt. You follow me into the woods and drag me to the ground and . . .'

'Rape you?'

'Sort of. I mean, it won't be real. But it will be fun. Drag me to the ground and fuck me.'

'OK, if that's what you want.'

'It is what I want, David. It's a shame you haven't got a friend here to join in.'

'You mean . . . God, Mandy, I . . . I don't know you at all.'

'I told you that I'm a slut, didn't I?'

'Well, yes, but . . . I have had group sex before. It was many years ago, but I have done it. Look, all I want is for you to be happy.'

'I'm asking too much,' Mandy sighed. 'It's not fair to treat you like this, and I'm sorry. It's just that my life has changed so much recently. I can't be faithful to one person, David. I like sex too much to commit myself to one person.'

'I just want us to go on seeing each other, Mandy. I'll do anything if we can still meet now and then. If you want me to ring a friend, I will.'

'Yes, I do want you to,' Mandy breathed. 'I know you must think me no better than a common prostitute. But that's the way I am.'

David took his mobile phone from his pocket and smiled at her. 'OK, you want to be chased through the woods and dragged to the ground and fucked by a stranger?'

'Yes, I do.'

'Go into the woods and wait. It may be a while before my friend arrives but when he does we'll come looking for you. We'll hunt you down, OK?'

'Yes,' Mandy breathed excitedly. 'Hunt me down – I like the sound of that.'

'OK, off you go.'

Walking along a narrow path through the trees, Mandy felt elated. This was possibly her last day of freedom, and she was determined to make the most of it. She felt a little guilty for wanting to play such a dreadful game with David, but she couldn't help herself. She didn't want to hide behind a screen of decency. She was no longer the sweet and innocent little girl that David had once known. She was a slut, and she didn't want to pretend otherwise.

Mandy found a small clearing amongst some bushes, sat on the soft grass and looked up at the trees. It was a beautiful evening, she thought, breathing in the scent of the pine trees. Her clitoris swelling, her pussy juice seeping into the tight crotch of her panties, she hoped that it was also going to be an evening of incredible sex. Wondering who David was going to invite to play the game, she wondered how many friends he had. He'd always been a loner, she reflected. Perhaps he was a dark horse.

After half an hour Mandy heard twigs cracking underfoot and the low murmur of voices. It was David and his friend, she was sure as her young womb contracted and her stomach somersaulted. Emerging from the bushes so that the men could find her, she looked around but couldn't see anyone. The voices grew louder and she noticed someone walking towards her. Had they seen her? she wondered, dashing back into the small clearing. Her heart racing, her hands trembling, she waited in anticipation.

'What have we here?' a man in his fifties breathed as he entered the clearing and gazed at Mandy. 'You're a sexy little thing.'

'I was just . . . just going for a walk,' she said, wondering where David was.

'Going for a walk?' he echoed, dropping a leather bag to the ground. 'A pretty little thing like you should be careful. Wandering around in the woods all alone . . .'

'What have you found?' David said, joining his friend.

'A little slut,' the old man replied. 'She was just going for a walk.'

'I'm not a slut,' Mandy retorted. 'I was just . . .'

'Just going to take your clothes off?' the old man said, with a chuckle. 'Here. Let me help you.'

Tearing her blouse from her young body, he tossed the garment into the bushes and gazed longingly at the pert mounds of her firm breasts, her ripening nipples. Mandy covered her naked breasts with her folded arms and begged the man to stop as he stroked her cheek. Forcing tears, she cried out as the man grabbed her skirt and tugged it down to her ankles. David stood back, watching the game as his friend tore her flimsy panties from her trembling body and held the garment to his face.

'I'll keep these as a souvenir,' he said, breathing in the scent of her torn panties.

'Please,' Mandy whimpered. 'Please, let me go now.'

'But I haven't fucked your hairless little cunt yet,' he replied. 'It would be a shame to let you go before I've fucked you.'

'No,' Mandy cried as he grabbed her arm and pulled her down to the ground.

David joined in, pinning her to the ground as the old man parted the hairless lips of her wet pussy and drove two fingers deep into her hot vagina. He massaged the creamy-wet flesh deep inside her tight sex duct, murmuring crude words as he abused her young body. *Dirty little slut, the whore needs her little cunt fucking hard, the filthy little tart needs it up her arse* . . . Mandy listened to his vulgar mutterings, her arousal rocketing as he forced all his fingers deep into her contracting vagina and stretched her open painfully. This was hard, cold sex, she mused happily. No love, no passion, just hardcore sex.

Mandy writhed on the grass, loving the game as the man slipped his fingers out of her vagina and began licking the full length of her dripping sex crack. She hadn't expected her clothes to be torn to shreds, but it was all part of the game. How would she walk back to the car without clothes? she wondered as the man sucked her solid clitoris into his wet mouth. She'd worry about that later, she thought as her clitoris swelled and pulsated within his gobbling mouth. Her orgasm welling from the depths of her young womb, her arousal soaring out of control, she closed her eyes and allowed her pleasure to come.

Pinned to the ground by David, her naked body shaking wildly, Mandy cried out as her orgasm erupted within the pulsating nub of her clitoris. She could feel her vaginal muscles rhythmically contracting, her lower stomach rising and falling, as he again thrust several fingers deep into her sex-yearning sheath. Sucked, fingered and licked by an old man, she mused dreamily. She didn't even know his name, had no idea who he was ... But he was playing his role perfectly. What was he thinking? she wondered as her orgasm began to fade. Invited to the woods to use and abuse a young girl, what were his male thoughts?

David held Mandy's arms tight as the old man took several lengths of rope from the leather bag. Securing ropes to her wrists, he pulled her arms out and tied the free ends to nearby trees. Securing her ankles, pulling on the ropes and parting her feet wide, he tied the ends to other trees and gazed at his handiwork. Spreadeagled on the ground, her arms and legs outstretched, Mandy could do nothing to halt the imminent violation of her young body. This was more like it, she thought as her vaginal milk streamed from her gaping sex hole and trickled down to the brown eye of her anus. This was real sex.

The old man chuckled wickedly as he slipped his trousers off. He was going to fuck her, Mandy thought happily, gazing at his erect cock as he knelt between her splayed thighs. Fucked by a total stranger, the ultimate sexual act. His knob slipping between the wet inner lips of her pussy, his huge shaft entering her tight duct, she gazed at David's solid cock as he knelt astride her head. Taking his swollen knob into her pretty mouth as the old man began his vaginal shafting, she wondered what David thought of her. A filthy slut, a common whore ... It didn't matter what he thought, she concluded. Besides, she wanted him to know what she was really like.

The two cocks repeatedly driving into her mouth and pussy, Mandy closed her eyes and listened to the sound of naked flesh slapping flesh, the gasps of debased male pleasure. Perhaps it *would* be a good idea to move in with David, she reflected as her vaginal muscles tightened and gripped the stranger's thrusting cock. If he had more friends like this and was willing to share her young body, perhaps she *should* live with him. They could turn a room into a sex den, she thought, imagining handcuffs and vibrators adorning shelves.

The man rested his weight on his hands, leaning over Mandy's tethered body and biting hard on her erect nipples as she gobbled on David's swollen knob. His teeth sinking painfully into the sensitive teats of her firm breasts, she moaned through her nose. She tried to protest as he bit her harder, but David gripped her head and rammed his bulbous knob to the back of her throat. This was only a game, wasn't it? she pondered fearfully as the man bit each erect nipple in turn.

The man's spunk jetting from his throbbing knob and flooding Mandy's spasming vagina, his swinging balls battering the rounded cheeks of her young bottom, he let out a low moan of pleasure. When Mandy's mouth flooded with David's spunk, she sucked and repeatedly swallowed hard while he held her head tight and rocked his hips. As the evening sun set and dusk fell, Mandy sucked the last of David's spunk from his deflating knob. Her nipples aching, she wondered how long the men would last. How many times would they be able to fuck her young body?

The old man's balls drained, he slipped his dripping cock out of Mandy's sperm-brimming pussy and clambered to his feet. Mandy thought that the game was over as he pulled on the ropes securing her ankles and untied the ends from the trees. Then, looking up, he threw the ropes over a couple of branches and pulled on the ends. Her feet wide apart, rising in the air, she grimaced as her naked buttocks left the ground.

'What are you doing?' she asked him as he pulled the ropes tighter and tied off the ends again.

'Hanging you by your feet so we can get to your little arsehole,' he replied, chuckling. He stood with his penis resting between her splayed thighs and grinned. 'Your arse and your little cunt are just the right height for a good fucking.'

'Someone's coming,' David said as voices came from the woods. 'Hang on, I'll take a look.'

'You're a dirty little slut, aren't you?' the man breathed, his cock stiffening again as he rubbed his purple knob over the wet flesh between Mandy's thighs. 'A right little whore. I'm going to fuck your tight little bum-hole and spunk in your bowels.'

'No, please . . .' Mandy breathed, loving the game. 'Please, let me go now.'

'We have company,' David said, leading two young men into the clearing.

'Who are they?' Mandy asked him, lifting her head and staring wide-eyed at the grinning teenagers.

'Friends of mine,' he said. 'OK, lads, she's all yours.'

The lads stripped naked and ran their hands over Mandy's nude body as David and the old man stood back. David hadn't said anything about bringing more people to the clearing, Mandy thought as one of the men slipped his bulbous knob between her wet inner lips and thrust his solid shaft deep into her hot vagina. Mandy was about to ask David what was going on when the other young man knelt on the grass and forced his ballooning knob deep into her mouth.

Her feet hanging from the ropes, her legs high in the air, Mandy's young body rocked back and forth as one young man shafted her tight pussy and the other pushed his huge knob to the back of her throat. Four cocks, Mandy mused as she gobbled on the salty knob bloating her pretty mouth. Was this her dream? she wondered. Was this what she wanted? Her mouth flooding with sperm, she'd hoped that the young men would have lasted longer. They were young and overexcited, she thought as her tightening vagina overflowed with creamy spunk.

The cocks left her trembling body and she lifted her head as the old man parted the firm cheeks of her bottom and pressed his swollen knob hard against the brown ring of her anus. His knob entered her, his shaft stretching her tight duct to capacity, and she watched as David knelt down and drove his solid cock deep into her spermed mouth again. They were going to take turns to use and abuse her tethered body, she thought as she listened to the young men whispering and chuckling. Jackie couldn't bring her such debased sexual pleasure, Mandy thought. Was this really her last day of freedom?

The cock pistoning her tight rectum pumped out its creamy spunk, lubricating the illicit union, and Mandy repeatedly swallowed hard as David flooded her gobbling mouth with his spunk. Breathing heavily through her nose as her mouth overflowed, she gulped down as much as she could as her tethered body rocked back and forth. She'd miss the taste of fresh sperm, she mused as she drank from David's throbbing knob. Jackie's girl-cream was heavenly, but there was nothing as delicious as fresh sperm.

Realising that her decadent sex session with four men wasn't helping her to decide what it was she wanted, Mandy considered her options. Paula was moving into her flat, so Mandy either would have to live at home with her parents, move in with David, or take Jackie up on her offer. Ruling her parents out, she tried to imagine living with David. Would it work, being next door to her parents? Back to Jackie, she mused as David slipped his knob out of her spunk-flooded mouth and the deflating penis left her bottom-hole with a loud sucking sound.

Her eyes closed, Mandy had no idea whose cock now drove deep into her rectal duct. The anal shafting once more rocking her naked body, she listened to the squelching sound of sperm and gasps of male pleasure. Her anal canal inflamed, her tight brown hole burning, she whimpered and writhed as the crude abuse sent her arousal soaring. Fingers driving into the neglected sheath of her pussy, massaging deep inside her young vagina, she knew that this was the ultimate act of decadence. Jackie could never do this. The girl had love to offer, but Mandy craved lust and sexual abuse.

Her rectum flooding again with male sex cream, her erect clitoris massaged by the thrusting fingers, Mandy shuddered as she reached her mind-blowing orgasm. Shaking uncontrollably as fingernails bit into the delicate flesh of her pert breasts, she wondered how many more anal fuckings she could endure. Her orgasm peaked and she grimaced as teeth sank again into the sensitive teats of her brown nipples and more fingers drove deep into the inflamed cavern of her aching vagina.

'No more,' Mandy finally managed to gasp. 'Please . . . no more.' The men ignored her. The fingers left her sex-drenched vagina, the deflating penis withdrew from her tight anal sheath, but another solid cock took its place and slipped easily into the wet heat of her sperm-laden rectum. Her eyes rolling, her head lolling from side to side, she breathed heavily and convulsed wildly as the solid knob repeatedly drove deep into the dank heat of her sperm-bubbling bowels. More fingers stretched her inflamed vagina open to capacity and she murmured incoherent words of sex in her delirium.

Sperm flooded her bowels once more, filling her to the brim as the men looked on and chuckled and whispered their crude words. The cock withdrew and was immediately replaced by another rock-hard organ. The ropes bit into Mandy's wrists and ankles as the enforced shafting commenced and she wondered again how much more her young body could take. Her holes would be bubbling with spunk for hours, she mused, listening to the sound of flesh meeting flesh. Would Jackie suck out the hot spunk from her tight bottom-hole and drink it?

Her thinking was perverse. She'd changed beyond belief in such a short time. Had she not bumped into Paula, had she not gone to the wine bar on that fateful evening . . . But it was the future that concerned her. She couldn't spend the rest of her life fucking strangers. Confused, Mandy didn't know what to do as another deluge of creamy sperm filled her hot bowels.

The men finally became exhausted. Mandy curled up in a ball on the ground as the ropes were released. Spunk oozing from the inflamed holes between her wet inner thighs, she watched as her abusers dressed. Would she be meeting them in the woods again? she wondered. Would David find more young men to use and abuse her young body? Grabbing what was left of her clothes, she managed to dress as the teenage lads slipped away. The old man said goodbye to David, and added that he was looking forward to the next time.

'Are you all right?' David asked her as his friend left the clearing.

'Yes, I . . . I think so,' Mandy gasped. 'God, that was incredible.'

'At least I now know what you want. I can give you anything you want, Mandy. If you move in with me, I can bring friends to the house and—'

'I need to get home,' she cut in. 'Please, David, take me home.'

As they walked back to the car, Mandy felt sperm streaming down her inner thighs. Her clothes in tatters, her young body aching, all she wanted to do was get home and go to bed. The people outside the pub gazed at her as she climbed into David's car. Her hair dishevelled, her blouse torn, they must have wondered what she'd been up to. They'd never know, she thought as David drove her home. No one would ever know what a slut she'd turned out to be.

Twelve

After a shower the following morning, Mandy
dressed in a miniskirt and T-shirt. Her body was still
aching from her time in the woods with four men as
she made herself a cup of coffee and sat in the lounge.
She was going to have to ring Jackie, she knew as she
checked her watch. Seven-thirty – the girl was bound
to be up and about. Dialling the number and pressing
the receiver to her ear, she had no idea what she was
going to say. Should she move in with her?

'Hi,' Jackie trilled like an excited child. 'I've missed
you. How are you?'

'I'm fine,' Mandy replied. 'Jackie, I . . . I think I've
come to a decision.'

'Really? OK, tell me the worst.'

'Actually, I haven't come to a decision. What I
mean is . . . God, I don't know what I mean.'

'OK, calm down. If you need more time, that's fine
by me. I don't want to rush you.'

'I said that I needed twenty-four hours . . .'

'Mandy, don't worry about it. Just take your time.
By the way, I rang you last night. I rang several
times.'

'Yes, I . . . I was out all evening. Look, can you
come and pick me up?'

'What, now?'

'No, no. Say, nine o'clock?'

'Er . . . you want me to take the day off work?'

'Yes, if you can.'

'OK. What's the plan, where are we going?'

'To your house, if that's all right?'

'Yes, no problem.'

'Thanks, Jackie. I'll see you later.'

Replacing the receiver, Mandy finished her coffee and checked her emails. Three more potential customers, she mused happily. A large company in London wanting a huge web site, an electrical wholesaler asking for a quote . . . Work was piling up, and Mandy knew that she had to clear her head and get down to business. This was what she'd always wanted, she thought. Customers building up, the money coming in . . . She switched the computer off, knowing that she couldn't concentrate on the business until her private life was settled.

She bounded up the stairs, grabbed two suitcases and began packing her clothes. 'That's it,' she breathed, emptying her wardrobe. 'I've come to a decision.' Realising how few clothes she had as she packed the cases, she gathered up the things from her dressing table. With money coming in, she'd be able to buy some new outfits. Perhaps Jackie would go shopping with her, she mused happily as she lugged the cases downstairs.

Opening the kitchen cupboards, Mandy gazed at the tins of beans. She hadn't been shopping for so long that there was very little food in the flat. Packing bits and pieces into cardboard boxes, placing the food she had into carrier bags, she worked for an hour. Finally, having packed up the computer, she was ready to leave the flat. It seemed strange to be leaving, she thought, looking around the place. Two years, she thought, recalling the day when she'd moved in. Two years of working hard on her business, struggling to pay the bills . . . That was all about to change.

'You're early,' she said, answering the front door to find Paula standing on the step.

'I'm on my way to work. I thought I'd call in and make sure it's still on.'

'Yes, I'm packed and ready to leave. I haven't been to the solicitor yet. I was rather busy yesterday and got tied up—'

'You're into bondage?' Paula cut in, giggling.

'No, I . . . I've worked out the rent,' Mandy said, taking a piece of paper from the hall table. 'Is that OK with you?'

'Yes, that's perfect,' the other girl replied, gazing at the figures scrawled across the piece of paper. 'I'm loaded, so money is no object. I'll move in this evening after work, if that's OK?'

'That's fine. There's a key on the table. I'll have my phone number changed later today and . . . God, there's so much to do. I should have prepared for this.'

'I get the impression that this was a last-minute decision.'

'You'll never know just how last-minute it was,' Mandy sighed. 'I haven't told anyone that I'm moving yet.'

'Not even Gary?'

'No, not even Gary.'

'What if he comes round? Where shall I tell him—'

'No one knows where I'm moving to, and I'd rather keep it that way. Paula, you're looking for a man, aren't you?'

'Several, if I can find any.'

'You can have Gary.'

'What?'

'Gary will come round here looking for me at some stage. He's married and likes a bit on the side, if you're interested?'

'Yes, but . . . will *he* be interested?'

'Of course he will. You're a very attractive girl, Paula. Gary will be only too willing to . . . There is one thing.'

'Oh?'

'Be honest with Gary. You won't have to dream up fantasies, Paula.'

'Fantasies?'

'I think you know what I mean.'

'Yes – yes, I do,' Paula sighed, hanging her head. 'I didn't think you'd fall for my lies.'

'You don't own the company, do you?'

'No, I don't. You see . . . when we met at the bus stop, I wanted you to think that I was successful. I was in the Mercedes and . . . I thought you must be doing well, so I exaggerated a little.'

'A *little*?' Mandy retorted. 'Owning your own company, travelling abroad, owning two houses . . .'

'I lied,' Paula confessed. 'I'm sorry, Mandy.'

'You don't have to apologise to me. I lied, too.'

'What do you mean?'

'Paula, when we met I was stony-broke. I'm doing very well now, but . . . Remember when I met Gary in the wine bar?'

'Yes.'

'I'd never seen him before. He chatted me up and . . .'

'God, Mandy, you're as bad as me.'

'Yes, I do believe I am.'

'You must be doing very well now. I mean, to rent the flat out and buy a house, you must be raking it in.'

'I'm doing OK,' Mandy murmured.

'So, when do I get to see your new house?'

'Er ... I don't know. We'll obviously keep in touch, so I'll let you know.'

'Right, I'd better get to work. Seeing as I don't own the company, I don't want to be late. I'm sorry that I made up all that crap, Mandy.'

'Don't worry about it. We all have dreams and sometimes they spill over and become a sort of reality.'

'I believed it myself at times. All that stuff about travelling abroad ... I'd better get to work. I'll see you around.'

'Don't forget the key.'

'God, yes. Thanks, Mandy. You've got me out of a real spot.'

'I'll see you soon, OK?'

'Yes, OK.'

Mandy shook her head as Paula left. At least the girl had been honest at long last, she thought. No doubt she'd lie about being rich to Gary and ... It didn't matter what Paula did, she decided. As long as she paid the rent, she could do and say what she liked. Taking one last look around the lounge, Mandy imagined Paula entertaining Gary on the sofa. Gary would satisfy the girl, and Mandy was sure that Paula would be more than happy with him. Everything was going to work out well, she thought.

Jackie arrived and gazed at the suitcases and boxes in the hall. Beaming, she realised that Mandy had come to a decision and was ready to leave. Mandy smiled, saying nothing as her lesbian lover helped her to load the car. She didn't know what to say – there were no words. Finally locking the front door and joining Jackie in the car, she reached over and placed her hand on the girl's slender thigh. Jackie squeezed her hand, her pretty face smiling as she pulled out into the traffic. Mandy still wasn't too sure about giving up her men, and she hoped that she wouldn't crave a solid cock and fresh spunk.

'Here we are,' Jackie breathed, parking outside her house. 'We're home.'

'Home,' Mandy echoed as she climbed out of the car and gazed at the huge house. 'It seems funny.'

'What does?' Jackie asked her.

'Well, this being my new home.'

'I hope you'll be happy here. I mean, I hope *we*'ll be happy here.'

'I'm sure we will. Jackie . . . I have a lot of work to do. I've got a web site to design, quotes to do and . . .'

'You have your own office, so that shouldn't be a problem. I won't disturb you, if that's what you're worried about?'

'No, I mean . . . I will need to be left alone when I'm working.'

'You worry too much,' Jackie said, giggling. 'Remember that I too have to go to work during the week. Come on, let's get your stuff into the house.'

After helping Mandy to lug her things into the hall, Jackie closed the front door. Mandy felt like a fish out of water. This wasn't her home yet. But she was sure that, given time, she'd settle in and feel more at ease. Passing Mandy a key, Jackie suggested that they should have coffee before taking the things upstairs. Mandy smiled, eyeing the girl's short skirt, her rounded buttocks, as she followed her into the kitchen. There was more to the relationship than sex, wasn't there?

'This is a dream come true,' Jackie said, filling the kettle.

'Yes – yes, it is,' Mandy murmured. 'It's going to be a whole new life, in more ways than one.'

'You're still worried about men, aren't you?'

'Well, not exactly. I mean . . .'

'Mandy, I do understand. Look, if you want to go out with a man . . .'

'No – no, I don't,' Mandy cut in.

'What I mean is, if you *do* want to see a man . . . I don't want to tie you down.'

'I thought that was exactly what you wanted to do,' Mandy said, giggling as Jackie poured the coffee.

'Mandy, I have a confession.'

'Oh?'

'I followed you last night.'

'What?' Mandy gasped. 'You followed me to . . .'

'To the pub, and the woods.'

'Oh, I see.'

'I went round to your place and I saw you drive off with a man. I wasn't going to follow you, but . . . well, I did.'

'So, you know everything?'

'I watched from the bushes.'

'God, Jackie. You must think me a right little slut.'

'I think that you were enjoying a last fling.'

'Yes, I was. God, if I'd known that you were watching me . . .'

'Come out into the garden – I want to show you something.'

Following Jackie through the back door, Mandy felt swamped with guilt and embarrassment. Her naked body tied with ropes, four cocks shafting her sex holes . . . What must Jackie have thought? she wondered as she followed the girl across the huge expanse of lawn to a wooded area. Would Jackie trust her now that she'd discovered that she was a complete slut? Was her love strong enough to survive?

'Take your clothes off,' Jackie said as she entered the wooded area.

'What, here?' Mandy asked her, looking down at the short grass.

'I have a surprise for you. Take your clothes off and lie face down on the ground.'

Frowning, Mandy slipped out of her clothes and took her position on the ground. This was going to be interesting, she thought as Jackie dragged four lengths of rope from the bushes and secured her wrists and ankles. Although she was face down, this was how Mandy had been tethered in the clearing with the four men, and she reckoned that Jackie was recreating the scene for a session of lesbian sex.

'There,' Jackie said, her pretty face beaming as she gazed at Mandy's naked body spreadeagled on the ground. 'You have a lovely bottom.'

'What are you going to do to me?' Mandy asked her.

'First of all, I'm going to give you a good spanking because you've been a naughty little girl.'

'I was hoping you'd say that.'

Kneeling down beside Mandy, Jackie raised her hand high above her head and brought it down across the smooth flesh of Mandy's tensed buttocks with a loud slap. Mandy let out a yelp and pulled against her bonds as the second slap resounded through the trees. Her arms and legs stretched out, her young body tensing with each slap of Jackie's hand, she buried her face in the soft grass as her clitoris swelled and her juices of lesbian desire oozed from the tight crack of her vulva.

'You like the rough treatment, don't you?' Jackie asked her as she finally halted the spanking.

'Yes,' Mandy gasped, her naked buttocks stinging.

'You like it *very* rough, don't you?'

'Yes, yes.'

Her face pressed against the short grass, her eyes closed, Mandy wondered what her lesbian lover was

237

doing as she heard the bushes rustling. Lifting her head as she heard a swishing sound, she cried out as the branch of a bush landed squarely across the glowing flesh of her rounded bottom. Again, the branch swished through the air and lashed her tensed buttocks. Jackie had gone crazy, Mandy thought fearfully as the rough leaves on the branch caught the backs of her slender thighs.

'No,' she cried as the branch lashed her tensed buttocks again. 'Please, no more.'

'What's the matter?' Jackie asked her. 'I thought you liked . . .'

'God, Jackie. That hurt like hell.'

'That was your punishment for being a naughty little girl last night. If I catch you with a cock in your mouth or your pussy again, I'll have to thrash you.'

'But you said . . . I thought you said that you wouldn't mind if I . . .'

'You can have cocks, Mandy. But you'll be thrashed after each time you go with a man. Now, it's time for your nappy.'

'Nappy?' Mandy echoed, lifting her head and watching as Jackie released the ropes.

'Come back into the house and I'll show you.'

Clambering to her feet, Mandy wondered whether she'd made the right decision as she followed the girl across the lawn. She was discovering a darker side to Jackie, she reflected, clutching her burning buttocks as she entered the kitchen. Perhaps Jackie wasn't the sweet little teenager she'd thought her to be. Following her into a small room off the hall, she looked around and frowned. The room was a nursery, she observed, eyeing a pile of nappies and pots of cream.

'Get onto the changing table and I'll do your nappy,' Jackie said.

'Is this . . .' Mandy began hesitantly, lying on her

back on the table. 'Is this some sort of fetish that you want me to get into?'

'You're my baby girl,' Jackie said, giggling and lifting Mandy's feet high into the air. She massaged cooling cream into her stinging buttocks. 'If you're a bad girl, I'll thrash you. If you're a good girl, I'll love you.'

'I don't know whether I like this,' Mandy breathed.

'Of course you do. Now, I'll put your nappy on and then your rubber pants.'

'Jackie, I . . .'

'Oh, your poor little bottom is very sore. There, the cream will make it better.'

Mandy frowned again as Jackie secured the nappy and slipped the rubber pants on. Leaving the table as Jackie passed her a short pink nightdress, she realised that she hardly knew the teenage girl. Perhaps this hadn't been such a good idea after all, she thought, donning the nightdress and following Jackie to the kitchen. She'd wanted to get her office sorted out and start work on the web sites, not play adult-baby games.

'Tell me when you've wet yourself and I'll change your nappy,' Jackie said, making two cups of coffee.

'Jackie, I'm not a baby,' Mandy protested.

'You're my baby.'

'But I have work to do. I can't . . .'

'You can work in your nappy, can't you?'

'Well, yes, but . . .'

'There you are, then. The material isn't bulky so you can wear it under a skirt or whatever.'

'You want me to wear it all the time?'

'Of course. I have to take the car in to be serviced and then I'm going to see my dad, so I'll leave you to unpack your things and get on with some work.'

'All right,' Mandy sighed, watching the other girl sip her coffee. 'Thrashing me with that branch was . . .'

'That was your punishment, Mandy. As I said, if I catch you with a cock in your mouth or your pussy, I'll have to punish you. The little spot in the trees at the end of the garden is the punishment area. I just hope I won't have to take you there again.'

Finishing her coffee, Jackie kissed Mandy's full lips before leaving the house. The punishment area? This was bizarre, Mandy thought, rubbing her stinging buttocks through the nappy. There again, it was only a game, she thought. She walked into the hall and lugged her cases up to the bedroom. After hanging her clothes in an empty wardrobe, she knew that the important thing was to get down to some work. In the office, she moved the new computer to one side and set up her old machine. Finally settling down, she began work on the web site for the large company.

After three hours, Mandy had done well on the web-site design. The office was heaven compared with her old dining room, she reflected happily. Switching the hi-fi on she listened to some classical music. She knew that she'd be able to get a lot of work done – if Jackie left her in peace, that was. An email arrived – she couldn't believe that yet another company wanted a quote for a web site. Where had Jackie got to? she wondered, as she worked out the price and replied to the email.

Leaving her desk, she was about to go to the bathroom when she realised that she was wearing a nappy. Might as well play along with the girl, she thought, squeezing her muscles and releasing a stream of hot liquid. Her clitoris swelling, her vagina tightening, she realised that her arousal was soaring as the nappy soaked up the golden liquid. Perhaps Jackie's baby fetish would be fun after all, she thought as the doorbell rang.

Bounding down the stairs in her pink nightdress and wet nappy, she reckoned that Jackie must have forgotten her key. Hoping that it wasn't the postman or someone else, she lifted the flap of the letterbox and smiled as she saw Jackie standing on the step. She had made the right decision, she thought, eyeing the girl's miniskirt, her naked thighs. Her stomach somersaulting as she opened the door, she held her hand to her mouth as she noticed Jackie's father heading her way.

'Jackie,' she breathed. 'I can't let your dad see me like this.'

'Why ever not?' the girl asked, giggling as she walked into the hall.

'Hello, Mandy,' Nick said, closing the front door and looking her up and down. 'You do look sweet.'

'Er . . . thanks,' Mandy said, flashing a frown at Jackie.

'Have you wet yourself?' Jackie asked her unashamedly.

'Jackie, please . . .'

'Go into the nursery and we'll sort your nappy out. Dad, you change her nappy and I'll make some coffee.'

'Right you are,' Nick said, taking Mandy's hand and leading her into the small room.

Mandy couldn't believe this was happening as Nick closed the door and told her to lie on the padded table. Taking her position, she thought that she'd better play along with the game. After all, to have a man rub cooling cream into her sore bottom would be rather exciting. Lifting her buttocks clear of the table as Nick tugged her rubber pants off, she rested her feet on the end of the table and opened her legs wide as he removed her wet nappy.

Cleaning the hairless lips of her pussy with a baby-wipe, Nick said nothing as Mandy began to breathe heavily. Parting her fleshy outer lips and wiping inside her crack, he massaged her erect clitoris as she opened her legs further and trembled on the table. This was Jackie's dad, Mandy thought anxiously. Did the girl know what her father was doing? she wondered as he slipped a finger deep into the wet sheath of her vagina. Was this part of the arrangement?

Slipping his finger out of her contracting sex sheath and placing her feet either side of the table, Nick pulled her towards him until her rounded buttocks were over the edge of the table. Mandy reckoned that Jackie had no idea what he was doing as he once more massaged the swollen nub of her sensitive clitoris. She heard the sound of his zip moving down and closed her eyes as he pulled out his solid penis and pressed his bulbous knob between the dripping inner lips of her vulva. Saying nothing as his huge knob slipped into her sex opening, she imagined Jackie walking in and catching her father in the illicit act. She'd go mad, she thought as the man's rock-hard cock drove deep into the tight duct of her vagina.

Mandy knew that she should have stopped Nick as he rocked his hips and began his fucking motions. But she couldn't deny herself the pleasure of a beautiful cock. If Jackie's dad called round now and then to fuck her, she'd have the best of both worlds. The arrangement was perfect, she thought as her orgasm stirred deep within her contracting womb. An illicit affair with the teenage girl's father? She couldn't have planned this better herself.

Her orgasm erupting within the pulsating bulb of her solid clitoris, she stifled her gasps of pleasure as Nick pumped his creamy spunk deep into her young vagina. His cock was huge, she thought dreamily as she clung to the sides of the table. His swinging balls battering the inflamed cheeks of her firm bottom, his sperm flooding her contracting vagina, he finally stilled his cock deep within her convulsing sex duct and allowed his knob to absorb the inner heat of her trembling body.

It was over all too quickly, Mandy thought as her orgasm faded and Nick slipped his deflating penis out of her pussy. Sure that Jackie knew nothing of her father's debauchery, she lay trembling on the table as he zipped his trousers and cleaned her sperm-dripping vulva with a baby-wipe. He said nothing as he lifted her buttocks and slipped a nappy beneath her. Securing the nappy and tugging her rubber pants up her long legs, he told her to get off the table. It was as if nothing had happened, she thought as she followed him out of the room with sperm draining into her nappy. Did Jackie know what he'd planned to do?

'All done,' he said as they joined Jackie in the kitchen.

'Thanks, Dad,' Jackie said. 'Was she a good little girl?'

'No trouble at all.'

'Would you mind babysitting now and then? Just on the odd evening if I have to go out, I mean.'

'I don't mind at all,' Nick replied, smiling at Mandy.

'You have a key to the house so, if you're passing during the day while I'm at work, you might look in on her. Just check her nappy and make sure she's OK.'

'Is that all right with you?' he asked Mandy.

'Yes, that's fine,' she replied, returning his smile.

Nick finished his coffee and then said goodbye. Mandy shook her head in disbelief as Jackie saw him out. Did the girl know nothing of his illicit act? Nick had slipped his cock into Mandy's pussy as if it had been expected, as if it had been planned. Perhaps it had been Jackie's idea to supply Mandy with a hard cock and keep her happy. Sipping her coffee, Mandy smiled as the other girl breezed into the kitchen.

'I like your dad,' Mandy said, waiting for a reaction.

'You don't mind him changing your nappy?' Jackie asked her.

'No – no, I don't mind.'

'I know I can trust my dad to look after you if I'm not around. I wouldn't trust any other man with a beautiful girl like you. God knows what they'd get up to. Are you OK with the nappy-and-baby idea?'

'Yes, I am,' Mandy said, smiling at the girl. 'I was rather shocked at first. No, not shocked. I was surprised. Do you have any other surprises in store for me?'

'No, I don't. I would have told you about the nursery earlier but . . . well, I thought you might not want to move in with me.'

'I like the idea, Jackie. In fact, I love it.'

'That's good. By the way, I have to go out at five to pick up the car. Dad said that he'd come round and look after you.'

'Oh, er . . . right.'

'You don't mind?'

'No, not at all. As I said, I like your dad.'

'That's good. When I get back, I'll cook a nice meal for the three of us. I think it's time for your sleep now.'

'Sleep?' Mandy echoed.

'Your afternoon nap. You go and have a lie-down and I'll call you in an hour or so.'

'Yes, OK.'

Climbing the stairs, Mandy was sure that Jackie knew nothing about her father's indecent act. Flopping onto the bed, she wondered why Nick had taken the liberty of pushing his cock into her pussy. Hadn't he thought that she'd protest? Hadn't he thought that she'd go running to Jackie? Nick was coming round at five, Mandy mused as she closed her eyes. He was bound to change her nappy and . . . Would he want sex again? The situation was strange, she thought as she drifted off to sleep.

'Mandy,' Jackie whispered. 'Mandy, it's time to wake up.'

'Oh, er . . . I must have dropped off,' Mandy said, opening her eyes and smiling at Jackie.

'I have to go and get the car. Dad will be here soon.'

'Oh, yes, of course.'

'When I get back, I'll cook dinner. Have you wet yourself?'

'Er . . . no, no, I haven't.' Slipping off the bed, Mandy stood in front of Jackie and frowned. 'Your dad . . .' she began, unsure how to put it. 'Do you know . . .'

'Do I know what?'

'That he . . . Nothing, it's all right.'

'OK, I'd better get going. Do try and wet yourself, Mandy. He likes to think that he's helping so he'll be pleased that you need your nappy changing.'

'Is this baby thing going to last for ever? I had no idea that your dad would be changing me.'

'You don't mind, do you?'

'No, no. It's just that . . . it's odd, that's all.'

'My dad likes to join in, Mandy. I'm his only daughter, he's alone in his big house . . . He likes to join in.'

'You don't think it odd, then?'

245

'No, not at all. Whether it will last for ever or not, I don't know.'

'Jackie, does he . . . Do you wear nappies?'

'God, no. And if I did, I wouldn't allow my dad to change me.'

'I just wanted to be sure of the situation.'

'Look, I have to go. I'll see you later, OK?'

'Yes, OK.'

Thinking again how bizarre the situation was, Mandy waited until Jackie had gone before wandering downstairs. In the lounge, she paced the floor and wondered about the future. She rather enjoyed the adult-baby game, but the situation with Nick was odd. If Jackie didn't know what he got up to, and she then found out and went mad . . . The last thing Mandy wanted was to cause trouble. The idea of the girl's father calling round for sex pleased her, but she didn't want to ruin her lesbian relationship with Jackie.

'Hi,' Nick called, letting himself into the house.

'I'm in the lounge,' Mandy said.

'Hello, Mandy. Has Jackie gone?'

'Yes – yes, she has.'

'The first thing to do is change your nappy,' he said, rubbing his hands together. 'You must be very wet.'

'Actually, I'm not.'

'I'll change you anyway. Come into the nursery.'

'Nick,' Mandy breathed, following him into the small room. 'Nick, does Jackie know what we did?'

'She knows that I change you. OK, up onto the table.'

'Yes, but—'

'Right, let's get this nappy off,' he cut in as she lay on her back.

Pulling her rubber pants off, Nick placed her feet on the table either side of her hips and parted her knees wide. Mandy stared at the ceiling as he slipped her nappy off and began cleaning her hairless pussy lips with a wet tissue. She loved the game, she mused dreamily as he parted her swollen sex lips and ran the tissue over her erect clitoris. With Nick to look after her and Jackie offering her lesbian love, Mandy would want for nothing.

After Jackie had witnessed Mandy's exploits in the woods with four men, the girl had obviously been trying to keep her happy by tying her down and thrashing her firm bottom. Jackie knew that she liked the rough treatment, and was obviously trying to cater for all her needs. Mandy wondered whether the girl had asked her father to fuck Mandy to keep her from straying and looking for men. It was a possibility, she thought.

As Nick slid two fingers into the tight sheath of her vagina and massaged her wet inner flesh, Mandy let out a rush of breath. Her clitoris emerging from beneath its pinken hood, her pussy milk flowing in torrents, she closed her eyes and relaxed completely as Nick attended her feminine needs. What would Paula think if she knew of her new life? she thought as her vaginal muscles tightened around the man's thrusting fingers. Hopefully, Gary would call at the flat and give the girl what she craved.

'I think you'd better pee yourself before I put a clean nappy on,' Nick said, withdrawing his fingers from her contracting vagina.

'All right,' Mandy breathed, squeezing her muscles.

Kneeling on the floor and parting her firm pussy lips, Nick pressed his lips hard against the pink funnel of flesh surrounding her love hole. Like father, like daughter, Mandy thought as her hot liquid jetted into his thirsty mouth. When she'd been struggling to pay the bills in her flat, she'd never have believed that she'd be in this situation, she reflected happily as Nick drank from her trembling body. Her life had changed incredibly since meeting Paula at the bus stop, but she hoped that there'd be no more changes.

Mandy was happy with her new life. Her web-design business was doing well, she had Jackie to love her, and now she had Nick to give her what Jackie couldn't. As Nick sucked her swollen clitoris into his hot mouth, Mandy arched her back and clung to the sides of the table. Crude sex was a way of life now, she mused. She craved the abuse of her young body and, with Jackie using a branch to thrash her naked buttocks and Nick to fuck her, she had everything she wanted.

Her orgasm erupting within the pulsating bulb of her erect clitoris, Mandy cried out as her pleasure rocked her young body. Nick repeatedly thrust his fingers deep into her spasming vagina and swept his tongue over the sensitive tip of her clitoris as she writhed and whimpered. This was her dream come true, she thought as she rode the crest of her illicit climax. Her orgasmic juices spewing over Nick's hand, her clitoris pulsing wildly, she lost herself in her sexual delirium as her pleasure peaked.

Before her orgasm had receded, Nick slipped his fingers out of her tight vagina and thrust his erect cock deep into her young body. Mandy once more gripped the sides of the table as he rocked his hips and battered her ripe cervix with his bulbous knob. His spunk came quickly, filling her contracting vagina and running down to the tight hole of her anus as his swinging balls pummelled the round cheeks of her naked bottom. She could feel her inner lips rolling back and forth along the veined shaft of his wet cock as he gasped. This was real sex, Mandy thought happily. This was her new and exciting life.

'I'd . . . I'd better put your nappy on,' Nick gasped, his spent cock finally sliding out of her sperm-bubbling vagina. 'Jackie will be back soon, so I'll have to get you cleaned up.'

'That was amazing,' Mandy said, her eyes rolling. 'You're fantastic.'

'I just want to make you happy, Mandy. Now, let's get you cleaned up and in a nappy ready for Jackie.'

Sure now that Jackie knew nothing of her father's illicit acts, Mandy relaxed as he cleaned her vaginal crack with a tissue. As the cold tissue ran over her sperm-drenched anus, she felt her clitoris swell again. Nick would have to call round several times each week and look after her, she thought as he slipped a clean nappy beneath her rounded buttocks. He'd have to babysit her regularly. Securing the nappy and pulling the rubber pants up her legs, he ordered her off the table.

'When did Jackie make the nursery?' she asked Nick as they sat in the lounge.

'The other day,' he replied, smiling at her. 'When the people were here doing the office, she had the nursery made for you. You've made her very happy, Mandy.'

'That's good – I'm pleased.'

'And you've made *me* happy.'

'Nick, does she know that we have sex?'

'I think that's her car now,' he murmured, ignoring her question and moving to the window. 'Yes, she's home.'

'Nick, does she know?' Mandy persisted.

'Put it this way. It's best not to say anything.'

'God, I wish you'd told me before. I might have said something to her earlier and . . .'

'Our little secret, OK?'

'OK.'

249

'Hi,' Jackie said, beaming as she breezed into the room. 'Have you been a good little girl, Mandy?'

'She's been very good,' Nick said. 'She's had her nappy changed and she's ready for dinner.'

'Thanks, Dad. Well, the car's all done.'

'No problems?'

'No, everything's fine.'

'Good, good. I'll make you a cup of tea,' he said, leaving the room.

'Are you happy?' Jackie asked Mandy, sitting next to her on the sofa. 'I mean, is everything OK?'

'Things couldn't be better,' Mandy said, kissing the girl's full lips. 'Your dad looks after me, you love me . . . Things couldn't be better. Oh, I must take you to meet my mum and dad.'

'Yes, I'd like that. Do you think they'll be OK with me?'

'I've already told them, and they're fine about it. There is one man I have to . . . I have to tell David that . . .'

'Mandy, you do whatever you need to do. By the way, I'll have to run Dad home after dinner. I just spoke to Jack, the young man from next door. He's happy to sit with you while I'm out.'

'Jackie, I'll be fine here alone.'

'I'd rather someone was here to look after you. He's eighteen and he's a very nice chap.'

'Jackie, I'll be fine.'

'I just want you to be happy, Mandy.'

'I *am* happy, with you and your dad.'

'Jack will come over anyway, just in case there's anything you want.'

'I don't need a teenage lad to look after me,' Mandy said, giggling.

'I just want to make sure that you have everything you need, Mandy. I mean, everything.'

The leading publisher of fetish and adult fiction

TELL US WHAT YOU THINK!

Readers' ideas and opinions matter to us so please take a few
minutes to fill in the questionnaire below.

1. Sex: Are you male ☐ female ☐ a couple ☐?

2. Age: Under 21 ☐ 21–30 ☐ 31–40 ☐ 41–50 ☐ 51–60 ☐ over 60 ☐

3. Where do you buy your Nexus books from?

☐ A chain book shop. If so, which one(s)?

_____

☐ An independent book shop. If so, which one(s)?

_____

☐ A used book shop/charity shop
☐ Online book store. If so, which one(s)?

_____

4. How did you find out about Nexus books?

☐ Browsing in a book shop
☐ A review in a magazine
☐ Online
☐ Recommendation
☐ Other _____

5. In terms of settings, which do you prefer? (Tick as many as you like.)

☐ Down to earth and as realistic as possible
☐ Historical settings. If so, which period do you prefer?

_____

☐ Fantasy settings – barbarian worlds
☐ Completely escapist/surreal fantasy
☐ Institutional or secret academy

☐ Futuristic/sci fi
☐ Escapist but still believable
☐ Any settings you dislike?

_____

☐ Where would you like to see an adult novel set?

_____

6. In terms of storylines, would you prefer:

☐ Simple stories that concentrate on adult interests?
☐ More plot and character-driven stories with less explicit adult activity?
☐ We value your ideas, so give us your opinion of this book:

_____

_____

_____

7. In terms of your adult interests, what do you like to read about? (Tick as many as you like.)

☐ Traditional corporal punishment (CP)
☐ Modern corporal punishment
☐ Spanking
☐ Restraint/bondage
☐ Rope bondage
☐ Latex/rubber
☐ Leather
☐ Female domination and male submission
☐ Female domination and female submission
☐ Male domination and female submission
☐ Willing captivity
☐ Uniforms
☐ Lingerie/underwear/hosiery/footwear (boots and high heels)
☐ Sex rituals
☐ Vanilla sex
☐ Swinging
☐ Cross-dressing/TV
☐ Enforced feminisation

☐ Others – tell us what you don't see enough of in adult fiction:

_____

_____

_____

8. Would you prefer books with a more specialised approach to your interests, i.e. a novel specifically about uniforms? If so, which subject(s) would you like to read a Nexus novel about?

_____

_____

_____

9. Would you like to read true stories in Nexus books? For instance, the true story of a submissive woman, or a male slave? Tell us which true revelations you would most like to read about:

_____

_____

_____

10. What do you like best about Nexus books?

_____

_____

11. What do you like least about Nexus books?

_____

_____

12. Which are your favourite titles?

_____

_____

13. Who are your favourite authors?

_____

_____

14. Which covers do you prefer? Those featuring:
(Tick as many as you like.)

- ☐ Fetish outfits
- ☐ More nudity
- ☐ Two models
- ☐ Unusual models or settings
- ☐ Classic erotic photography
- ☐ More contemporary images and poses
- ☐ A blank/non-erotic cover
- ☐ What would your ideal cover look like?

_____

15. Describe your ideal Nexus novel in the space provided:

_____

_____

_____

_____

16. Which celebrity would feature in one of your Nexus-style fantasies? We'll post the best suggestions on our website – anonymously!

_____

THANKS FOR YOUR TIME

Now simply write the title of this book in the space below and cut out the
questionnaire pages. Post to: Nexus, Marketing Dept., Thames Wharf Studios,
Rainville Rd, London W6 9HA

Book title: _____

NEXUS NEW BOOKS

To be published in March 2008

AMERICAN BLUE
Penny Birch

American Blue takes a light-hearted but unashamedly perverse look at the American porno industry from the perspective of an innocent young model. When Penny Birch discovers that her niece Jemima has been seduced into making a working tour of some of the USA's most notorious pornographers, she feels she has no choice but to save her from the clutches of these dangerous men. But Jemima is not to be dissuaded, and as aunt and niece travel west from New York they get themselves into all kinds of kinky trouble . . .

£6.99   ISBN 978 0 352 34169 3

To be published in April 2008

LEAH'S PUNISHMENT
Aran Ashe

Leah – a petite, brave and comely slave – innocently attracts the covetous attentions of the jealous steersman on her master's boat and precipitates a chain of predicaments over which she has no control. Following a night of punishing retribution by her obsessive mentor, she is abandoned to the depravities of strangers at the mysterious Tithe Retreat. But her attempted escape serves only to propel her even deeper into the bizarre and exacting realms of intemperate sexuality.

£6.99   ISBN 978 0 352 34171 6

NEXUS CONFESSIONS VOLUME 3
Various

Swinging, dogging, group sex, cross-dressing, spanking, female domination, corporal punishment, and extreme fetishes . . . Nexus Confessions explores the length and breadth of erotic obsession, real experience and sexual fantasy. This is an encyclopaedic collection of the bizarre, the extreme, the utterly inappropriate, the daring and the shocking experiences of ordinary men and women driven by their extraordinary desires. Collected by the world's leading publisher of fetish fiction, this is the third in a series of six volumes of true stories and shameful confessions, never-before-told or published.

£6.99   ISBN 978 0 352 34113 6

If you would like more information about Nexus titles, please visit our website at www.nexus-books.co.uk, or send a large stamped addressed envelope to:
Nexus, Thames Wharf Studios,
Rainville Road, London W6 9HA

NEXUS BOOKLIST

Information is correct at time of printing. To avoid disappointment, check availability before ordering. Go to www.nexus-books.co.uk.

All books are priced at £6.99 unless another price is given.

NEXUS

☐ ABANDONED ALICE	Adriana Arden	ISBN 978 0 352 33969 0
☐ ALICE IN CHAINS	Adriana Arden	ISBN 978 0 352 33908 9
☐ AQUA DOMINATION	William Doughty	ISBN 978 0 352 34020 7
☐ THE ART OF CORRECTION	Tara Black	ISBN 978 0 352 33895 2
☐ THE ART OF SURRENDER	Madeline Bastinado	ISBN 978 0 352 34013 9
☐ BEASTLY BEHAVIOUR	Aishling Morgan	ISBN 978 0 352 34095 5
☐ BEING A GIRL	Chloë Thurlow	ISBN 978 0 352 34139 6
☐ BELINDA BARES UP	Yolanda Celbridge	ISBN 978 0 352 33926 3
☐ BIDDING TO SIN	Rosita Varón	ISBN 978 0 352 34063 4
☐ BLUSHING AT BOTH ENDS	Philip Kemp	ISBN 978 0 352 34107 5
☐ THE BOOK OF PUNISHMENT	Cat Scarlett	ISBN 978 0 352 33975 1
☐ BRUSH STROKES	Penny Birch	ISBN 978 0 352 34072 6
☐ CALLED TO THE WILD	Angel Blake	ISBN 978 0 352 34067 2
☐ CAPTIVES OF CHEYNER CLOSE	Adriana Arden	ISBN 978 0 352 34028 3
☐ CARNAL POSSESSION	Yvonne Strickland	ISBN 978 0 352 34062 7
☐ CITY MAID	Amelia Evangeline	ISBN 978 0 352 34096 2
☐ COLLEGE GIRLS	Cat Scarlett	ISBN 978 0 352 33942 3
☐ COMPANY OF SLAVES	Christina Shelly	ISBN 978 0 352 33887 7
☐ CONCEIT AND CONSEQUENCE	Aishling Morgan	ISBN 978 0 352 33965 2
☐ CORRECTIVE THERAPY	Jacqueline Masterson	ISBN 978 0 352 33917 1
☐ CORRUPTION	Virginia Crowley	ISBN 978 0 352 34073 3
☐ CRUEL SHADOW	Aishling Morgan	ISBN 978 0 352 33886 0
☐ DARK MISCHIEF	Lady Alice McCloud	ISBN 978 0 352 33998 0
☐ DEPTHS OF DEPRAVATION	Ray Gordon	ISBN 978 0 352 33995 9
☐ DICE WITH DOMINATION	P.S. Brett	ISBN 978 0 352 34023 8

NEXUS CLASSIC

------ ✂ -

Please send me the books I have ticked above.

Name   ....

Address   ....

                  ....

                  ....

                  .... Post code ....

Send to: **Virgin Books Cash Sales, Thames Wharf Studios, Rainville Road, London W6 9HA**

US customers: for prices and details of how to order books for delivery by mail, call 888-330-8477.

Please enclose a cheque or postal order, made payable to **Nexus Books Ltd**, to the value of the books you have ordered plus postage and packing costs as follows:

   UK and BFPO – £1.00 for the first book, 50p for each subsequent book.

   Overseas (including Republic of Ireland) – £2.00 for the first book, £1.00 for each subsequent book.

If you would prefer to pay by VISA, ACCESS/MASTERCARD, AMEX, DINERS CLUB or SWITCH, please write your card number and expiry date here:

....

Please allow up to 28 days for delivery.

Signature ....

Our privacy policy

We will not disclose information you supply us to any other parties. We will not disclose any information which identifies you personally to any person without your express consent.

From time to time we may send out information about Nexus books and special offers. Please tick here if you do *not* wish to receive Nexus information.   ☐

------ ✂ -